The G.I.'s Daughter

The G.I.'s Daughter

By

C. E. Hollingsworth

Nashville

This novel is a work of fiction. References to historical events or real people and places are used fictitiously. Other names, events, characters, and places are products of the author's imagination, and any resemblance to actual events or places or persons, living or dead, is entirely coincidental.

Copyright © 2017 by C. E. Hollingsworth

All rights reserved, including the right to reproduce this book or portions of this book in any form whatsoever, without the prior written permission of the author.

First paperback edition

Manufactured in the United States of America
25 24 23 22 21 20 19 18 17   1 2 3 4 5

ISBN 978-0-9996924-0-0 (hardcover)
ISBN 978-0-9996924-1-7 (paperback)

This book is dedicated to my parents, whose lives, like characters in this story, were disrupted and thrown into disarray by the turmoils of World War Two.

Also in honor of the gallant men and women of the Greatest Generation in both the USA and the United Kingdom

Contents

Saturday, May 21, 1943 – Somewhere in Libya, North Africa.... 1

Tuesday, September 14, 2004 – Thorpe Beauchamp, England.... 6

Friday, September 17, 2004 – Honeypot Hill................ 21

Saturday, September 18, 2004 – Honeypot Hill.............. 29

Monday, September 20, 2004 – Honeypot Hill............... 38

Wednesday, September 29, 2004 – Honeypot Hill 42

Friday, October 1, 2004 – Honeypot Hill 48

Saturday, October 2, 2004 – Honeypot Hill 59

Monday, September 25, 1944 – Royal Engineers
    Temporary Quarters, Naples, Italy 74

Saturday, October 9, 2004 – Honeypot Hill 82

Saturday, September 30, 1944 – Naples, Italy 90

Sunday, October 8, 1944 – Honeypot Hill 96

Saturday Afternoon, October 9, 2004 – Honeypot Hill....... 104

Sunday Morning, October 10, 2004 – Honeypot Hill........ 114

Monday, October 9, 1944 – Honeypot Hill................ 121

Friday, October 13, 1944 – Honeypot Hill 137

Sunday Lunchtime, October 10, 2004 – Honeypot Hill 141

Wednesday, October 20, 2004 – Honeypot Hill 145

Sunday, November 5, 1944 – Honeypot Hill............... 150

Thursday, November 11, 2004 – American Cemetery,
  Madingley, Cambridge............................... 162

Thursday, February 2, 2005 – Nashville, Tennessee, USA 177

Tuesday, April 19, 2005 – Nashville International Airport,
  Nashville, Tennessee................................ 187

Wednesday, April 20, 2005 – Franklin, Tennessee, USA 204

Friday, April 22, 2005 – Franklin, Tennessee 221

Sunday, April 24, 2005 – Old Hillsboro Pike,
  Franklin, Tennessee................................. 230

Monday, May 30, 2005 – American Cemetery,
  Madingley, Cambridge............................... 239

Wednesday, June 29, 2005 – Honeypot Hill 246

Tuesday, July 12, 2005 – The Quinn Galleries, London....... 258

Ten Years Later, Wednesday, September 15, 2015 – Video
  Conferencing, GPDS Partners, London................. 268

Saturday, May 21, 1943 — Somewhere in Libya, North Africa

A blistering hot wind was blowing off the Sahara Desert. Jeremy and his driver had each eaten the stale sandwich that the cookhouse had come up with for their lunch and were now resting underneath their Jeep, the only place they could find a square inch of shade. While the Cockney corporal snored gently, Jeremy was lying on his back on the dusty ground, sweating and trying to conjure up a nice damp, cold, misty November day in the Fenlands of eastern England from where he hailed.

"Oh, Lord," he kind of prayed, "just a tiny cloud no bigger than a man's hand and a few drops of rain would more than satisfy me."

It was now three years since the then Second Lieutenant Jeremy Lisle had kissed Rebecca goodbye as his final few days of leave drew to a close. All he knew was that he was to be shipped out to God knows where, although by a process of elimination it was obvious their final destination would be the North African theatre of operations. He had always longed to visit Africa, but would have preferred to have been a tourist on his way to see wild animals in Kenya than a soldier heading for what would certainly become a chain of bloody desert battlefields.

As he lay in the sandy heat unable to conjure up rain, his thoughts went back to that agonizing morning at the Royal Engineers' Depot in the army town of Aldershot, where a tearful Rebecca clung to him weeping, terrified she would never see him again. Her fear was well-founded. Holland and Belgium were at that moment collapsing before the Nazi blitzkrieg, and France's defenses buckled. He had wondered then if there would be an England to come back to, or if their troopship would disappear beneath the forbidding waters of the Atlantic, hunted down and sunk by one of Hitler's U-Boats?

Corporal Tommy Docherty, his driver, wisely used their lunch-break to catch up on sleep, but for Jeremy siestas had become moments when he could allow his imagination to wander. For the ten thousandth time his thoughts drifted back to the last day of leave when he and Rebecca had been together at their home in the modest village of Thorpe Beauchamp on the edge of the Fens, not far from Cambridge. They had been married less than nine months and Jeremy hated leaving her, but he was now a newly-minted army officer, a man under orders.

A couple of days before their wedding in late August 1939 Jeremy Lisle had received orders to report to the local Territorial Army barracks. Jeremy had joined this reserve unit the previous year when Hitler had focused his sights on Czechoslovakia, and it had appeared increasingly likely that war was coming. His obligation then had been to turn out for weekly training and occasional exercises. He knew that, although a mere corporal at the moment, his background meant that it would not be long before he was sent for officer training as the size of the army was significantly expanded. Now that moment of patriotic commitment had come back to bite him just as he was about to get married.

After talking with his senior officer he was given compassionate leave to wed and have a couple of nights of honeymoon. On the second Sunday of his married life, two days after Germany's invasion of Poland, the couple was stretched out together on the sofa in each other's arms, dreading the worst. A warm September breeze gently lifted the net curtains around the open French window. With the rest of the British people they waited with foreboding for the Prime Minister to speak to the nation. His words were greeted with tears and instant anxiety. "I have to tell you now... that this country is at war with Germany."

Jeremy had handed the reins of the family's modest engineering business back to his father, donned his uniform, and become a soldier. He and Rebecca were to find themselves apart more than together in the following few months as he received a crash course of officer training. After the passing out parade, one pip now on his khaki shoulder, embarkation leave gave them a morsel of time before he would be spirited away. They had talked about making a baby, but afraid what the winds of war might do, they decided against it. On their last day together, Jeremy kept his promise to his bride, and went up to cement in place the charming chimneypots she had chosen. Then his last task was to complete the wooden sign that bore the name of their new home – *Honeypot Hill*.

The stories of Christopher Robin's teddy bear, Winnie-the-Pooh, enchanted Rebecca. It was published in the 1920s not long after she had learned to read. Having received the book as a Christmas present her ten-year-old self had then spent hours reading to younger cousins. After that the book was never far from her, and to Jeremy's amusement she was able to quote verbatim huge chunks from both *Winnie-the-Pooh* and *The House at Pooh Corner*. That funny old bear so beguiled her that in his honor she had wanted to name their home *Hunnypot Hill*, using Pooh's eccentric spelling of the word 'honey.'

Jeremy so adored his wife that he readily gave Rebecca her own way on just about everything, but, while happy with the name she chose, he put down his foot on the spelling. Pooh sayings regularly dripped from his wife's tongue but now, after being briefly furious with him for being so mannishly pompous, she left a lipstick smear when she kissed him on the tip of the nose and scolded him for being such "a silly old bear". Wrapping her arms around his middle, she lay her head on his shoulder and told him for the umpteenth time how much she would miss him.

Rebecca willingly let him get away with this conceited piece of male stupidity because he was off to war, and she hated there being an unresolved argument on the last day they were together... perhaps forever. She had a vague idea where he might go, but meanwhile was increasingly worried for her own safety as they had been watching the Nazis corner the British Expeditionary Force on the French coast. They would soon be licking their lips at the juicy prospect of invading England. For all she knew, within weeks she could be a childless widow, and much worse could follow. Inside she was petrified. She had found the best man in the world, but now that perturbingly evil Mr. Hitler was taking him away from her.

However, to the very end of her life she thought of her home as *Hunnypot Hill* and even had personal letterhead printed with that spelling!

After Jeremy had screwed the house's name to the wall by their front gate, the pair stood back arm-in-arm to admire their handiwork. Their home, a four-bedroom 1930s box, was too new to have yet developed much character, but it was theirs and they were fortunate to have it. On that sunny May afternoon both it and their garden looked perfect, the only cloud in their sky being whether Jeremy would ever see it again. If he didn't come home, he wondered, what would happen to this woman nestled against him? She was always talkative but now was so nervous that she couldn't stop chattering away like a little house sparrow. Rebecca's garrulousness was in marked contrast to her man's quiet reticence, yet despite the endless flow of words he loved the sound of her voice.

Their romance had been hurried along due to the uncertainties of the times, moving rapidly from a chance encounter when Jeremy had run into her after a meeting at her father's office to marriage a mere ten months later. They had met in the autumn of 1938 just after the Prime Minister returned from Munich waving his paltry piece of paper and bleating about "peace in our time"; they became husband and wife during those late August days when telegrams were being delivered to call tens of thousands into military service. Then, for the second time in their lives, Britain was again at war.

Before hostilities had broken out Jeremy had not been much of a churchgoer, but since that May morning in 1940 when he and Rebecca had kissed each other goodbye he had been assiduous about his attendance at church parades, praying every day for their home where the land gradually rises at the edge of the endless flatlands of the Fens and for the woman who was living there, his beloved wife. Often she would not be alone. At the outset of hostilities children evacuated from London had come, stayed for a while, become homesick and gone back home. Later she would rent a room to another military wife, the pair of them cycling together each morning to the office that administered the distribution of food where they both worked.

As he prayed all through those years, Jeremy readily promised God the sun, the moon, and the stars to be spared so when this terrible ordeal was finally over he could return to their modest brick-built abode nestled beside the old churchyard wall in Thorpe Beauchamp. Here they would raise their family, and he pledged that never again would he venture into the world without his wife at his side. His happily-ever-after plan was to remain there for the rest of his life. He was determined that he would not leave *Honeypot Hill* until they carried him out feet first.

And this is precisely what happened, although the story is a lot more complicated than that.

Tuesday, September 14, 2004 — Honeypot Hill, Thorpe Beauchamp, England

Amanda's voice had a bossy irritable edge, "Really Mother, it isn't safe for you to go clambering up there at your age."

My tall, elegant daughter, Amanda, was standing at the bottom of the rickety folding stair, scolding me as I did my best to scurry up to the attic at least as well any woman approaching sixty could manage. We were in *Honeypot Hill*, my parents' home, the place where I had done all my growing up. Since my mother's recent death the house had become mine, although in the last couple of years my mother had needed me with her much of the time; with probate now sorted I could begin making *Honeypot Hill* what I wanted, selling the London house where my children grew up.

I turned and grinned at her apprehensive face, wiggled my nose, stuck out my tongue, and said with a smile, "My darling girl, I'm not yet ready to be consigned to my dotage. I'm sound in wind, limb, and mind, could still walk more miles a day than you, and, as you discovered yesterday, am still perfectly capable of trouncing you on the tennis court. For heaven's sake stop fussing. Besides, I'm itching to see what Gran has salted away up here."

Amanda's face had become a picture of self-righteous annoyance as I tried nonchalantly to hoist my posterior through the tight little hatchway. Landing on the dusty attic floor with a bump followed by a grunt, I then broke into gales of laughter. Having brushed myself off I switched on the lights to find myself in a grubby space where, since early in the Second World War, the family had consigned every conceivable piece of junk or left-over. Gran Lisle had never been a pack rat, but Granddad more than made up for her – although his neat and orderly hoarding was the product of his tidy engineer's mind.

With only a couple of low wattage light bulbs, it took a few moments for my sight to adjust. The first thing I set eyes on was the sled Daddy had made when I was little and on which I first experienced snow – this had been so cold and unpleasant that when growing up I could never get excited about winter sports. Friends went off to ski in Scotland, Switzerland, or Austria, while I stayed home, rode my bike, and talked my mother into taking me to as many art galleries and museums as possible. Leaning against the toboggan was my father's last set of golf clubs, abandoned when he could no longer ignore the agonizing protests of knees and back several years before he finally died.

When finally Amanda's head popped through the attic opening, the first thing she glimpsed was me cuddling my dear old teddy bear whom I had loved passionately, and with whom I had as a three-year-old once run away from home in a fit of frustration with my mother. I got as far as the Village Shop before Mrs. Aitcheson, the shopkeeper, gathered me up, bribed me with a sweetie, and taking my hand had walked me home to my distraught parent who had hardly had time to miss me.

Initially, Amanda could make no sense of the waves of nostalgia sweeping over me as I rediscovered first this and then that. She kept muttering dire threats as she cast around with her eyes and then would see something that interested her so that she, too, was drawn into this scavenger hunt. On knees and bottoms we slowly progressed together down the center aisle of bare planks, kicking up clouds of filth and getting caught up like oversized flies in ancient cobwebs, steadily gathering a thickening layer of grime. Unexpected items reawakened long-forgotten memories as we made mental notes about what should be recycled, what should go to the church rummage sale, items for charity shops, and things that were little more than fire hazards and no longer of any earthly good.

We inched forward for several hours, finally reaching the chimney breast at the far end of the attic against which were stacked several cardboard document boxes. These had clearly been accessed more frequently than the rest of the clutter. Glancing inside the top one I discovered letters, photographs, and a peculiar mixture of odds and ends. Alongside them sat an elderly brown leather suitcase, obviously part of this same stash.

Pulling the last clean tissue from my jeans' pocket I wiped from my usually spotless daughter's pert little nose a fetching smudge, murmuring, "Well, Sweet Pea, I think we have seen about all there is, most of which has no value at all. When your brother and sister-in-law come down at the weekend we can cart this lot into the garage, which would be a good place to separate sheep from goats."

She laughed, "Mumsie, you really don't expect David and the Lady Millicent to dirty their hands with all this? He's happier in up-market sales rooms, schmoozing with an artist's agent or discovering some lost Canaletto rather than ferreting around his late grandparents' attic."

"Maybe," I answered, "but it's worth a try... besides, wouldn't it be fun just this once to see Millie dressed in grubby jeans, tee shirt, a scarf tied around her hair and grimy marks all over her face." We both laughed. My daughter-in-law was an absolute darling, but her aristocratic upbringing had been such that even her everyday clothes made Amanda, no slouch when it came to dress sense, look shabby. "Besides," I muttered, "I suspect these boxes and suitcase contain the mother lode."

Hardly a mother lode, more an unexploded bomb!

• • • • • • •

An hour or so later, with itchy eyes and runny nose but having washed my hair, we had both showered, changed clothes, and were settled in the little conservatory clearing the dust from our throats with the help of hot cups of tea. The conservatory had been the focal point of Mummy's life in her final years. The light scent of our shampoos hung in the air, and we allowed the late afternoon sun to dry our wet manes. The boxes had proved too heavy and awkward for us to drag from the attic, so we had foraged for interesting-looking papers and files, not entirely sure what had been in my mother's mind when she had salted away this hoard.

My mother's last years had not been easy. She had managed to hold mental deterioration at bay until that moment, a couple of months after their sixtieth wedding anniversary, when Daddy's unexpected fatal heart attack had robbed her of most of her cogency. She had barely been on the same planet as the rest of the congregation at his funeral service in the crowded village church, and never again would she fully emerge from the fog of dementia.

For as long as I could remember Daddy had insisted he be buried in the churchyard that backed up to *Honeypot Hill*. His wish was granted.

In the months following, the mental fog that hung over Mummy's mind grew ever thicker. After one particularly distressing episode when I had had to drop everything at work in London and dash down to Thorpe Beauchamp, I finally came to terms with the reality that radical changes were necessary. In the wake of endless sleepless, tearful nights I decided to pass the daily management of the business to my son, David. Mummy now had to be my priority. She had taken good care of me in childhood and it was now my turn to care for her in old age.

The zest with which David settled into his new position confirmed my instinct to begin preparing him to take over The Quinn Galleries as soon as he had graduated from university. Initially, he made me apprehensive, and I stood ready to jump back in if needed. He started off leaning heavily on me, but in a relatively short time the flood of panicky phone calls diminished to a trickle, and within a year you would think he had been in charge all his life. I had never asked to run the business; I had been dropped into it by my husband's sudden death. I had no option if I was to keep a roof over our heads, food on the table, and my son and daughter properly educated.

The wheel had now come full circle. In my heart of hearts I knew I no longer belonged in London – the time had come to pull up my roots and move back permanently to *Honeypot Hill*. Initially, we rented the house in Belsize Park fully furnished while I moved back to my childhood bedroom so I could be with my mother 24/7. Mine had been a happy, secure childhood – and now I was coming home to where I truly belonged. Well-heeled friends, all incurable Londoners, were appalled. How on earth could I walk away from a respected position directing a successful art gallery to spend my days with a frightened old lady whose mind drifted and whose schedule revolved around mealtimes, her lunchtime glass of Bristol Cream Sherry, and the BBC Evening News?

Occasionally Mummy would potter in the garden, even getting down on her knees to pull a few weeds, but otherwise she roosted in the conservatory, watching the seasons change and forever re-reading the *Daily Mail*, never absorbing much of its content. She took copious naps and would be in bed asleep by nine o'clock, giving me the space I needed. At first this was a relief after the rough and tumble of London, but the novelty gradually wore off. I missed dressing up in nice clothes and the daily discipline of going to work, yet I was immensely proud of David's growing success, sometimes feeling just a tiny bit jealous – although never letting on.

The three years of my mother's decline were much harder than I ever expected, and there were times when being the faithful daughter irked me, but my son was sensitive enough to keep me marginally involved with the gallery, recognizing that I needed something more than the company of an elderly woman with a vanishing memory. Besides, he would say, my role was vital because I was the institutional memory of the business.

Mother's ramblings often made little sense. She would sometimes talk as if Daddy was out messing around in his greenhouse, or she would treat me as if I was one of her favorite girlfriends from her twenties dropping by for gossip and a cup of tea. While she recognized me most of the time, the boundary between fantasy and reality was crumbling.

One morning as she sat in bed drinking her first cup of tea of the day, out of the blue she asked, "Sarah, darling, have the B-17s left yet this morning... I had hoped Robbie and Chuck would drop by so we could wish them good luck and warn them against doing anything stupid over Cologne or which other secret place they have been sent to bomb today."

On another occasion, as the sun was setting at the end of a short winter afternoon, she asked me why I had not drawn the blackout curtains properly. "There's enough light coming from these windows to give the enemy a straight run at our airfield."

The wartime airfield had finally closed during my second year at the village primary school, after which the abandoned buildings gradually fell apart, with weeds sprouting through what had been hastily paved concrete runways. "Our airfield" had been RAF Thorpe Beauchamp during World War Two, home to several dozen B-17 Flying Fortresses of the US Army Air Forces and their crews. It was during my childhood that the rich farmland had been restored, although a handful of the buildings which remained had become storage space for the farmer.

Mummy and others who had been around the village would talk about American construction crews and their heavy equipment arriving as if from nowhere during the second half of 1942. Within weeks several hundred acres of fertile fields on this edge of the village were converted from fertile agricultural land into runways and taxi ways. Necessary buildings had then been thrown up, and no sooner had the concrete set than brand new bombers would fly in from the USA and with them gangs of young men, many of whom had seldom strayed from their home State, let alone across the Atlantic. Overnight the local population doubled, and Thorpe Beauchamp would never be the same again.

Looking out from *Honeypot Hill* across what had once been the airfield there are few clues that the verdant fields and pastures had once been the launch pad for tens of thousands of tons of high explosive. Just one old Nissen hut could be seen from my bedroom window as it rusted away in the distance. What had once been the airfield's entrance was now almost swallowed up by weeds and brambles that hid a modest plaque announcing to a forgetful world that the Eighth Air Force Bomb Group (H) 991 had once been stationed here.

Some of the first pictures Amanda and I stumbled over in the attic boxes were little black-and-white Kodak snapshots taken by Mummy during wartime from what would eventually be my bedroom window. Planes were being serviced for their next mission, while everything around them looks either military or muddy. Until we found those boxes I was oblivious to the vital role the airfield had played in my mother's life and the manner in which it had shaped my own.

On the last day of my mother's life, as she was drifting in and out of consciousness, a light plane of some kind flew quite low over the house. Her eyes fluttered open for a moment, then she mumbled her last words. "That sounds like a Flying Fortress... the boys are coming home to tell me goodbye."

• • • • • • •

I had been sitting on the edge of her bed and holding her hand when she had spoken. In my weariness I had unthinkingly dismissed my mother's words as the lost meanderings of her worn-out old brain, yet they were to be her very last words. A handful of moments passed, there was an inaudible sigh, then she just stopped breathing. She and I had always been close, and I wept as grief swept over me. Only now have I come to realize that at the very end she was reliving what had probably been the most important episode of her eventful life.

When Mummy had been laid to rest alongside Daddy in the village churchyard, friends started making overtures. They were eager for me to return to London, pick up my old life, and at the very least help David and Millicent with the gallery; but there could be no going back. As my emotions steadied I acknowledged that I no longer craved the noise, the smell, the rush, the crush of people. Country living had somehow flushed this from my system, and I was content to be reintegrated back into this close-knit community in which I had grown up. There was a garden to care for, books to read, dresses to make, fields across which to walk, birds who needed to be watched, butterflies to identify, blackberries that would go begging if I did not pick them, and the rediscovery of village friends with whom I had sat in class on my first day at school.

During these initial years back in Thorpe Beauchamp while Mummy was still alive, I found myself being drawn into church life for the first time since university; I was able to improve my flower arranging skills and delighted in membership of the little Mothers Union group. I was coopted onto the boards of a couple of charities Daddy had favored, played some tennis, and was now engaged in recasting the style of the house to reflect my tastes rather than those of my mother. Only now that everything was getting to be more or less as I wanted had the time come to tackle the attic.

"Attic? Why on earth would you want to go up to the attic?" the eminently sensible Amanda had asked in horror on one of our regular evening phone calls.

"I don't think I've been up there since I was a little girl," I had unenthusiastically shrugged, "but I need to see what's lurking there –

and I'm certain the jumble of books, toys, and furniture must be a fire hazard."

"Mumsie," my daughter commanded in no uncertain terms, "I don't want you going up there on your own."

Amanda had since her teens been prematurely consigning me to my dotage. "If you're so concerned then come and help, or I'll get up there on my own whether you like it or not." I was being mischievous because I knew this would sound alarm bells of responsibility, coaxing her away from London's bright lights so she would dash down, spend a night or two in deepest Fenland where her mantra would be that she was grateful she had never been forced to grow up in such a godforsaken place.

· · · · · · ·

That Amanda was in her early thirties and continued to be single was a mystery to me. I had been married ten years by the time I was her age and had two children. My daughter had no animosity to the married state, but despite an ongoing procession of boyfriends she seemed either unable or unwilling to pull it off. Her intelligence, good looks, cheerful personality, and the pleasure males took in her company seemed the right ingredients – but men would hang round for a while, then move on. When I tried talking to her about this she made it perfectly clear that it was none of my bloody business. Her ferocity wounded me while at the same time raising my antennae. For the moment I held my peace.

Any man interested in my daughter would have to learn to play second fiddle to her lifelong passion for art and its history. She developed this passion honestly as it was a family obsession, but by her undergraduate years it had become all-consuming. After gaining a fistful of degrees her life now revolved around the Courtauld Institute of Art in London, her post-doctoral work, some teaching, researching, and constantly scratching around to find the funds needed to write what she believed would be a ground-breaking book – the book that would make her reputation.

I was convinced she was more than capable of bringing this off. Framed and in a place of honor in my little home office at *Honeypot Hill* was a lovely profile of *Dr. Amanda S. Quinn* taken from a respected art world publication, complete with a gorgeous picture of her being awarded her doctorate.

• • • • • • •

Elegant designer jeans accentuating her long shapely legs, Amanda finished her tea, placing the mug on a small occasional table before sliding from her chair and tucking her feet neatly beneath her. She then spread across the floor those items we had brought from the attic. We intended this to be an appetizer of what my mother had salted away.

There seemed to be little rhyme or reason behind Mummy's boxed collections, but our curious hands riffling through them had only added to the confusion. Mummy had deliberately kept this stuff but had never organized her hoard, something that was very much in character. She had always attacked life with a verve that left a messy trail in her wake for others to clear up.

Poking through these odds and ends, I found myself wondering if disorder might actually be her organizing principle. Why on earth had she held onto a bill dated 9th September, 1944, from George Cunliffe, the local grocer and Air Raid Warden, or for what purpose did she hold onto a wartime food ration card? For some incomprehensible reason these had meant something. There were pre-war copies of *Vogue*, a booklet given to American service personnel to help them understand the bizarre ways and language of the British, and alongside these a delicate pair of white silk evening gloves. Holding onto these items was out of character for Rebecca Lisle, my mother, who normally had little patience with sentimentality, never keeping anything very long, blithely tossing it out when it had outlived its usefulness – whether old letters or exotically expensive evening gowns.

How different from Daddy. Mother's way to stay tidy was to get rid of anything she no longer wanted, yet he held onto everything, keeping meticulous track of his hoard with a regimental measure of order. Just looking through these boxes I wondered if the contents might have been deliberately unsystematic, thereby discouraging my father from snooping into something she did not believe concerned him. A good engineer and excellent manager, the tools in his workshop were always spotlessly clean and lined up like soldiers on parade. He kept the family accounts in well-ordered ledgers, the top of his desk was seldom untidy, shirts and suits in his wardrobe were fastidiously color-coded. When documents were no longer immediately relevant they found their way into one of the rank of four-drawer filing cabinets standing against the back wall of our large, dry garage.

This was what made mother's trove so intriguing. While Daddy was a methodical pack rat, Mummy lived for the moment, assiduously covering her tracks by destroying evidence from the past. The question was, why on earth had she held onto the contents of these particular boxes?

My father would have been unlikely to poke his nose into them because they were his wife's private realm. He had grown up in a houseful of four sisters all drumming into his head, sometimes violently, that it was a capital offense to compromise a woman's privacy. He was wonderfully old-fashioned in that sense, and even when I was a small girl he respected my space by always knocking on my bedroom door when asking to come in. Besides, in the last years of his life his knees had become so wobbly that it was impossible for him to get up into the attic, which was probably when Mummy finally realized her secrets were safe.

Amanda pensively browsed over the odds and ends scattered all over the rug at my feet, occasionally commenting on something she ran across.

"Did you ever see Gran wearing any of these?" she asked as she emptied the contents of a large manila envelope onto the carpet, scattering small brooches and costume jewelry across the floor.

I shook my head while at the same time reaching for a tiny American flag lapel pin.

"I wonder where this came from?" I said to myself. The pin was a strange thing to find among my mother's personal effects because, despite liking certain American ways, she had always shown impatient disdain for the ways of our transatlantic cousins. For Mummy the damned Yanks, as she always called them, had four strikes against them before they started: they had been overpaid, oversexed, over here, and spent the early Forties messing up her precious view with their airfield. In light of what I now know I ought to have remembered the words spoken of Lady Macbeth, that 'the lady doth protest too much.'

Amanda took the little flag from my hands, looked at it, then shrugged. "Given dozens of US bombers parked almost on her doorstep, I suspect this is one of those little things gullible Americans scattered round the community as part of a clumsy public relations exercise. But why did she keep it?"

I was not so sure. Perhaps that was when I first thought there might be mysterious reasons why she had hung onto this debris from the past. A ridiculous idea began to nag, but irritably I shoved it to the back of my mind. Beside memorabilia from the 1940s were family pictures and documents that were all new to me. I always wondered why my mother had so few pictures of herself and her parents, but here they were jumbled in with everything else.

As I perused a yellowed envelope of fading snaps, obviously a seaside holiday of long ago, Amanda's inquisitive nature quickly got the better of her; she jumped up and disappeared back into the roof. I could hear her sailor-like curses as she shuffled heavy boxes across the attic floor until they were close to the opening before calling for my help.

Those elegant jeans and pretty yellow top into which she had changed after our first expedition were now caked in dust and smothered with cobwebs, but with both of us wishing we were physically a little stronger we had maneuvered the boxes and their contents down the rickety folding steps to the conservatory floor.

"Well," my daughter remarked with a shrug, "I've spent more time than is probably decent combing through dusty documents researching the minutiae of English art during the late Middle Ages and Renaissance, even prying into the private lives of those who created it, but I never expected I'd be doing something similar amongst a topsy-turvy set of odds and ends left by my own grandmother."

Gratified by my daughter's investigative abilities, I sat back and let her take the lead. A dusty cobweb hung from the ponytail into which she had bunched her hair, and her slightly upturned nose once again sported a fetching smudge. However, Amanda's blue eyes were alight with fascination, leading me to silently puzzle why men seemed so oblivious to her qualities. I suspected she might be too assertive as she was never happier than when she could, as now, take charge. I became her audience.

We started by working through what we had already found; by doing so we stumbled across more trails than might be expected. A plenitude of faded black-and-white photographs came to light, everything from my parents' wedding pictures to an eleven-year-old Mummy posing in a tutu against the backdrop of a flower garden. There were bundles of notes, cards, and missives, unworn silk stockings, obviously American and still in their packages, a wartime London bus ticket, and so forth. Towards the bottom of one box were three jeweler's padded boxes containing a brooch, a necklace, and a diamond ring I had never seen before. For some reason a chill ran down my spine, yet I had no idea why.

An attention-grabbing wad of documents then caught my eye. Amanda handed them to me and I carefully slipped off the pink ribbon, flicking through the contents. Here was another strange mixture – a West End theatre ticket, a May 1944 invoice for a dress from Bourne and Hollingsworth's, then a fashionable department store on Oxford Street, more clothing ration coupons, written instructions on the use and maintenance of a vaginal cap for birth control, and so on. These seemed to be left over from the latter part of the war, around the time my father had come home. There was nothing unusual about the cache, but my intuition sensed they were hinting at something I might not want to know.

It was slightly embarrassing blundering into Rebecca Lisle's secret world, a hoard of documents and mementos holding clues to her war. The afternoon sky darkening as evening approached, I joined Amanda on the floor on my hands and knees. There were diaries, correspondence, photos, keepsakes, more envelopes tied in pink ribbon, and a bundle of letters from Daddy – each written on a miniscule military regulation correspondence sheet from North Africa or Italy, the pages filled to overflowing in the tiniest crabbed handwriting so he could say as much as possible while avoiding upsetting the censors. It was a wonder that any relationship could survive for so long with such minimal contact. Theirs was a tough generation!

As I have said already Rebecca Lisle's instinct was to throw away not to amass, but this appeared to be a cherished collection she had ferociously protected for decades. Even into her eighties, Mummy had been exasperatingly out-with-the-old-in-with-the-new, a lifetime's habit. Now, in this higgledy-piggledy mishmash that had deliberately been saved from fire or landfill, we were digging into a side of her life that had been resolutely hidden from prying eyes.

It felt bad enough that we were snooping, but this was heightened by a mounting sense of foreboding that I kept trying to push away. My daughter was obviously in her element. As I watched I said nothing; besides, she seemed to know instinctively what was and what was not of value as we continued poking our meddlesome noses into this private corner in which my mother had hidden her secrets away. An inner voice was whispering to beware. Amanda had found a notebook and was carefully categorizing our finds. I just grazed, fighting disquiet, fearful of an unwanted ghost from the past being exhumed.

Eventually hunger overtook us and I made an executive decision to go hunting for hot food and cool drinks. The evening had turned chilly, so after we had wiped yet another layer of dust from ourselves, we put on our woollies and walked to the Lamb and Flag, where we ordered cheap and cheerful pub food and sat by a roaring log fire sipping glasses of Pinot Grigio.

Friday, September 17, 2004 — Honeypot Hill, Thorpe Beauchamp

I was grateful for beautiful weather while Amanda was with me, a veritable Indian summer, so during the following few days we put the adventure in the attic on hold. We worked together in the garden, chattered endlessly, went for walks, and only once in a while dipped into the boxes. Amanda helped me prepare for the weekend visit of my son and daughter-in-law, David and Millicent Quinn. I was so looking forward to seeing them. David, now in his mid-thirties, was revealing instinctive talent for the family business, obviously passed down from his forebears. There was inevitably criticism from certain onlookers who thought him too young and immature, but I knew better and the balance sheets backed me up. The Quinn Galleries, strategically located in an appropriate and fashionable corner of London, are highly respected, the business having been founded by my late husband's grandfather during the reign of King Edward VII.

The day before David and Millie were to arrive, Amanda and I walked the footpaths that crisscrossed the fields that had once been the Thorpe Beauchamp US Army Air Forces base, enjoying the trees, hedgerows, and sweet musky smell of autumn. These were my favorite walks, and it was especially lovely having Amanda tag along, spotting things of which she had previously been unaware.

The old airfield had been restored as fertile farmland; the wheat, barley, and oilseed rape had been harvested weeks earlier which meant most fields were already plowed and sown with winter wheat as the farmers waited for potatoes, beets, and other vegetables to continue ripening for several more weeks. The hedges were a-twitter with birds gorging themselves on the plump elder and bright red hawthorn berries, preparing themselves for the hardships of winter; I made a mental note that the time had come to gather berries to make my famous elderberry cordial, always a Christmas favorite. My mother had brought me up with this autumn routine when I was a child, and now that I was home I had restarted the tradition – for her sake as much as my own.

The landscape had matured massively since I was little. Back then agriculture was in the process of reclaiming the fields from their wartime role. The concrete had been broken up and hauled away to provide fill for the foundations of new buildings replacing those blitzed in London. The fields were then plowed and quickly became highly productive after lying fallow beneath the runways. Hedges were replanted and saplings set at odd intervals in the hedgerows had now grown into sturdy oaks, rowans, and ashes – the elms, alas, having disappeared when Dutch elm disease had swept Europe in the Sixties, one of the less pleasant imports from the New World.

Lounging under an oak tree's shade while taking a breather, we basked in the unexpected warmth of the autumn sun and shared a bottle of water. Amanda mused, "It's difficult to imagine this place alive with Flying Fortresses and noisy Americans yelling ceaselessly at one another, isn't it?"

I laughed. "If a time machine could take us back to those days we would be sitting in the middle of a runway!"

"It's hard to believe, isn't it?"

My thoughts exactly. I pointed to the cluster of decaying buildings at the far corner of the field near the rural road that meandered from Thorpe Beauchamp then wandered across the Fens vaguely in the direction of Peterborough. The control tower was still standing, having been thrown up in record time using the ugliest, cheapest Fletton bricks. Its asbestos roof had long since disappeared, and the whole structure together with a few ancillary buildings was fast becoming crumbling ruins.

"That's about all that's left," I told her. "While she protested vehemently when they were constructed in 1942, your grandmother got even more agitated when they tore down almost all the secondary buildings after the war; then some of the Nissen huts were moved elsewhere when the airfield was decommissioned."

"What's a Nissen hut... anything to do with Nissan cars?" my astonished daughter asked. Only then did it occur to me there was no reason she should know.

"Oh, darling, Nissan cars were made by the enemy, the Japanese," I chuckled. "I didn't see my first Nissan car until the early Sixties and it was driven by a distant cousin who was a car dealer. We all wondered whether such rattletraps would ever catch on. I wish I had been old enough to buy stock in the company in those days – Nissan cars were called Datsuns back then. Besides, Nissan cars have an 'A' in their spelling while Nissen huts have an 'E.'"

"Thanks for the history lesson, Mumsie," said Amanda with a sly smile, "but you haven't yet told me what a Nissen hut is."

"You've probably seen old corrugated metal buildings shaped like a huge half a barrel – in fact, Robert Wright at Home Farm had one until recently." She nodded. "That was a Nissen hut... prefabricated buildings that could be erected in a rush. Not very comfortable but serviceable as offices, messes, sleeping quarters, for meetings, and so forth. They were excruciatingly cold and damp during the winter and like roaster ovens in the summer sun."

My daughter shrugged and asked another question. "Which direction did the runways go?"

We got up and walked around as I showed her where the runways had been, and, depending on prevailing winds, which were the flight paths for most takeoffs and landings. She was immediately able to see that planes would inevitably fly directly over *Honeypot Hill*, whose white walls and red-tiled roof surrounded by trees and shrubs could be seen in the distance glistening in the sunshine.

Amanda laughed. "I'm sure Gran wasn't too pleased about that."

"Old timers still impishly tell me just how hopping mad she was," I half-laughed. "In a few weeks she went from having the most fabulous rural view across Fenland to having a ringside seat overlooking acres of concrete and mud, with a clutter of the ugliest buildings nestled in the midst. Planes came and went at all hours. Some of my earliest childhood memories were of an occasional plane taking off or coming in to land over the house… the noise was terrifying. I sometimes hid in the cupboard under the stairs where Gran kept her ancient vacuum cleaner."

Occasionally I had found myself chatting with some of the long-time inhabitants of the village, old men and women who back then had been young adults. They told me how the land had been requisitioned with no ifs, ands, or buts from the then landowner, the Earl of Lynn, a close friend of King George VI, who considered releasing it his patriotic duty – but *he* did not have to put up with the racket of takeoffs and landings at all hours. Besides, they would have commandeered his land whether he liked it or not, so it looked better to volunteer.

In October 1942, after the harvest was in and before plowing for winter wheat could begin, surveyors suddenly appeared with theodolites and measures; they were followed by American army engineers with heavy equipment and big vehicles far wider than narrow English roads could handle. Within days vegetation, trees, fences, and hedgerows were torn down. Despite a lot of rain, by New Year the initial wave of B-17s was flying in. Then began tens of thousands of landings and takeoffs right over *Honeypot Hill.*

"Your mother was like a fire-breathing dragoness," big old Bill Cartwright had told me over a drink at the Lamb and Flag. He shook his head and carried on in his rich East Anglian burr. "That was before she became chummy with some of the American guys."

Despite being eager to make friends old Bill had grunted, "For the longest time your mum refused to have anything to do with 'damned Yanks,' as she called them. She stayed away from the pub for months as it speedily became a favorite watering hole for GIs and the local folks who wanted to get to know them. When walking or out on her bike, it took forever for her to acknowledge their friendly greetings. By and large the Yanks were a cheerful bunch, very generous too."

As Amanda and I lay against the bole of a sixty-year-old oak tree staring into middle distance she said softly, "Rebecca Anne Johnson Lisle was a funny old woman, wasn't she, Sarah Charlotte Lisle Quinn?"

"Sweetie, she was young, desirable, good looking, and quite the social butterfly by all accounts. She also had a lot to worry about. As you know, by the time the Americans got here there had been the Blitz and other air raids, as well as three years of almost constant battlefield setbacks. She once told me that by late 1941 and early 1942 she was burying her head in the sand, no longer able to bear listening to radio news because it made her feel so ill – despite the BBC trying to put a positive propaganda spin on it. Her remedy was to ignore the wider world, then work and play at a frenetic pace."

"Tough times."

"Yes, my darling, more than we can understand. Food, fuel, clothing, and just about everything that made life worth living was getting scarcer, which just intensified gnawing anxieties. Folks around here knew all about London, Coventry, Bristol, Birmingham and the other cities that had been bombed, with ordinary people, women and children, homeless or killed by the thousand. Some had been turned into little more than refugees in their own country. When the Americans came on board in December 1941 there was a glimmer of hope after a long, dark, stormy night. Things didn't change immediately, but I understand that when Churchill went tootling off to Washington, DC, to spend Christmas with Franklin Roosevelt people were heartened to see something happening, but it was a close thing."

"But Gran didn't welcome the Americans?"

"I suppose not, and neither was she flattering about local women who, to use a popular word from that time, fraternized with American men."

"Fraternized?"

I laughed. "You can load that word with almost everything you like, girl, it was all probably true. Lots of Land Army girls conscripted to work on the farms adored GIs, dated, tumbled in the hay with them, and received stockings and often became pregnant as a reward. Both married and single girls succumbed."

"But Gran refused?"

"She never talked about it..."

We chattered amiably, a mother and daughter merely enjoying each other's company. The sun was warm and there was a gentle breeze. From the branches pigeons cooed while squadrons of swallows had gathered along telephone lines preparing for their annual commute to warmer climes. Blackbirds, chaffinches, goldfinches, yellowhammers, robins, and wrens all chattered away in the hedgerows, yet sixty years earlier this would have been the time of the afternoon when Flying Fortresses returning from their sorties would have been putting down their wheels on this very spot after a long day's work over Europe, their controllers and ground crews apprehensively worrying and wondering who would or would not make it home.

Hundreds of planes would have departed from the sixty-seven American airfields in Eastern England as the day had been breaking. They would have completed their daytime bombing raids, and then came the hazardous journey back, dodging the Luftwaffe who were determined to take down as many of them as possible. At the same time the RAF would have been getting ready to rain down terror on the Nazis during the night hours. Agitated senior US officers would have scanned the afternoon skies, chain-smoking Camel cigarettes, and then would gather information on the day's tally. During 1943, their first full year of daytime bombing, American casualty rates were often close to catastrophic. Yet, eventually the tenacity and might of the allied English-speaking peoples paid off.

I have a childhood memory of Mummy helping me into my little black wellington boots and overcoat, and then, trotting along as I held her hand, we joined a sizeable group of villagers at the end of the runway where we watched the last few planes set off home for the USA and waved them goodbye. Only a few GIs ever came back to visit, but they left a permanent mark on Thorpe Beauchamp.

As Amanda and I lounged in the sun, I idly wondered how many children I was at primary school with might have been the result of a hasty coupling in the back of a Jeep. Mother had made clear to Daddy that day the last Americans left just how relieved she was that the 'bloody Yanks' had at last gone, not least because the skies were quiet above her home for the first time in eight or nine years. 'Good riddance' were her precise words, but was that really what she meant?

Making our way home Amanda said, "Mumsie, I hope you don't mind, but I need to be back to London. I'm way behind on work, and you know how burdensome I find my sister-in-law."

We sauntered on in silence and then I sighed. "I just wish you two girls would get on better. She's nowhere near as deadly as you imagine."

Amanda shrugged. "Maybe, but she always looks down on me from aristocratic heights… and remember how impossible she was when I was one of her bridesmaids."

I conceded. "Yes, that was quite a performance – but even the nicest women have a tendency to be ferociously impossible as they prepare for their wedding day. Both of you said things that I'm sure you've since regretted."

More silence, then "I know, but I wish she wasn't a damned blue blood."

"You can't blame her for that, she didn't choose her parents."

"No, but…"

I took my daughter's hand. "Darling, you may be the one in our little family with left-wing leanings, but you can't blame Millie that her father was born an Earl; she had no more control over that than you have over your father and grandfather being engineers. Your political convictions may differ from David, Millicent, and myself, but don't let them tear the family apart."

"Hmph."

I linked my arm in hers as we approached the house. "Reconsider," I asked.

She was uncomfortably quiet then said, "Mumsie, darling, you know I love you to bits. You know I think David is an awesome businessman and wonderful brother, but, truth be told, Millie and I are chalk and cheese. If we are around each other too long God knows how intense the storm would be… Besides, Tristan Mountford emailed and asked if I would be his partner at a stuffy dinner tomorrow evening."

"When will I see you again?"

She grinned as we walked up the path toward the house. "I'd love to come back in a couple of weeks and see how far you have got with Gran's boxes."

I thanked her then and said, "You really don't want to see Millie at all, do you?" She made a face and shook her head. "Then why don't you get away before she and David arrive… we would probably all be happier."

"You are a brick, O Mother of Mine," she whispered, kissing my cheek. Amanda went up to pack her bag and after sharing a cup of tea I drove her to the train station, but not until I had extracted the promise that she would be back within the next couple of weeks. As I drove home I sighed as I wished my children were able to get on a little better.

Saturday, September 18, 2004 — Honeypot Hill, Thorpe Beauchamp

I was upset that Amanda did not stay because the weekend with David and Millie turned out not only to be fun but also unexpectedly wonderful. David and Millie had arrived late Friday night, and then on Saturday morning my son filled me in on the latest from the gallery; we went over the financials and how the next few months were shaping up in the context of our larger long-term business plan. That afternoon, while Millie excused herself in favor of lounging in the conservatory with a book, David came for a walk with me after which we went for dinner to my favorite restaurant in the shadow of the ancient cathedral in Ely. Our round table was in a quiet corner, affording some privacy.

Millicent was several years younger than David and Amanda and found her way into our life when I hired her to be a summer intern at The Quinn Galleries. Her academic credentials were solid if not stellar, but she was attractive, affable, well turned out, and had a reputation for hard work. When I interviewed her she was charming, and I sensed she had what it takes to succeed in the quirky world of retail art. She proved me right; I marveled at her qualities, as well as her knack for making everyone who came through our door feel special. When her internship ended and she had finished her degree I hired her on a permanent basis but was not aware that she had caught David's eye.

They had now been married six years, and Millie had become in every way her husband's partner and equal at the gallery, her people skills being a huge asset. She had also managed to soften David's rough edges and could lovingly deflate his sporadic bubbles of pomposity. They were a well-matched couple, in many ways a younger version of what we might have been if my late husband had lived.

While sipping coffee at the end of our meal David squirmed in his chair and gave the impression of awkwardness – a characteristic he had had since a little boy when something significant needed to be said.

Millie also read the signs. Her eyes sparkled as she looked into mine, reached for David's hand, and said, "Sarah… Mumsie… David and I were so looking forward to this weekend because something rather delightful has happened… by this time next year, God willing, you'll be a grandmother."

She grinned at her husband. He squeezed her hand, looking like that cat that got the cream. Her face was radiant, and I realized her youthful prettiness was turning into something more mature and lasting. Her face was framed by carefully tended honey-colored hair, blue eyes shone, her cheeks were flushed with happiness, and David was as puffed up as a rooster in a barnyard.

"Yes, Mother," he said softly, "isn't she clever. I have never loved Millie so much."

I sighed. "Oh, David, darling, you're so like your father."

He looked quizzical. "How do you mean, Mumsie?"

I leaned over the table and touched his cheek. "When I told him I was pregnant with you he was as delighted as you two are now! You would have thought no other woman had ever conceived a child – he tried to treat me like a piece of Dresden china." I got up, came around the table, gave Millie a cheek-to-cheek hug, and kissed her saying, "My darling Millie, I can't tell you how pleased I am for you – and the whole family... the next generation of gallery proprietors is on the way."

Millie had reached a point where in some ways she was closer to me than my own daughter. When she joined the business, she had been a little girl lost. Her elder sisters appeared innately more talented but, having been spoiled, had squandered their university years. Their present claim to fame was their regular appearance in the gossip pages. Millie had struggled academically, her consolation prize being a hard-earned place at an unfashionable university. She studied hard, eventually earning a reasonable degree in business administration, thus bringing with her vital skills to our family store.

Her father was one of a dying breed, a charmingly well-bred man who haunted his club and whose title opened doors to 'do something in the City.' Her mother was a barefaced snob who, having elbowed her way into this aristocratic family, made sure everyone knew she was a Countess. She doted on her elder daughters but treated Millie like Cinderella.

The Earl and Countess seldom seemed to think of their afterthought daughter, so it was not surprising that following marriage Millie had been fully absorbed into the Quinn clan, Amanda notwithstanding. Nearly thirty, after a few teething problems, she and David had established a secure, happy marriage. As the Chair of The Quinn Galleries I had insisted she become a full member of the board rather than just sitting at the table taking minutes. While her sisters played up to the paparazzi, she had made a life and career for herself, being respected by clients and staff alike. There was also a very soft spot for her in my heart.

I had not noticed while hugging my daughter-in-law that David now stood behind me; as I turned to return to my chair I walked straight into his arms. Taking my hands in his he said, "Mumsie, I want to tell you what you sometimes told me when I was that nervous little boy – you are the bestest in all the world. You are the bestest mother a man could have. Thank you for raising me and for entrusting the gallery to me, I just wish Dad was here now."

At that moment I would have done anything in time and eternity for Timothy to be there; the scars left by his sudden death still occasionally ached. I had never had the chance to say sorry and goodbye.

• • • • • • •

Timothy and I had met during our first year at Cambridge in the mid-Sixties and had fallen impossibly in love while flirting with the hippie fringe of university life. Despite parental misgivings we married before our final year – our first home being a squalid flat in a down-at-heel neighborhood just off Cambridge's Newmarket Road. Over the Easter vacation, while preparing for finals, our sex life intensified and we fumbled the birth control with the result that, by exam time in late May, morning sickness prevented me from getting the sort of degree of which I would have been capable. Despite this we graduated reasonably well, and as I went into nesting mode Timothy joined the family business – Quinn Gallery and Antiques as it was then known.

Parenthood rapidly turned Timothy and me into adults; my father regularly crowed that it was the making of us, Mummy always nodding energetically in agreement. As students we had half-heartedly experimented with drugs and occasionally consumed too much alcohol, but when we moved to London and a nicer flat in the Swiss Cottage area babies and the demands of real life almost overnight turned us into health and fitness fanatics.

House prices back then were nowhere near as iniquitous as now, which meant that after three or four years we were a couple with two small children who had managed to put down the deposit on a solid but run down Victorian pile at the scruffier end of Belsize Park, a house requiring years of work to make it a comfortable family home. To keep himself fit and save money Timothy always cycled the few miles to work. At weekends the house became our labor of love and a regular bone of contention. We were almost at the end of renovations when one morning, in the gloomiest part of winter and after a particularly bruising battle, Tim slammed out of the house, jumped on his bike, taking out his temper on the busy road between home and the recently rebranded The Quinn Galleries. I went to soak in the bath hoping warm water would help me relax.

Wednesday, February 14, 1979, turned into my worst Valentine's Day ever. Just after ten that morning as I was stretching out my toilette the doorbell rang. I tried to ignore it, but whoever it was kept ringing until finally I pulled on my old terry cloth dressing gown and stumbled downstairs muttering curses, only to open the door to a male and a female police officer.

"Mrs. Quinn?" the woman asked.

I nodded. "Is there anything wrong?" I asked, this awful upheaval starting deep inside.

"I'm WPC Charlotte Johnson," answered the woman, introducing herself. "May we come in?"

In the sitting room, I perched myself on the edge of my chair, shivering with cold and anxiety as the male officer, PC Donald Gascoyne, lowered his voice and said as gently as he could, "I'm sorry, Mrs. Quinn. There is no easy way to tell you this, but this morning as he was cycling down Portland Place your husband, Randolph Timothy Quinn, was hit by a delivery van when the driver, attempting a sudden U-turn, did not look where he was going."

"Where is he now?" I gasped. "I have to get there."

"Sarah," Charlotte Johnson said softly reaching out for my hand, "your husband was dead by the time the ambulance got him to the Middlesex Hospital."

A widow at thirty-three, from now on it was my job to raise David and Amanda on my own. If that was not enough, I had hardly begun juggling home and what had been Tim's job at The Quinn Galleries when my father-in-law, who was orienting me into the business, unexpectedly suffered a major heart attack. He was game to get back to the gallery as soon as he could, but both his doctors and his wife persuaded him that this was likely to be a death sentence. While he continued to provide occasional helpful advice, his early retirement made me feel as if I was very much on my own.

At Cambridge I had studied History and the History of Art; having worked occasionally at the gallery I knew enough not to make a complete idiot of myself, yet with tons of help from all sorts of people we managed to pick up the pieces – but it was a close run thing. I *had* to do it because my children needed feeding, clothing, and educating. Back then I supposed I had only taken the position until we found an appropriate Managing Director. Never did I think the eleven-year-old boy who was determined to walk behind his father's coffin at the funeral would turn out twenty years later to be the one who would be my successor.

• • • • • • •

Recovering from David's kind accolade, Millie then stretched out her hand and took mine. "Your face told me you are thinking of Timothy, Mumsie."

I nodded, rummaging for a tissue. Millie knew more than most how much my husband had meant to me, having in the most sensitive way gradually gathered information about Tim, how we had met, and why our son's first name was Randolph and not David! (His grandfather who had founded the business had been Randolph and thus a silly family tradition had been born). Every Valentine's Day she sent me a little card remembering me on what she knew to be a difficult day.

She grasped better than anyone how, because our parting disagreement that February morning had been unresolved, there were the hidden scars of unfinished business. This may be why I still wear wedding and engagement rings and have, despite opportunities, never remarried. Millie's own upbringing as an almost unwanted child gave her sensitivities many others lacked. Perhaps this added to Amanda's disdain.

I gave Millie her first real job at the bottom of the totem pole, mentored her in the business, became her friend, and even introduced her to my son. In due course I would be her mother-in-law. Sometimes when working together late on some project we would exchange confidences; she never betrayed my trust, nor I hers.

Sent off to boarding school in North Wales because she was in the way, as far as her parents were concerned she was a colorless drone. No wonder the girl had been wrestling with issues of self-confidence when she found her way into our little clan.

What her family had not bothered to take notice of was her resolve, her ability to get on with people, and her enviable knack of making friends. She enjoyed creating genuine and lasting relationships with clients, which brought in new clients, all the time improving our balance sheet. Millie loved getting to know not just the works of art we were selling but also what was in the minds of the artists who created them. She could then explain a complex picture or sculpture, enticing potential buyers to dig deeper and see what the artist was getting at, until they fell in love with it. Millie's star was rising, yet she kept her head down and the paparazzi never discovered that the Earl and Countess's youngest daughter was entirely more interesting than her narcissistic siblings.

Her gentle stubbornness was a prerequisite for handling David. My wretched son had been so full of himself that he left university imagining he was God's gift to women and that his work was so fascinating that he was a so-called 'chick magnet.' Those years he spent late nights hanging out in the right places in the company of what he considered the right women, finally hitting rock bottom when an attractive but astonishingly silly young thing made an utter fool of him. He even contemplated running away, taking a year out, sailing round the world as part of the crew of a tall ship, or the like.

Millie did not throw herself at him but scrutinized David from a polite distance. He treated her amicably but had little interest in the runt of the Earl's litter! She was good-looking but never as glamorous as the willowy creatures who fascinated him. Rather than being obvious, Millie shrewdly provided opportunities for him to get to know her better, often volunteering that extra pair of hands when they were needed. One evening David was at my house putting his dirty clothes in the washing machine and enjoying home cooking. In the course of the conversation he mentioned nonchalantly how well he thought Millicent Fitzpatrick-Evans was coming along.

"She's marvelous," I commented as I tossed a salad. Then he did what he always did when not yet ready to talk about something; he immediately changed the subject.

At the end of the afternoon some weeks later David sheepishly sidled into my office. I looked up and asked him what was wrong.

He shrugged. "I've asked Millicent if she would like to accompany me to that event at the Tate next week. She made the lame excuse that she might have something else on."

I put down my pen and stared at him. "So what do you think that means?"

He shrugged, slumping down in one of the comfortable chairs by my desk. "I guess it means she doesn't like me."

I knew better. Getting up, I quietly closed the door then sat down beside him. "My son, have you ever watched the movie *Gigi*?"

"I've never even heard of it."

"It came out when I was quite young, 1959 I think, so that doesn't really surprise me. It is about a dashing man about town in *Belle Epoque* Paris who chased women left, right, and center. Gradually it dawned on him that the little girl, Gigi, granddaughter of a longtime family friend, had grown gorgeous right under his nose and was now not only a captivating young woman, but he enjoyed her company far more than the vaunted clothes horses he'd been escorting around town."

"So?"

"So, my boy, you should be ashamed about the silly shallow

women you've been wasting time and money on. They don't think you're anything special, more an easy meal ticket. Meanwhile here's a young woman who's been waiting patiently for the penny to drop. You are an idiot, Davey. Millie is worth a dozen of the girls you have been breaking your neck to snare. She'd make you a wonderful wife and is exactly what this gallery needs."

David looked nonplussed. "You've got to be kidding. You're laying it on because she's your little protégée, and you think it would be nifty for her to marry me."

"Think that if you like but keep an eye on Lady Millicent Fitzpatrick-Evans, she will yet surprise you." Then I smiled. "You are so like your father… he was such a perceptive man but would regularly miss the obvious as it stared him in the face. Persevere with Millie, she's worth the effort."

Almost a year to the day later, at a modest ceremony in the village church near the Fitzpatrick-Evans' stately pile, Millicent happily discarded her aristocratic double-barreled name, becoming plain Mrs. Millie Quinn. She never had liked the courtesy title of 'Lady' that went with being an Earl's daughter. Now, as we sat around the table after David and Millie's baby announcement, my son looked across at me and said, "Mother, regularly you tell me that I'm just like my father. I wish I'd known him better…"

"So do I, my darling, so do I."

"Well," David continued, raising his glass and looking heavenward, "to my father. I wish you were here, Dad, because I'd love to introduce you to your grandson…"

We drank and then Millie chuckled. "Granddaughter."

I agreed by giving Millie a big wink. Her hand went to her mouth and giggles erupted, which got me going too!

Monday, September 20, 2004 — Honeypot Hill, Thorpe Beauchamp

    The lovely old cherry wood table in my dining room had belonged to my Lisle grandparents and when fully opened could comfortably seat twelve people. I had put in both the extenders so I could spread a large selection from the attic boxes over its surface. This gave me a better idea of just what my mother had salted away. David had spent Sunday morning heaving most of the junk from the attic for disposal in one way or another; he also helped me get the boxes and suitcase into the dining room.

    A contented couple returned to London around teatime on Sunday afternoon, leaving me feeling warm fuzzies for my first grandchild; but even as I celebrated there was this sad ache that the little one's grandfather would never see the child. Sentimentally I wondered if perhaps he had met him or her already. Before David and Millie departed, my son promised that before Christmas he would get the attic space completely sorted out, clear and tidy.

I did not often weep over Timothy these days, but that night lying in bed thinking over the weekend tears flooded my eyes; only after I had put out the light again and was trying to get to sleep did a long ignored emotional dam burst. How I wished with my whole heart that he were here for the good news, he would have been proud.

Waking on Monday morning I discovered that the bedtime upset coupled with the darkness of the night had totally flushed that sense of wellbeing from my system, its place being taken by a sense of foreboding that refused to evaporate. So instead of pouncing on the boxes first thing as I had originally intended, I put it off with chores that needed doing, like sheets to wash and beds to make. Finally, I sat down at the table hoping my late morning cup of coffee would give me renewed vigor while persuading me that I was imagining things.

The first hour into the task, I laid out what seemed relevant, sorting everything into a theoretical chronological order. Then, after an even stronger cup of coffee and chatting on the phone with Millie, who called to thank me for the lovely weekend, in trepidation I set out to climb the mountain of papers and other odds and ends scattered across the surface of the table.

Why had the seemingly irrelevant been stored alongside the obviously important?

It did not seem significant that in early 1944 my mother blew months of clothing coupons and eight guineas, a small fortune in those wartime years, on a cocktail dress at Pettigrew and Robertson in Cambridge. Mother was infatuated by lovely clothes, but I wondered why she needed an expensive new cocktail dress in the middle of a war – and how she had managed to discover one given clothing shortages. Were not stockings in such short supply that women were prepared to go to almost any lengths to get hold of them? Then why keep the yellowing booklet giving advice on caring for the family car during wartime or details of birth control – although with Daddy away fighting why did she need it? I suspect I was in denial.

After another little break and a couple more phone calls I worked assiduously until mid-afternoon, keeping hunger at bay by grazing on weekend leftovers. I was about to call it quits and take a bracing walk before it was too dark when I came across an unusual envelope that had somehow wedged itself into a wad of bank statements.

Opening it I found a short message:

Somewhere in Norfolk
February 18th, 1944

Rebecca, Honey,

We need to take a rain check on the tea dance at the Savoy and our weekend in London. The ship took very heavy flak as we were leaving the target area around lunchtime, and it was one heck of a job for Danny and me to get the old girl back to friendly soil.

We put her down at the first airfield we came to and it will take days for the folks here to get her airworthy again. Danny, Marvin, and myself elected to stay with our battered old bird. Jerry Jankowski, our tail gunner, got shot up quite badly and picked up a touch of frostbite. He is now in the local hospital wishing the nurses were younger and better looking. They tell me it looks worse than it really is, but I suspect it is his ticket Stateside. I am sending the others back to Thorpe Beauchamp in a truck; as Snuffy Smith will be cycling past your house on his way to his girlfriend's place, he will put this in your mailbox.

Sorry, sweetheart, I know you were looking forward to it as much, if not more, than I was, buying that gorgeous dress for the occasion.

It was quite an ordeal today, so I'm going over to the officers' mess to drink myself paralytic – other than going to bed with you I can't think of any better way to deal with my nerves.

Your very special friend,

Chuck

I sat back in my chair and wrapped my arms around myself. "Oh dear God... Mother, how could you?" was all I could say – and I kept repeating these words. Leaving everything as it was I threw on my coat and fled from the house, walking until long after dark; I arrived back with muddy feet and having cried my eyes dry while letting myself be soaked to the skin by heavy rainfall.

Wednesday, September 29, 2004 — Honeypot Hill, Thorpe Beauchamp

"Good God, Mother, you look dreadful."

I woke with a start. It was almost dark. For days I had lived like a hermit with my nerves permanently on edge, sleep having been almost an impossibility. That lunchtime I had taken a short walk across the fields, wandering around the one remaining Nissen hut on the site of the old air base. Was this the place where they had first set eyes on one another? Getting back home I made myself a cup of tea, which was now sitting stone cold on the small table beside my chair. My dozing had been abruptly interrupted by the light coming on, and I opened my eyes to see the tip of my daughter's nose barely inches from the end of my own.

"Oh, you gave me a shock, darling," I gasped, my heart missing a beat and my hand going to my chest. "You could have given me a coronary."

"Mumsie, I was getting ever so worried about you. Every time we've talked on the phone these last couple of weeks you've sounded, well, not quite right... Finally, I managed to talk my boss into letting me have a few days away to finish writing a research paper, so I've brought my work with me and wanted to give you a nice surprise... but, well, you look ghastly."

She did not have to tell me. Since discovering that little note my life had been spinning out of control, and the implications of the arithmetic was impinging upon me. I had hardly eaten and was scared even to look at myself in the mirror. Just that morning it had been impossible to disguise the black shadows around my eyes, and clothes that a week or two before had fitted a little too snugly were now hanging off me. The whole secure bubble of my life had been burst.

As Amanda closed the curtains, forever a neat-nik, she exclaimed over the untidiness of the dining room, cluttered as it was with stacks of papers and items from the boxes and suitcase. I had spent even more hours in the attic unsuccessfully searching for anything else my mother might have secreted away. Further hours were then spent in the garage with my father's filing cabinets where I found notebooks and letters that had been half-helpful and I had thought might shed some light on the enigma of Rebecca Lisle's early married life.

Each night following that initial discovery I had been dropping into bed exhausted, but sleep evaded me and I would just toss and turn. I found myself wondering if everything had been left in the attic as they were because there were things she longed to tell me, or which she wished to hide from me. Had she missed the opportunity to say anything years ago but then had not been able to bring herself to talk of at the end – was this a deliberate scavenger hunt? She knew me better than anyone and must have realized how dangerous it would be for such a tsunami to break over me. Mother loathed any kind of discomfort, so perhaps she left things as she did knowing she would be dead by the time there was fallout.

Amanda marched officiously into the kitchen and was soon

clattering around. Shivering as I arose from my chair, I wrapped my beloved blue shawl around my shoulders and went to the doorway. She was checking cupboards and refrigerator while exclaiming about the dirty dishes in the sink.

"What on earth have you been eating for the last couple of weeks?" she demanded. "There's nothing here?"

I made a face. "I haven't been at all hungry, darling."

She walked over to where I leaned against the door frame and reaching down put her finger in the waistband of my slacks. "When I was with you the other week you were complaining that your clothes were far too tight." She then thrust her whole hand inside my waistband and tugged at it, declaring, "Now you appear to have shed at least half a dozen centimeters from your waist."

Being a product of the days of Imperial linear measure it took a moment for me to convert that into inches while she stared at me, a worried look in her eye. She then gently put her hands on my cheeks. "There's no color in your face, your eyes look as if they are bruised, and this is the first time I can remember seeing your hair so unkempt that the gray is showing."

I gave her a wan smile. "Guilty, as charged."

"Oh, Mumsie," she whispered, wrapping her arms around me. Before I knew it I was in tears – this was the first time anyone had touched me in days. Finding those damned boxes in the attic had been like falling down a deep dank well-shaft and being unable to get out.

After feeding us from the few scraps she had brought from her own fridge, Amanda supervised my going to bed; knowing she was here helped me sleep a little, although I was still roaming the house by four in the morning. After she was up I listened while Amanda phoned her senior colleague exaggeratedly reporting the state in which she had found her mother. She told him there was nothing pressing at the office, that she had brought a pile of work with her, and although the Internet connection wasn't great at her mother's home she was accessible; besides, it would be irresponsible to leave me by myself at the moment.

There was obviously a sharp response to which she replied and an edge in her voice. "Oh, I have a carful of those research documents with me, I won't be frittering away my time – but I have to get Mother to the doctor for a checkup." Her manner suggested this was the rather awful man who at that moment happened to be her boss, a bachelor who knew nothing of the responsibilities adult daughters so often take on when parents are ailing.

My children had started calling me Mumsie soon after their father died. Only when in formal company or talking to people outside the family, like the doctor's surgery, did they revert to Mummy or Mother. Millie had picked up on this habit when she married David, and I had already made up my mind that my grandchildren would call me Mumsie, too, as I was not sure Grandma or Granny or Gran quite suited me.

That afternoon we found ourselves in the doctor's surgery. Dr. Eva Baumann had been able to work me in due to an unexpected cancellation but only after Amanda had become unnecessarily strident with her receptionist. I was furious at my daughter's bad mannered tactic. She had steamrollered her way to an appointment, and I bit off her head as if she was a naughty child, insisting on an apology for both Karen, the receptionist, and Eva.

"I'm sorry, doctor," she said in that innocent little girl lost voice she perfected years ago when she was in a fix, "but as you can see Mummy's not in good shape, and I was worried."

Eva and her husband, Bruno, hailed from Bavaria in southern Germany, not far from Munich; for years he had been an eminent figure in some obscure specialty at Addenbrooke's, the university hospital in Cambridge. They had lived in Britain for the whole of their married life, their children had been born here, and they had moved to Thorpe Beauchamp when their offspring had flown the nest. In the last couple of years Eva, a general practitioner, had joined the local medical practice.

She turned to me, took off her attractive red-framed reading glasses, and said with kind but Teutonic sternness, "So, what have you been up to, Sarah, my dear. You're usually such a together lady?"

I had never before felt embarrassed with Eva. Perhaps I was anxious because my father had been in North Africa fighting Rommel, and on the opposite side had been Eva's father at the second and decisive Battle of El Alamein, where he was seriously injured, was captured, and spent the duration as a prisoner of war. We had talked about it some months earlier at a social gathering, but now I felt so ridiculously self-conscious because it was almost as if I was intruding on our parents' war.

Eva carefully checked me out finding nothing appreciably wrong, yet constantly repeating that a woman my age should be a bit more responsible in the way she looks after herself. She prescribed vitamins and some sleeping tablets, recommending regular healthy meals and exercise, then praised Amanda for staying on for a few days.

"Oh, Sarah," Eva said as we prepared to leave, "at Janice's house a few months ago you told me you would walk with me round the perimeter of what used to be the airfield – we haven't done that yet, let's make a date to do it."

I almost lost it when Eva said this and was in floods of tears by the time we got into the car. I was glad Amanda was driving. During the next couple of days I slumped, letting my daughter make decisions and keep the household running. Having hinted to Amanda the nature of my discoveries, she did not return to that business but instead made sure I was cuddled, exercised, fed, watered, and sent to bed at a reasonable hour as if I were a naughty child.

A couple of evenings later, after dinner as I was dozing in my chair, I heard Amanda getting adamant with her brother on the phone.

"Damn it, David, she's your mother just as much as she's mine, for God's sake…" There was a pause as he obviously broke in, then she became more assertive. "…and you wouldn't have had that wretched business to worry about if it hadn't been for her. You owe this to her, you effing bastard."

There was a pause and then she spoke again. "Look, she's spent most of the last couple of weeks worrying over things she had found in those wretched boxes from Gran's attic. She has been uncovering information that has upset her even more than when Daddy died, if that's possible..." An interruption. "No, I don't know every detail, I'm not entirely aware of everything that is eating at her, but I mean to go through some of the papers scattered over the dining room table this evening."

At that point, as the telephone row between my two irate children escalated, I quietly rose from my chair, slipped into the dining room, gathered the documents that told the heart of the story, went upstairs to my little office, and locked them in one of my desk drawers to which only I had the key. I was not yet ready for the whole family to know everything. Then I went off to bed where Amanda found me, deciding to dose me with some new 'improved' sleeping tablets she had somehow got hold of.

Friday, October 1, 2004 – Honeypot Hill, Thorpe Beauchamp

"Hello, Mother, I've brought you a cup of tea." A male voice came echoing from what seemed a great distance, breaking into the fog of seemingly endless sleep.

I opened my eyes as the curtains were being drawn, revealing the insipid light of a dreary autumn day. "David, what on earth are you doing here at this time in the morning?"

He laughed. "Oh, David, how lovely to see you…"

I smiled sheepishly as I hoisted myself up in bed. "I'm sorry, darling, you've taken me by surprise."

He sat down on the bed and handed me my tea.

"What time is it?" I asked.

He looked at his watch. "Oh, just after three…"

"In the afternoon?"

"It wouldn't be light, neither would you see me here, if it was three in the morning," he joked. Then continued, "Amanda and Millie are gabbing in the kitchen, and I was commanded to deliver a cup of tea, because that is the only thing I am useful for."

"Good grief, I've slept away a whole day." My brain was feeling vague and fuzzy.

He gave me a quizzical little grin that so reminded me of his father. "Well, Mumsie, you have that darned sister of mine so well trained. She read the riot act on the phone last night and stipulated that if I didn't come she'd do something so bloodcurdling that there would be no more grandchildren. But what she told me has me worried. We made sure the gallery is covered for the weekend, then Millie and I headed out of town before weekend traffic on the M11 reached its usual Friday afternoon standstill. Millie and Amanda are now like a couple of cats circling one another and trying to be nice."

I sighed as the warm liquid quenched my thirst. "I do wish those two could get on better."

David shrugged. "So do I. I can't tell you how many times I feel trapped in this feud between two of the three women I love most in the world... I don't think it actually has anything to do with Millicent having an aristocratic background and Amanda being incapable of abiding what she considers to be a life of unwarranted privilege. I'm sorry to say this, but I think it is more to do with you taking Millie under your wing at the gallery – and Mandy Pandy being jealous."

I sighed. Things had to be bad for him to revert to his childhood name for his sister. She was obviously driving him up the wall. He had evidently had enough.

I sighed. "Maybe, but Millie was such a lost little soul. I'd go so far as saying that her supposedly advantaged background meant growing up with something akin to child abuse."

He looked wanly at me. "You've told me that before, and you're right. There's little doubt they spent time and money on the Ugly Sisters, and what a bad investment that has turned out to be."

"Is that what you are calling them now?" I gasped.

"Well, they are, aren't they? Millie doesn't like me to talk in those terms…"

"You're dead right about that, Quinn," came Millie's voice as she walked into my bedroom. "You have been utterly impossible all day. I've a good mind to make you to do at least fifty push-ups."

David's face instantly turned beet red as he looked across at his wife standing hands on hips, wearing a white roll-neck sweater and jeans, but unsuccessful in her attempt to look ferocious. "I'm sorry, darling, but they *are* the Ugly Sisters, and doesn't that makes you Cinderella?"

Millie faked a braying laugh. "Flattery will get you nowhere, Quinn."

He smiled, about to say something more when, looking at her face, he thought better of it.

She chuckled, walked to the bed, sat down beside me, leaned over and gave me a lovely kiss. Taking the cup from my hands she put it down on the bedside table, kicked off her shoes, and curled up beside me with arms around my neck, purring softly, "I'm so worried about you, Mumsie."

Wrapping my arms around her as she nestled against me I replied, "Sweetheart, I'm worried about me, too, but I'm also anxious about you and your baby."

I was glad that by the time Amanda joined the gathering in my bedroom Millie was only sitting on the bed holding my hand.

"Mumsie, you've been quite a sleepy head," my daughter laughed. "It's so unlike you. You're usually up with the lark."

I suspect my eyes twinkled a little as I responded, "I'm not sure whether larks are early risers at this time of the year… besides you're to blame. How many of those sleeping tablets did you give me?"

She grinned. "I texted a doctor friend in London and she told me what she thought might be a good dose to keep you from wandering around the house in the wee small hours; yesterday evening that's what I gave you – I'm surprised you didn't notice. You needed the seventeen hours sleep you have had, didn't you?"

"Bravo, Amanda," Millie praised. "Someone has to take responsibility for this woman's health."

Millicent Quinn was trying her level best with her sister-in-law. I hoped sometime she would get more than the tight-lipped look she received. Amanda has always had a bossy streak, but during recent years of striving with a career in the dog-eat-dog arena of academia, she had shed too much of her innate generosity. I could identify from her response to Millie one reason there had been such a revolving door of men through her life. I prayed to God my girls could sort out their differences.

"David," I bade when I discovered they had yet to think about food for the evening. "Slip over to Harry Martin's farm shop and get one of his free range ready-prepared chickens for dinner, oh, and maybe some new potatoes."

Glad to escape, he kissed my forehead and did as he was told. As the door slammed I managed a giggle and said to the girls, "That gets rid of him for at least half an hour; men accuse women of gossiping, but he and Harry are capable of talking forever about rugby and their beloved Northampton Saints and what might be England's chances in the Six Nations and the rest of international rugby this season, so we can have a nice chat while I wallow."

Without needing to be asked Amanda, still determined to mother me, slipped to the bathroom and started running the bath while I pattered down the hallway to the other toilet, before being supervised by my daughter as I lowered myself into the scented water as if I was already in my dotage. Meanwhile, Millie went downstairs, found a bottle of white wine in the fridge, and came up bearing a tray with cheese, nibbles, two stem glasses with wine, and a glass of water for herself.

By the time David arrived home, gales of giggles and female laughter emanated from the bathroom so that when he tapped on the door his sister told him in no uncertain terms this was a testosterone-free zone.

Millie shook her head knowingly and said, *sotto voce*, "That is not the right way to get David to do as he's told."

I smiled, "Which is probably why these two siblings have always loved each other but can be the most vicious fighters."

"Men," my daughter had muttered angrily, slamming the door in his face, a move designed to further offend. Millie winked at me, then slipped out to talk to her husband. There were quiet voices followed by a girlish titter; having calmed the savage beast, he did as he was told, went downstairs and began preparing the evening meal.

"My goodness, Millie," I gasped. "You have him well trained."

She smiled beatifically. "You prepared the ground when he was young, I'm reaping the benefits."

Amanda scowled but found it impossible to maintain the visage of a thundercloud for long. We were soon chattering away again while David got the chicken in the oven, then sat morosely watching the evening news. Letting my hair down with the girls was the best tonic imaginable.

• • • • • • •

As we were finishing our evening meal around the kitchen table, David's curiosity finally got the better of him. "Why this royal summons, Mother?"

I gave a little grin, then replied, "Sweetheart, I didn't summon you. Blame your sister for that; but I'm glad she did… if only for the lovely evening we're having together."

"But she must have had some reason for calling the clan from the four winds," David answered, turning to look at his sister.

"Don't be so ridiculous, Davey," Amanda retorted. "When I got here the other evening Mumsie was in a terrible state and not taking care of herself, so I got frightened. Intuition told me she needed us just as much we needed her when Daddy died."

I reached out and put my hand on my son's forearm. "David, darling, I'm over the moon Amanda got hold of you and Millicent. I've had the worst couple of weeks I can remember. To have all of you around the table, including the little one…"

"What little one?" Amanda blurted out.

Millie smiled at her sister-in-law, reached across and took her hand and motioned with her eyes to David to explain the meaning of my statement.

David reddened. "When we were here the other week we'd literally just found out that Millie's pregnant. We told Mumsie but were going to wait a few more weeks before telling anyone else just in case anything went wrong."

"We haven't even told my family anything, Amanda, so you haven't been left out," Millie added. Amanda looked astonished at the very idea of her brother being capable of fatherhood and hurt that she had been left out.

Having a shrewd sense an emotional scene might be brewing I told them, "Look, girls and boy, we've had enough excitement for one day. I am so, so appreciative you're all here, and thank you, David and Millie, for taking several days away from the gallery to come and visit this feeble old woman."

"Now you're being stupid," David gasped. "You're not yet properly old – and the last thing in the world I would call a lioness like you is feeble."

I shrugged. "Well, I'm hardly a youngster, and going through all your grandmother's documents has been traumatic enough to age me at least twenty years. I've been discovering things that have upset me every bit as much as your father's death. An earthquake has shaken what I once thought was my life's sure foundation." I paused, swallowing back tears, then went on. "But let's gather as a family tomorrow morning and I'll lay out the facts."

We all cleared the table, stacked the dishwasher, and prepared the kitchen for the morning. I could see Amanda was barely holding herself together. When all was done she said goodnight and went to her room. I looked at David and Millie and shook my head. "I am sorry, you hadn't told me it was a secret."

"It wasn't really," Millicent replied. "It's just that I have two girlfriends who told the whole world but within weeks had miscarriages. I wanted to be sure our child is well locked in place before making it public… I wanted you to know because you're David's mother and because you've been far more of a mother to me than, well, you know."

"I shouldn't have let the cat out of the bag, but I thought you would have probably told everyone else, not only me. My mind has been on too many other things."

Millie came and hugged me. "Don't fret, Mumsie. No harm done."

I shook my head. "I hope not, but you know how fiercely competitive Amanda is. She may be a career woman, but she's always longed for children."

"Well," growled David, "She shouldn't chase away eligible men."

I made a warning face at him. He took the hint and said no more.

We chatted a little longer, then, a few minutes after I had locked the doors and David and Millie had gone up, I went upstairs and listened at Amanda's door. It seemed quiet, but as I was turning to leave there were muffled sobs. It was quiet for a moment, then more sobs. I tapped on the door, heard her groan, and decided to interpret that as an invitation to come in.

Amanda was curled up in a fetal position on the bed, wearing a pair of powder blue cotton pajamas. I went and lay beside her, wrapping my arms around her.

"Oh, Mumsie," she choked, nestling against me.

"Are you upset because Millie didn't tell you, or are you upset because you're jealous, or is there another reason?" I whispered, stroking her long auburn hair.

There was a seemingly endless silence until, finally, she propped herself up on an elbow and dabbed her eyes with some soggy tissues. I gave her a fresh Kleenex from the box on the night stand so she could blow her nose.

"It was another reason," Amanda finally responded in a tiny little voice.

"Go on."

"You're probably going to hate me for this, which is one of the reasons I've never said anything." She was as wary as a cat. Then she moaned, tears dribbling down her cheeks; for a moment she was lost for words. At last she whispered, "Do you remember several years ago when I was so utterly objectionable that we were out of touch for a while and I didn't want to talk to you?"

I nodded, remembering only too well, already sensing what she might say next. Everything had seemed wonderful, and then she became downright uncommunicative, holding me at arm's length. Without warning she disappeared off to France, eventually sending me a postcard saying she was doing research. Instinct told me something else was going on, that it probably had to do with a man, and one of whom I would disapprove.

"Well, I was sort of living with Julian and accidentally fell pregnant. A big bit of me was delighted," she muttered in a snuffling sigh. "I've always, always wanted to be a mother, and even if it was on the wrong side of the blanket that dream was coming true. The idea of carrying a baby obliterated all other dreams and ambitions. But Julian was furious – even accusing me of trying to blackmail him into marriage. In a desperate attempt to hold onto him I had… I had…" She could not finish the sentence.

"You had the pregnancy terminated?"

"Oh, Mumsie, after all you've taught me, how could I have been so hardhearted? I had thought your rigid views on the sanctity of life were so old-fashioned and narrow-minded, something to do with your generation, until I did *that* to my child. I tried to dismiss it as disposing of unwanted tissue that had for a time inadvertently become part of me… but I've cried buckets over that little scrap ever since. I've steered away from children, given up babysitting for friends, and made it impossible for any man worth his salt to get too close. Mumsie, darling, I've been eaten up with guilt, and now David and Millie's news has brought it all back."

I took her in my arms as if she was herself a baby, held her close, and we wept together for the child and grandchild that had never had a chance. While I had had a shrewd notion something unpleasant might have happened a year or two back, there is a difference between sensing and knowing. Yet another emotional whammy was being thrown at me, and as my stomach churned I wondered how much more I could take.

"What happened with Julian?" I finally asked.

"Filthy bastard," she muttered from between clenched teeth.

I had only met Julian a few times, the last being when he accompanied Amanda to her grandmother's final birthday party. I said nothing at the time but did not like him one little bit. He was charming, shallow and self-absorbed – spurning anyone who thought differently from himself, especially conservative countrywomen like me. I am sure some of the distance between Amanda and myself had been because he disdained a business like ours which served an affluent and influential clientele – reinforcing Amanda's left wing scorn of us.

"What did the bastard do?" I asked, my own dislike of the man echoing her words.

"I paid for the summer together in France with that little bit of money I get from the gallery. While I mourned alone in this dreary rented apartment in a depressing corner of Paris, he was not going to allow me to slow him down. Only after he told me bye-bye did I find out he had slept with several questionable women without using protection. I killed my child for him, and in return he treated me like filth – but maybe I deserved it. He could charm birds from the trees and had this obnoxious gift of being able to beguile a woman out of her underwear. He was a repellent little alley cat. Thank God he moved to Australia... If some woman has the sense to push him off the Sydney Harbour Bridge, I'd pay my own way to Australia to be star witness for the defense at her trial."

"Why have you never told me this before?" I asked.

"Oh, Mumsie, I was too ashamed. I didn't want you to know the mess I was making. Neither did I want you to know how much I had come to loathe Julian… and myself for opening the door to him. I may look as if I am a together kind of female on the right trajectory, but it's all an act. I'm ever so lonely. If I could start over I would do a lot very differently."

"Doing what?"

She snuggled close. "Mother darling, I guess I'm now mature enough to say that, having discovered I can survive and prosper in the big, bad world of careers and academia, deep down I want more, which means I want to be more like you."

Tears were the only legitimate response to such a compliment.

A little while later, as I was getting into my own bed, there was a light tap on the door and Amanda's head poked around it. "Can I come and sleep with you tonight like I used to when I was a little girl?"

I said nothing, just patted the empty space beside me. She scampered across the room like the child she had once been, hopped under the covers, and cuddled up beside me. Utterly exhausted she was soon asleep. Meanwhile, having slept for the best part of the day, I merely dozed, lulled by my daughter's gentle breathing.

It may have been two or three hours later when I was aroused by the bedroom door opening again, and then Millie was whispering in my ear.

"Mumsie, can I spend the night with you, please. David's snoring like a pig. I can't sleep with the racket he is making." She then saw Amanda and whispered, "Oh."

"Don't worry about her, sweetie, it's a good thing I have a decent-sized bed." I moved into the middle, lifted the covers, and she snuggled up on the other side of me. How ironic, I thought, my daughter and my daughter-in-law who had been daggers drawn now sharing the same bed – perhaps some good might come of all this.

I was up very early in the morning, leaving these two sleeping beauties to discover their proximity to one another when they awoke. A while later, I was sitting in the kitchen with my cup of tea and reading the morning newspaper when there was a creak on the stairs and a moment later David, looking flustered, came into the room.

"Oh," he said, looking around and not seeing his wife. "Do you know where Millie is?"

I smiled, said nothing, and taking him by the hand led him upstairs again, quietly opening my bedroom door. The dim landing light illuminated the bed just enough for us to see Millie and Amanda still sound asleep together.

"How did you manage that?" he asked in amazement.

I shrugged. "David, my son, I did nothing, but I suspect the stage might have been set by the women-only conference I conducted from my bath. Your sister was so upset that she wanted to be cared for like a little girl, so spent the night in my bed like she often did after your father died."

"Was it the baby that upset her?" He looked distraught.

"Partly, but there was a lot more to it than that. Knowing about the next generation of Quinns lining up to enter the world pried the cork off a very unpleasant bottle for her."

He showed no interest in what I might have been hinting. "But Millie?"

I grinned. "A bit later Millie also appeared complaining that you were keeping her awake. I'm hardly surprised, your snoring was rattling the rafters!"

"You do exaggerate, Mother," he laughed.

"No she doesn't," came Millie's voice from under the bedclothes. "You always snore like that when you drink too much wine. I watched… Mumsie and Amanda each had a glass and *you* then finished the bottle."

Much more than an hour later, when David, Millie, and myself were around the kitchen table drinking coffee and eating toast, a bleary-eyed Amanda appeared wearing my red dressing gown. Not a morning person, it was vital she absorbed at least two huge cups of coffee before she could imagine there was a day that needed facing.

Saturday, October 2, 2004, — Honeypot Hill, Thorpe Beauchamp

We were all up by 10:30 on that unseasonably raw October Saturday morning, having showered and dressed. A large pot of steaming hot tea was there to lubricate us as we all gathered round the papers from Rebecca Lisle's boxes, now set out in neat orderly piles on the polished surface of the huge old cherry wood table. Almost as if it was a board meeting at The Quinn Galleries, Millie sat down beside me with her notebook. David was opposite her, with Amanda beside him and opposite me.

Getting up well before everyone else had allowed me to get the table tidy, retrieve the critical documents locked in my desk, get my ducks lined up, and be ready to share what I had found out, which had been so upsetting. My stomach was doing flip flops, and I was feeling slightly nauseous, but my family did not need to know this.

Looking around the table I was obviously not the only person feeling one degree under. Pregnancy had sent Millie rushing away from the breakfast table, Amanda was sallow and withdrawn, while David was distracted, probably wondering what he was doing here when he should be delighting customers as Mine Host at the gallery. I had not the slightest idea what the outcome would be.

"Come on, Mother," David grumbled irritably as he watched me shuffling papers, trying to work out where to begin. "We don't have all day."

I shook my head. "No, we don't, but you have to realize, David, this something that has been festering; I just didn't know about it until I started delving into your grandmother's boxes."

He made a face. "You obviously found something you considered highly unpalatable."

"Shocking is a better word."

"What sort of shock, Mumsie?" Amanda asked, ignoring the tea and cradling a glass of water in her hands.

I frowned. "One which has thrown my life into turmoil, and has me asking who on God's good earth am I? I'm not sure of its long term impact, but there has been a tidal wave crashing over me, sweeping aside what I thought were life's certainties."

"Don't keep us in suspense," said my son, getting impatient.

I sighed and responded by taking from the stack of documents before me what I considered one of the initial clues that things I had been told about what happened, as the war was moving toward its conclusion and peace was approaching, were little more than fairy-tales. This was the letter about the postponed tea dance at the Savoy Hotel written in early 1944.

I pushed it across to David, who frowned as he read it. He silently passed it to his sister, who, having read it herself, slid it back in my direction so I could hand it to Millie, busy scribbling away on her notepad and, out of habit, taking minutes of this important family meeting.

There was silence after they had all looked at it. Then David cut in, "So, Gran had an affair while Granddad was in North Africa. Big deal. From what I've heard an awful lot of married women bounced from bed to bed, and American servicemen were special favorites because they were strong, healthy, elegantly turned out, rolling in money, and could shower women with gifts – preferably nylon stockings. Besides, if she had been several years without a man in her bed, well…"

"I won't allow you to be so crude, Quinn," David's wife scolded, wagging her finger at him from across the table, a distasteful look on her face.

"Yes, Davey, like most men you've always had this rather nasty habit of reducing everything to the lowest common denominator – sex," added Amanda, momentarily emerging from silence. Then she continued, "But, Mumsie, one swallow doesn't make a summer, and one little missive about a flirtation can't mean that Gran was head over heels and in the sack with this Yank."

"No, darling, you're right. But I went through these documents time and again with a fine-toothed comb. It was like uncovering the provenance of a picture; there's far more than just one swallow. I've discovered a whole flight swooping around all over the place."

With the three of them listening intently I methodically laid out theatre programs, the wrapping from a 1944 birthday present, bus and train tickets, a rather simple home-made Valentine card, unworn American-packaged nylons, and so the list went on.

Millie scribbled hard, every now and then looking across at David and with her eyes telling him to keep his big mouth shut until his mother had finished her presentation. Amanda sat primly, hands in lap, until I finished then said, "OK, there's circumstantial evidence but nothing that says in so many words these weren't just two lonely people doing no more than seeking consolation in one another's company, while separated from spouses and with their lives on the line."

"I know," I responded, "but have patience, there's more to come – besides, as far as I have been able to work out, the American wasn't married."

I had pulled from the collection of papers a quantity of letters, postcards, and notes that had passed between Rebecca Lisle and her male friend; these now went round the table. Here was more solid evidence that these two people, who had met during this horrendous world crisis, every day facing the possibility of death, had fallen into each other's arms.

In these notes were, among other things, the names of men who had taken off over the roof of *Honeypot Hill* on sunny or rainy mornings and whose B-17 Flying Fortresses never came back. Some spent the duration as prisoners of war, many more were lost over the North Sea or were incinerated as their aircraft tumbled from the sky, unable to escape or get parachutes to open. My feelings had become ever more fragile and raw as I had pieced together the course taken by this relationship; there were gaps I wished I could fill, and while evidence was incomplete it pointed inexorably in one direction.

Captain Charles Andrew Vanderhoven had come with his crew in the autumn of 1943 across the Atlantic following the completion of almost a year of flight training. They were bringing a replacement for one of the planes from Thorpe Beauchamp that had been shot down on a bombing raid over Germany. This was to be their ship as they commenced active service. Then, with only one mission under his belt, Vanderhoven had managed to damage his left arm in a pick-up game of touch football that turned a little too rough. The cottage hospital decided to keep him under observation, then, because he needed time to heal, after being discharged he was given administrative duties until declared fit for flying duties again. As the weather was almost consistently terrible for most of that month he missed little if any real action.

This was the start of a chain of events that brought together Mrs. Rebecca Lisle and Captain Chuck Vanderhoven. Rebecca's day job was at the government's local office handling food distribution. She was occasionally working as a minion in the administration of a warehouse, a food depot that had been established just a few miles away. Given how few German sorties there were over Thorpe

Beauchamp her position as a community air raid warden was pretty nominal, which was why she added visiting patients at the cottage hospital to her war work.

As my brood passed around the various missives I had pinpointed as evidence, I drew from the very full notes I had taken and now had open in front of me, explaining the background to each item – and how it seemed to me they all fitted together.

"How do you think she went from volunteer hospital visiting to, well, sleeping with an American airman?" asked Millie, a frown on her face.

"I'm not sure, darling," I conceded, "but I doubt he'd have been in hospital more than a day or two. I suspect he would have been kept under observation to make sure he was OK, then was sent back to the airfield…"

"… and the airfield is only a short walk from *Honeypot Hill*," added Amanda, still looking pale and drawn, no doubt due to the admission she had made to me the previous night; but I sensed she was starting to warm up to my detective work. "I suspect this airman was lonely, had time on his hands as he recovered, and Gran must have been a gorgeous young woman, so they stayed in touch – despite the fact that she was married and until then had been anything but friendly towards Americans, by all accounts."

"You're probably close there, Amanda," I responded, "But your grandmother was always capable of being beautiful, charming and witty, even when she was covering up that she couldn't abide someone."

"But who was this bloke?" David cut in, irritated by feminine prattle.

"That I have managed to uncover," I retorted. "Captain Charles Andrew Vanderhoven was known by everyone as Chuck… Good American nickname. He volunteered for the US Army Air Forces as it was then known in 1942, not long after the balloon went up for the Americans when Roosevelt declared war. I'm almost certain from what I have seen that he grew up in Nashville in Tennessee."

"Isn't that the place where Johnny Cash and all those Country musicians come from?" Millie broke in with a giggle.

I nodded. "Yes, but I don't think Chuck lived in that sort of world. From what I've been able to work out he was more likely to have come from a privileged background, perhaps he could have been a banker or a lawyer."

David had been sitting, simmering, and now repeated what he had said earlier. "Mother, I can't see why you're so upset. OK, Gran had an affair with an airman during the War. God knows, they were the only decent-looking males around in a lot of places because such a huge proportion of younger British men were off fighting, and, from what I've heard, those years were a pretty sexy time. I hope I haven't wasted a weekend so I can mourn my grandmother's unfortunate wartime lapses."

"David," I said sternly, "humor me, please." My son looked nonplussed, then having nodded his head, I continued. "I'm simply setting the scene, there's more to come. I hope you don't think I'm so narrow-minded that I'd be sitting here worrying what people might think of your grandmother's moral failures a lifetime ago – it goes further than that."

"There's more?"

I glared at him and responded sharply, "A lot more. Now, young man, just for once in your life, zip up your mouth, sit on your hands, and *listen* to what your mother has to tell you. Your sister, who asked you to come, rightly felt there was good reason to drag you into the wilderness of Cambridgeshire and away from your native habitat where there's a Starbucks on every corner, your favorite wine bar for lunch, and all the so-called civilities of upmarket London."

Amanda reached across the table and picked up another letter that had caught her eye. This was the one that had been my undoing. It was sitting on the top of the pile in her line of sight. My mother had always had this infuriating habit of keeping letters in their envelopes, and this letter was in an envelope so tatty that it had obviously been borne around, treasured, and re-read endlessly.

When delving through the boxes some days earlier, I had discovered this envelope and instantly recognized it from my childhood but could not remember precisely where I had last seen it. That incomplete memory gnawed at me all day. That night, awaking from a brief snatch of uneasy sleep, it all came back to me. When small I loved delving into my mother's handbag as most little girls do, wanting to try out lipstick, makeup, or to spritz my wrists with her perfume, perhaps dreaming of having a real handbag of my own one day. Back then and before I could read, I had seen the envelope poking out of one of the private pockets in her various bags, obviously carried wherever she went. I suspect she deposited it somewhere safer when I had learned to read because I was nosy enough to have opened and read it, resulting in endless questions she would then have refused to answer.

Stumbling across this letter had accelerated my emotional spiral downward, its content making my blood run cold. My heart had pounded and I had felt so disoriented that I had needed to take a long walk to steady my nerves before even attempting a re-reading. It was in a man's handwriting and dated Monday, August 28, 1944.

I motioned to Amanda who read the letter aloud. I would have been incapable of doing so myself and would have collapsed into a weeping heap before having gone a few sentences. It had been the last thing Chuck wrote to my mother.

My darling Rebecca,

I crept out of Honeypot Hill early this morning long before dawn. You had felt so warm and delicious beside me, our bodies entwined and you looking serenely beautiful. You were sound asleep, left arm stretched across the pillow, my ring twinkling on your finger in the dim light that came from the hallway. Your breasts rose and fell gently as you breathed. I wanted to get back in beside you, but dropping destruction on Adolf is the order of the day.

I felt the luckiest man in the world and find myself loving you more than I would have thought humanly possible. You are my good luck charm as the boys and I set out today on our final mission over Occupied Territory. I won't be sorry to have this chore out of the way. It is less than a year since you came into my life, but having you has kept me sane through all the goddamned terror, probably killing men, women, and kids whose only sin has been their misfortune to be citizens of Hitler's sordid tyranny. I often think of you when we are dodging the flack over wherever we are bombing, and in a funny sort of way you always seem to come to our rescue.

By the time you are awake, bathing, and preparing for your day in the food office, The Rebecca Anne will be revving her engines for my last stint at the helm. I pray you will be our guardian angel again today. When the plane bearing your lovely name lands back at Thorpe Beauchamp this evening, then you and I can stop dreaming and pretending and begin planning the rest of our life – together. I'm glad I wrote my younger sister, Emily, told her about you, and asked her to give you an idea of what life is like for a woman in our little circle in Nashville, so far away from your English home. I'm delighted she replied and now you two are in touch.

But as I fly out across the North Sea today my heart will be ringing with the promises we made afresh to each other last night. I cannot tell you how much I admire your courage. Only a spunky broad would willingly break her ties in England to make a new life on the other side of the wide, dangerous Atlantic Ocean.

Part of me can't wait for that, but part feels horribly guilty about poor old Jeremy. What the hell is the man going to do when he receives that letter you read to me? I am never likely to meet him, yet I cannot help but feel sorry for the poor bastard.

As you have told me about him I realize what a fine and honorable man he is, someone who has selflessly given of himself, answering the call of King and Country to defend our freedom, spending four and one-half precious years overseas and away from you. In different circumstances, I suspect he and I could have been good friends. He has not complained but has done his duty believing he was fighting to raise a family in freedom so that you two could grow old together. But after all these years, as you have told me, you have become strangers. The circumstances of war have drawn a line under your past and brought us both together. This will be a fresh start.

As you repeated so many times, the Jeremy you married could well be someone you would hardly recognize now. You had only been his bride for a handful of months when he shipped out, and since then contact has been so minimal; you haven't even been able to talk to him for 53 months – what sort of a marriage is that? What chance does it have? He does not deserve to lose you, but in all those years since you last set eyes on each other a great gulf has been fixed.

I will never forget that evening earlier this year when you wandered into the cottage hospital to cheer the boys up, this mad fool lying there having made an ass of himself playing touch football. We met, we became friends and then lovers, a man and woman somehow destined for one another. I love you, honey, with all my heart, and the crew of The Rebecca Anne will make you proud today.

Your Lifelong Loving Slave,

Chuck

As Amanda finished reading she put her hand on her chest and then, as she gasped, the hand covered her mouth. She now looked even paler than when trailing down the stairs this morning. David silently gazed at the table, while Millie was shaking her head, not sure what to say.

The letter had stunned me when I first read it. While the initial shock had moderated there remained an inner ache that was beyond words. So my mother had been planning to leave my father for another man, an American airman. I found myself recalling, as if it was yesterday, my father and mother broadly grinning and arm-in-arm at their 55th wedding anniversary party some years earlier and remembering all the wonderful things that had been said about their lifelong devotion. But it seems there was one dirty little secret neither they nor anyone else was prepared to reveal. Surely, this was not possible?

My mother at times had hinted at how confusing the war years had been, but I never imagined they would include an affair of such intensity, more like something from a bodice-ripping paperback romance than something that could have happened in a staid middle-class family like ours. I had no idea who this Chuck was, but he must have been very special for Mummy to be prepared to throw caution to the wind. I immediately branded him as a scoundrel for trying to take her away from Daddy. Did the winds of war really obliterate commitments made in church before God until death them do part?

As we all sat at the table I passed around several black-and-white snapshots. The first showed my mother girlishly wearing a gorgeous full-skirted cotton sundress, stylish for those austere times when so-called utility fashions were the norm, but very 1940s. She was obviously wearing stockings, an item almost impossible to get hold of – unless, of course, you had an American boyfriend. She was nestling up against a gangly airman, a dashing figure, his short blond hair flopping over his forehead. They were standing in front of the nose cone of a Boeing Flying Fortress on which had been painted a reasonable likeness of my mothers' face and the name *The Rebecca Anne*. That's how much this man adored her.

I had wondered again and again if this might have been just one more of those silly impulsive wartime romances where hormones ran ahead of good judgment, destined to crumble immediately as peace was restored and a sense of reality about the long haul of recovery became the agenda. However, as I had delved further into the disorganized collection my mother had thrown together there had been other heart-stopping moments.

Among this muddle of paper I had found an official brown manila envelope dated a few days later and bearing the crest of the US Army Air Forces.

Dear Miss Lisle,

(Interesting, I thought, Mummy would have been Mrs. Lisle for some years at that point. I looked back at the photo and despite it being small and grainy I could clearly see that on her left hand she no longer wore her rings. That was so unlike her – for as long as I could remember it was as if her wedding ring, engagement ring, and later an eternity ring were welded to her finger.)

It is with a heavy heart that I must officially confirm that Captain Charles Andrew Vanderhoven and his co-pilot, Lieutenant Daniel Gonzales, were lost somewhere over the North Sea and must be presumed dead. Wreckage from his B-17 has not been sighted.

Captain Vanderhoven's plane was damaged by flak when completing what had been their ultimate daytime mission on Monday, August 28, 1944. He managed to coax his ship as far as the Dutch coast, then instructed all but his co-pilot to parachute to safety into what they presumed was Allied-controlled territory. Clearly, the damage was too extensive for Chuck and Danny to keep the plane aloft across the Channel.

On behalf of the President and People of our grateful nation we grieve with you in the loss of your fiancé.

On a personal note, Rebecca, I mourn with you, aware of the plans you and Chuck had been making. I am sure he went to his death with your name on his lips and your love in his heart, yet that is but little consolation. Chuck and Danny will be posthumously honored for gallantry. That hardly ameliorates your loss, but does illustrate the high regard in which his memory is held by our nation and his colleagues.

Your friend,

Marty

COL. MARTIN C. ROBINSON, JR.
UNITED STATES ARMY AIR FORCES

On first reading this letter I had jumped up from my chair feeling so sick that I did not know whether I would vomit or just run away. Even reading it physically hurt; I was dizzy from the spinning in my head. Slipping on a cardigan, I stumbled through the kitchen and out of the back door. A moment later I had clambered over the garden wall into the village churchyard where my father had lain buried for some years, to be joined more recently by my mother. Tears burning my eyes, momentarily I hated her and wondered whether she even deserved to share a grave with Randolph Jeremy Lisle, my sainted father.

The day's start had been chilly, but now the churchyard was bathed in the late afternoon sunshine of a perfect autumn day. On reaching my parents' grave I had spread my cardigan on the grass, sat down on it and pulled my knees up under my chin, wrapping my arms around them while staring at the headstone.

Randolph Jeremy Lisle
1912-1997
and
his loving and faithful wife
Rebecca Anne Lisle
1916-2002

We had chosen these words for Mummy because until the end the pair of them had seemed so utterly inseparable, but at that time we knew nothing of Chuck Vanderhoven. How unfaithful had my mother actually been? All couples have ups and downs – in our marriage Tim and I had been champions at falling out, but no third party had ever been able to elbow his or her way between us, despite ungentlemanly attempts by a couple of Tim's so-called friends.

I will never forget the ferocious clashes between my parents when I was a child and am certain these agonizing recollections were so lodged in my memory that I have always been chronically averse to conflict. There had been nights when I had lain in terror upstairs in my little bed, tightly cuddling my now threadbare teddy bear, listening to the raised voices and the ghastly things they said to one another. More than once Mummy had screamed fearful, blood-curdling abuse, grabbing the car keys, slamming the front door thus shaking the whole house, and driven off into the night. In those immediately post-war years, on several occasions they must have been within a whisker of splitting.

"Oh, Mummy," I sighed as I transferred my hug from knees to gravestone, a dull ache at the back of my head that I knew would soon turn into a blinding headache. "What am I to think? Daddy was not as dashing as your bomber pilot, but he was a good, kind, loving, faithful, honorable man. Yet you were preparing to walk away from him because some over-paid hunk of a Yank crossed your path… I know things weren't easy during the war years, with all sorts of strange temptations, but couldn't you have stood by your man? Now the pair of you are buried in the same grave less than a hundred yards from the home you shared since the 1930s, your earthly remains wrapped up in one another until time ends. But Mother, I have to ask you, do you deserve to be there?"

There was no reply, of course, and my ache intensified. This was the first of a number of trips up the little hill to their grave since I made my discovery, each evoking a bleak monologue. My windpipe felt constricted and I was momentarily short of breath. How on earth would I tell my family?

Finally I sighed, "You know you've left us a terrible conundrum – perhaps now is the time to get to the bottom of it… But I want you to know, Mummy, you've managed to scare me out of my late middle-aged wits."

I tried to pray, but my soul was frozen and brain numb; all I could do was groan. So I sat quietly and grieved over my parents in God's little acre, a fog of trepidation settling over me for days and nights to come.

I had always loved my Christian names, as we called forenames when I was growing up. I had been Sarah Charlotte Lisle, and when I married I became Sarah Charlotte Quinn. When I was old enough to understand I think it was my grandfather who told of Daddy going with the Eighth Army across North Africa, to Sicily and then Italy, and how while he was there he had made up his mind that his eldest child should be named either 'David' or 'Sarah'. I had sometimes wondered why mother had chosen Charlotte as my second name. The reason seemed unclear and I never got a straight answer out of her. Now I wondered if it had anything to do with this Charles, and where did he fit into this conundrum?

Monday, September 25, 1944 — Royal Engineers Temporary Headquarters, Naples, Italy

It had been four and a half seemingly endless years since Major Jeremy Lisle had feasted his eyes upon the green fields, wooded hills, streams, and countryside of England, especially that corner of the land where he had been born, bred, and of which he dreamed and for which he ached during the sweaty sleeplessness of Mediterranean nights. There had been periods during his long exile in North Africa, Sicily, and now Italy when he thought his heart would be crushed by homesickness. A few days earlier as he had sat smoking his pipe sitting outside the Officers' Mess in the cool of the evening, he had found himself wishing he had kept a journal of his thoughts and feelings throughout this long interlude when serving his country had kept him so far from it – it would certainly have helped him digest and understand the world-changing dramas in which he had been a minor player, and how it had changed him.

Worn out, all he craved was to be back where he belonged. Over these years other men had come and gone. Some had been promoted upward, disease had taken others home, while others still had been killed, injured, or permanently maimed – their memory haunted him. Jeremy was not sure how much more his bruised soul could take. His body was beset by minor physical ailments made worse by months of stress, an inadequate diet, intermittent dehydration, and the continual grinding anxiety of warfare. Try as he would, he did not know how he would brace himself for the long grueling haul up the spine of Italy and over the Alps. The Germans had already engaged in ferocious rearguard actions that could delay the Allied advance for months.

Jeremy's blues were deepened by the irregular arrival of Rebecca's letters despite his father and sisters managing to write with clockwork regularity. He tried to blame it on the military postal service while telling himself that the turning tide of war should have speeded things up, but, as he tossed and turned on his uncomfortable camp bed, he failed to stifle the budding conviction that his wife was no longer interested in him. His morale had hit rock bottom, something he manfully tried to hide.

• • • • • • • •

Second Lieutenant Jeremy Lisle left Britain as spring 1940 was turning into summer. At that time ordinary people were only just becoming alarmed by their peril. The tight corner in which the British Expeditionary Force in France now found itself was front page news, but to those keeping their eyes and ears open it was patently obvious hundreds of thousands of men were trapped between the Nazis and the sea. The miracle of the next three weeks was just how many of those British and French troops would be swept off Dunkirk's beaches and pulled back across the English Channel. Dunkirk snatched honor from disaster, but, as the new Prime Minister, Winston Churchill, was quick to point out, wars are not won by evacuations.

After having dodged U-Boats while being shipped halfway round the world, Jeremy and his men had ended up in North Africa. Soon after this the newly promoted Captain Jeremy Lisle was settling into his wartime exile in Egypt. The news from Britain and every other theatre of action was incessantly grim with the Axis seemingly unstoppable. From shortwave broadcasts of the BBC and London newspapers that arrived weeks late, his heart ached as he learned of ancient landmarks disappearing as the Blitz decimated London and other British cities. He found himself emotionally way out of his depth as he tried to comfort men receiving devastating news of homes destroyed, wives and children injured, parents, babies, and siblings bombed to Kingdom come. Jeremy had then begun worrying for his own wife when in 1942 she had written to tell him that their home was now directly beneath the flight path of an American airfield – could she be blown to smithereens by retaliatory German attacks?

His first months were spent in the relative safety of the Nile delta around Alexandria and Cairo. But when the Germans became so exasperated by the ineptitude of the Italian army and sent in Rommel to take command, the military landscape in North Africa became a nightmare. At the eleventh hour General Bernard Montgomery was given command of the Eighth Army, of which Jeremy's Royal Engineers were part; Monty led them out into the desert to face the foe. There were assorted skirmishes all over the place, then Jeremy found himself in the thick of things in late October and November 1942 at a God-forsaken place called El Alamein where they fought things out.

He and his Royal Engineers worked on logistics, roads, landmine clearance, bridge-building, and the like. As they did the earthmoving and engineering to keep troops advancing, heavy fighting swirled around them. Having won, these Sappers were responsible for after-battle cleanup before the whole outfit, through the winter and into the spring, slogged hundreds of miles west, all the way nipping at German and Italian heels. As planned, they met up with the Americans coming eastward from Morocco. Eventually they were to meet, cross to Sicily, and finally up the boot of Italy and northwards toward Rome.

But the war was far from over back home. The imminent threat of Hitler's invasion diminished, yet he still feared for his lovely wife's safety, given the proximity of the Thorpe Beauchamp air base. His anxieties about Rebecca were morphing again by the time he reached Naples. Could a couple so recently married, separated from each other for so long, their relationship under such constant stress, survive as husband and wife? His war weariness, a combination of physical, emotional, and spiritual exhaustion, together with a touch of shellshock, fed his apprehension. To himself he seemed to be a mere shadow of the man who had kissed his wife goodbye at Aldershot. Was this why the arrival of letters from Rebecca was now so spasmodic?

Major Jeremy Lisle lounged alone in a rickety old deck chair after a less-than-appetizing dinner at the Officers' Mess tent. His pipe smoke curled upward into the still humidity of the Neapolitan sky as he looked over the roofs of the city at the smoky swirl still drifting upward from the fairly recently-erupted Mount Vesuvius. He had been trying to remember the details of the lanes and footpaths back in the Fens that he had once known like the back of his hand, but the details evaded him. Even England, it seemed, was slipping away. Naples was lovely, yet its glory faded when compared to his own corner of England, especially the very ordinary house on that gentle hillside and the lovely woman living there. Besides, the drains of Naples stank! He longed for home and to hold his Rebecca in his arms. He didn't care if at this moment their farmland view was marred by an airfield, he just wanted to be back where he belonged.

Jeremy had been proud to serve his country when Britain and their Empire had stood alone against Hitler's scourge. Now he was attempting to brace himself for mammoth changes at home about which newspapers and letters spoke; while there might always be an England, as the old song put it, it would never be the same again. He had enjoyed working alongside the Americans and even appreciated the company of several German and Italian prisoners of war he had come to know, always wondering how such intelligent men could have been so hoodwinked by Hitler and Mussolini. But with Occupied Europe giving way to Allied might, he felt drained, a sense of emptiness made worse by several spells in military hospitals with bugs his immune system seemed ill-equipped to beat, topped off by a bout of malaria.

No longer in the vanguard, he was now part of the supply chain feeding the army from the rear. His minor shrapnel injury sustained at El Alamein was not enough for him to be sent home but was one reason why he was so far from the front line. He was glad not to have to watch the death and dying first hand any longer, but he wondered if being back here he was still doing his duty. It unmanned him that his younger sister, a nurse in the medical corps, was far closer to the front than himself, yet in honest moments he knew that even if he was there he could no longer handle it. Someone had to supply the boys fighting the ferocious Nazi rearguard further north. He was good at managing logistics and had been promoted, but despite the bigger paycheck he felt a fraud.

After having chewed over all his worries his thoughts always came back to Rebecca. He wondered if they still had anything in common, whether there was still a marriage to salvage. He was nearly thirty-three and there was nothing he wanted more than to settle down and start the family they promised themselves. Another of his terrors when he lay awake in the sweaty southern Italian nights was that when he got home it would mean starting literally from scratch and looking for another wife – there never could be another woman like Rebecca.

It had been several weeks since their unit had reached Naples, but yesterday evening he had received a note to report to Headquarters at 1100 hours the following morning. He had no idea what it was about. Had something gone amiss and was he going to be skewered for it? He promised himself he would get up early and spent several hours preparing reports and looking for ways to protect his rear.

• • • • • • • •

Jeremy finger-combed his hair and knocked apprehensively on the office door, opening it on hearing Colonel Reeves's "Come".

"Ah, Jeremy, old man, thanks for being so prompt, pull up a pew," said the Colonel, looking up from his desk. Toby Reeves was a conscript who turned out to be a natural soldier. Several years younger than Jeremy, his ability had put him on the fast track from second lieutenant to full colonel. He and Jeremy had served as lieutenants together, but as Reeves admitted on several occasions, the war had saved him from floundering as a schoolteacher in a third-rate Public School and helped him discover his true vocation. Jeremy suspected he would be at least a brigadier when he retired.

"Well, old friend, any idea why you've been pulled in?" the Colonel asked, pouring two glasses of whisky, putting one in Jeremy's hand. This was not the sort of treatment Jeremy usually expected from a senior officer.

"I have no idea, sir… Toby… I presumed some idiot in my command has done something stupid and you want me to sort out." He laid his reports on the Colonel's desk. "These summarize where things are right now."

The Colonel laughed. "Good God, man, I wouldn't waste several drams of my decent single malt just to haul you over the rug. No, you've won the lottery, old boy, the War Office has decreed that blokes with more than 54 months overseas, and who have borne the heat of the day, are to go home, get some leave, and then either be de-mobbed or given some cushy number back in perfidious Albion. Given all you've been through you're at the top of my list."

Jeremy was stunned. "Are you sure?"

Toby picked up some papers and tossed them in Jeremy's direction, then propped his bottom on the desk to watch him read them.

Having gone over them twice he handed the papers back to the Colonel, a stunned look on his face. "Well, that's my name. There aren't too many Randolph Jeremy Lisles and probably no other soldiers of the King who share my service number." He was dumbfounded. It was as if nearly five years of Christmas and birthday presents had been delivered all at once, and he had no idea which to open first.

"Why am I first?"

"Because, dear boy, you deserve it. Besides, the paper-pushers know you have skills vital for rebuilding the country, and now, since the Normandy landings, we find ourselves in the third scene of the final act of this mess. While I doubt they'll allow you to resign until Victory Day, which I hope will be sooner rather than later, I suspect you'll be given something that could let you begin finding your way back into that business of yours. Who's been running that show while you've been away?"

In his mind's eye Jeremy could see his father's face. These years had been stressful, so he expected Pops would look more stooped and wrinkled than when he had last seen him. He had virtually retired when that revolting little specimen, Adolf Hitler, had set global disaster in motion. When Jeremy had gone off to officer training in Aldershot, his father had moved back into the Managing Director's office, picked up the reins, and started to deal with the flood orders of from the War Office. He had not had a holiday ever since.

"Oh, the Old Man, Randolph Reginald Lisle," Jeremy mumbled. "I'm sure he'll be pleased to hand the whole shooting match back to me."

"Ready for it?"

"Not sure, but it's my duty whether I want it or not. Pops would have a fit if I bailed out."

The Colonel laughed. "I understand... our generation of fathers is all the same... thank God my old man is happy for me to stay in the army – that is, if they will keep me."

Jeremy grinned, downed his mouthful of Scotch, put the glass on the desk and said, "They'd be fools to send you back to Civvy Street. You're a natural at this lark."

Toby smiled. "Thanks for that vote of confidence, old chum." Then, looking down at the papers on his desk, he began instructing Jeremy. "It seems you have a berth on a troop ship leaving Naples latish on Sunday. It's one of those old Cunarders, the *Georgic*, I think. It stops at Gib on the way home, and you'll be well set up for a choppy ride across the Bay of Biscay in the autumn storms, although now the Jerries have lost those ports all down the French coast there won't be packs of U-Boats to contend with. You should be in Southampton by next Friday or so. Transport will meet you at the dock to take you and the other Engineer officers to Aldershot to be mustered out." He ran his eye down the orders then continued. "It looks as if they are promising you at least a month's leave during which you will receive details about what next. How does that sound?"

There was a chuckle. "I spent yesterday evening and early this morning worrying about how to cover my backside over something having gone wrong, but, instead, I'm getting my gold watch… a man can't hope for better than that. I'm flabbergasted, but I'll rise to the challenge."

The first thing Jeremy did on leaving Toby's office was to fire off a telegram to Rebecca telling her what had happened, that he was on the way home, and when roughly to expect him.

Saturday, October 9, 2004 — Honeypot Hill, Thorpe Beauchamp

Our little family wrapped up the morning's conversation by passing round the telegram Major Jeremy Lisle had sent from Italy telling Rebecca that he was coming home. Paper-clipped to it was a scribbled note on which my mother had reminded herself that he wanted to get home by train from Aldershot, traveling through London, hoping to get to Thorpe Beauchamp by Saturday evening or Sunday at the latest. In pencil she had doodled a little flowery circle around the date – 6th October.

When we broke for lunch it was clear that we had a lot more to talk about during the afternoon.

Millie and David took charge of the kitchen while Amanda, her earlier doldrums now behind her, decided I needed fresh air. She set about walking me around the village as if I were an aging family dog! We picked up extra milk at the village shop, decompressing by chattering about everything in general and nothing in particular – the morning's conversation was not revisited.

As we opened the door of *Honeypot Hill* I was glad I had taught my son a little about cooking when he was younger. The smell of his gourmet-style macaroni and cheese wafted out of the kitchen, David's *pièce de resistance*. I was thankful to have fulfilled Daddy's dream of a grandson – and my father had always lavished David with affection, doing his best to fill the gap that Timothy's sudden death had left in his grandson's life. One of David's prized possessions had always been a small picture of his grandfather, then in his thirties, wearing army uniform and seated atop a camel with the Great Pyramid in the background. David had it extravagantly framed so he could display it properly in the miniscule room that doubled as spare bedroom and study in their tiny London flat.

Instinctively, I reached for the kitchen door in order to help, but Amanda barred my way, steering me toward the sitting room while Millie appeared, as if by magic, with a glass of a fruity dry white wine on a tray, which was thrust into my hand.

"There you are, Mumsie," Amanda cooed softly, having put her arm around my shoulder to nudge me in the direction of the easy chair beside the roaring fire that David had lit. "You just sit there, relax, and enjoy your Pinot Grigio."

I gave her a peck on the cheek. "I have a wonderful daughter, a magnificent son, and a lovely daughter-in-law."

She grinned. "We used to be over the moon whenever you'd say that when we were kids. I can't speak for Davey, but you know just how to make me feel special."

There was a little less tension as we gathered around the kitchen table for lunch. Laughing and joking allowed us to decompress following our morning session. Only after lunch while sitting over our cups of strong coffee did Millie look in my direction and half ask, half prod. "There's more, isn't there?"

I let out a long sigh. "I wish I could say no, but what has been left unsaid is for me the most wrenching part of the story."

"Well, let's not hang around, let's get it out and onto the table," she responded. "It always seems far easier to look what you dread in the eyes, rather than trying to hide it away and pretend it does not exist."

There was no need to repeat the morning's formality of the dining room table because there were no more documents or pictures to pass around, so with cups in hands, and me ensconced in what had been my mother's favorite rocking chair, I told them how on the night after I had uncovered the irrefutable evidence of my mother's infidelity I had not slept at all. Such was the confusion churning up my mind that, even when I did manage to doze off, moments later I would be wide awake as yet another uncomfortable impulse surfaced and slammed into me. Eventually I gave up on sleep altogether.

Slipping out of bed I had stumbled barefoot down to the conservatory where that old brown leather suitcase lay on an ancient ottoman. I had in mind to check something that had flitted across my nighttime field of vision, with the intention of hustling back to the warmth of my bed; I was chilly, just wearing a light cotton nightgown. Despite occasional shivers, curiosity got the better of me. The case had been shut fast for so long that I had yet to open it.

The locks were a bit corroded but were so old and inadequate that only a few tweaks with a kitchen screwdriver flipped them. I pulled the reading lamp towards the case, then knelt and began rummaging around the assortment of clothing. Initially it appeared no more than a jumble of stuff Mummy had packed away for safe keeping, yet that was so out of character.

Rebecca Lisle's passion since girlhood had been lovely clothes. Coming to adulthood in the Thirties she had begun to read *Vogue* assiduously, the bible of fashion for women aspiring to dress elegantly and well. She had always spent an inordinate amount of time taking care of every item of clothing she possessed. Yet when something had outlived its usefulness or could no longer be considered chic, it would be ceremoniously tossed on one side. Under normal circumstances these items in the suitcase should have been bundled out decades ago.

Poking through what had accumulated I found a long white silk scarf made of parachute silk that flyers loved to wear with their sheepskin jackets. Digging deeper I unearthed a pretty cotton dress, recognizing it immediately as the one Mummy was wearing in that snapshot taken with her American airman. Pinned to the bust was a little note in her girlish handwriting, *My Favourite Dress.*

Reaching the bottom of the case, carefully wrapped in tissue paper, I unearthed an officer's dress uniform from the US Army Air Forces, smart light khaki trousers and a darker waisted jacket. Pinned to the lapel was another note, *The Uniform of Captain Chuck Vanderhoven, the love of my life, lost over the North Sea in August 1944. He left it in my wardrobe.* I shivered involuntarily, all the things I was discovering were chilling me to the core. Chuck would have been sleeping with Mummy, this and all the other clues suggested he had been more or less living here; *Honeypot Hill* would have been far more comfortable than a drafty, damp or overheated Nissen hut on the airbase. I suspected his belongings would have been scattered around the house much as Daddy's had always been when I was growing up.

Without thinking I lifted the garments to my nose to see if any of Chuck's natural scent remained. Alas, there was only that old clothes' mustiness, the inevitable outcome of decades spent in the attic. I wondered how often Mother would creep up there when she had the house to herself so that she could touch, look at, and even smell traces of Chuck on his clothing. I had done that time and again with several of Timothy's shirts that I had clung onto, each still buried in my own drawers, occasionally to be brought out and appreciated.

Returning to the hoard of clothes scattered round me, I picked out an impressive long pale pink quilted silk dressing gown, richly embroidered and with a luxurious shawl collar. It was breathtakingly beautiful. I sensed it was from the States, a suspicion confirmed by the label. I held it against myself and trembled uncontrollably. Being cold I put it on. I shivered and shook as I wrapped it around myself. I was a little taller than my mother, but this did not matter as it seemed to fit me perfectly. Before I had been widowed there was no money for such feminine fripperies, and since Timothy's death I had not bothered. Yet this was special. I skipped into the hallway, turned on the lights, and admired myself in the full-length mirror.

But there was this nagging suspicion that I had seen it before. Casting back in my mind I wondered if my memory was playing tricks. Despite her lifelong addiction to nice things, as far as I could remember this had never hung in my mother's wardrobes; I should know, I went through them times without number when I was a little girl.

Despite her every effort Mummy had never managed to pass on her passion for lovely clothes to me. I was content to be presentable because, as a single mother raising her children, there were too many more important things than being a clothes horse. As a small girl, my mother had loved dressing me up like a living doll, and often she would sweep me off to London on the train for a mammoth shopping expedition. We would 'do' the West End, always lunching at her favorite little restaurant just off Regent Street, a place I was later to find out had been a favorite haunt for wartime G.I.s. Afternoons were for Knightsbridge before Mother hauled me home utterly exhausted. I came to adulthood in the Sixties and was more comfortable in jeans and tee shirts, later graduating to Mary Quant with occasional dashes of Laura Ashley. It disappointed Mummy that Christian Dior would never float my boat.

I stumbled back into the sitting room and slumped in my mother's easy chair, luxuriating in the soft warmth of the garment wrapped around me, still racking my brain in a state of sleepy wakefulness trying to recall where I previously encountered the robe.

Just as I was dozing off it came to me. My mother occasionally found excuses for a day or two away without either Daddy or me. Sometimes it would be a tennis tournament with girlfriends, a day at Wimbledon, or shopping with the London-based women she had been close to growing up. As a child I had been fascinated by the pots, potions, perfumes, and cosmetics strewn across her dressing table and was still fascinated enough by her clothes, aching to grow up to be like her. I would watch with eagle eyes as she prepared to go out or packed to go away. It was in these mother-daughter moments she sought to shape my tastes and desires, without any lasting success.

When getting ready for trips she would lay out on the bed all she wanted to take. There was one occasion, at least, when I recalled seeing this delectable dressing gown together with some of her prettier things going into the elegantly soft-sided powder blue leather suitcase that always accompanied her. I guess I had always assumed then that when Mummy went away that there was nothing surreptitious about it, but now I was having serious doubts.

Finally, I drifted into restless sleep, the lovely robe still wrapped around me, and found myself tumbling into a complex labyrinth of dreams about my mother, flirting, American airmen, tea-dancing at the Savoy, and other questionably bizarre fantasies dredged from the unexplored recesses of my subconscious. It would be superstitious to think the seeds had mysteriously clung to the folds of the silken robe, but putting it on had perhaps triggered something buried deep inside, addling my already mangled emotions.

When I had finished explaining this to my family there was a long silence, Then David suggested, "Mumsie, I still think you're making too much of this. So Gran has an affair during the war and the evidence may be incontrovertible that it was hot and heavy. It ended sadly when Captain Van What's-His-Name ditched his bomber in the drink and has never been heard of again. Not long after that Grandad came home, you were conceived, and while the pair of them may not have lived as happily ever after as we might like to believe, their life wasn't that bad."

I sighed. "David, darling, I'm just setting the scene... I haven't got to the most difficult bit."

"How do you mean?"

"This whole business has been like solving a jigsaw puzzle

because since we opened these boxes fragments that were scattered all over the place have been coming into focus, joining up with one another."

"What sort of fragments?"

"For a start, arithmetic," I answered.

He shook his head. "Now you're talking in riddles."

"Hardly, sweetheart, I'm merely trying to put six decades of life into perspective."

There was a moment of silence and then Amanda gasped, "Oh my God," banging her forehead with the palms of her hands and letting out a little shriek. She glanced at Millie whose surprised look meant she was also reaching the same conclusion at that precise moment. Without saying another word my daughter and then my daughter-in-law slipped from their chairs and knelt on the rug at my feet, each taking one of my hands.

David sat mystified. "Can one of you ladies please tell me what on earth is going on?"

His wife looked across at him and said softly, "Darling, you should be able to guess this one – how long will it take for the gestation of our baby?"

"What has that got to do with this conversation?"

"Everything," his sister answered.

"It is thirty-eight weeks give or take a few days either side."

"Precisely. At least you know roughly when to expect your daughter to arrive."

"Son," David snorted assertively. Obviously this was the ongoing argument between the pair of them.

"I'm her mother," Millie retorted, sticking her tongue out at him, "and I know for certain that this is a little girl baby I'm carrying, although she's still ever so tiny."

"Now, children," I cut in, "you can carry on this argument when you are together in bed tonight, but right now we are back in 1944 and 1945…"

David looked stymied as three female faces gazed intently in his direction. He was blank for what seemed like an age, then the penny dropped. "Oh... Oh... Now I can see where you're going."

I smiled, shaking my head. "My, you are a clever boy, although I suppose it isn't surprising the girls get there first as this cycle is so deeply engrained in the female psyche. We are used to counting off months, missed periods, and so forth, something I expect Millie has been teaching you in the last month or three."

Amanda spoke in a sarcastic tone, "Brother, dearest, what do you think Mumsie has been trying to tell us?"

"If it's what I think it is," he shrugged, "then I'm not sure I want to know."

It was my turn to speak again. "Darlings, I'd been led to believe that Granddad got his orders to return home in late August, arriving back in mid-September. Even then the very first thing he and Gran would have had to do was leap into bed and conceive me, and despite that I would have screamed my way into this world some days too early." They nodded. "But as I've been unpicking your grandmother's jumble of papers and letters it's clear that I was deliberately misled. Granddad arrived home a good month later than the earliest possible date for a normal conception and delivery."

"Yes," Millie piped up, "but what if you were premature?"

I smiled wanly. "Don't think I haven't thought of that, sweetie, but a premature baby girl is highly unlikely to weigh the eight pounds, two ounces I did when I arrived on VE Day, especially during wartime when even pregnant mothers were on short rations and there were vitamin supplement shortages. No, my darlings, I was conceived late August or early September, some days before Granddad even knew he would soon be on his way back to England after four and a half years away."

You could have heard a pin drop. The only sound was the light patter of rain on the window panes. The fire had reduced itself to a few smoldering embers; I shivered, wrapping my cardigan more tightly around myself, my innards feeling unsettled despite the fact that I had now told my family all that I had discovered.

Saturday, September 30, 1944 – Royal Engineers Temporary Headquarters, Naples, Italy

Jeremy's younger colleagues in the Officers' Mess, aware that their Major Lisle was, at the best, a one pint of beer man, what else could you expect from an old fellow in his thirties? They were determined to give him a send-off neither he nor they would ever forget. The man who dragged himself up the old cruise liner's gangplank on Sunday afternoon, October 1, 1944, had been legless when his colleagues had hauled him from the mess and put him to bed as the dawn was breaking. He did not know with what they had spiked his drinks, stumbling up the gangplank of the boat with the mother of all hangovers.

The first of the three officers sharing their cabin, he shed his clothes in a pile on the floor, fell onto the first bed he came to, and slept most of the way to Gibraltar. As they arrived after he had disappeared into the arms of Morpheus, Jeremy was unaware of the other two men until well into Monday. They told him later when he apologized for being so unwelcoming they had come on board in similar states of intoxication.

The Bay of Biscay was as gruesome as the Colonel had promised. Barely had the ill-effects of the alcohol begun working themselves out of his system than rolling autumnal seas had the men in that cabin evacuating their aching innards. When the seasickness had begun Jeremy was scared he was going to die; by the time they entered the Western Approaches he was terrified that he was *not* going to die. No one was more grateful than Jeremy when they steamed up the relative calm of Southampton Water. Dawn had yet to break when they disembarked, but if he had been less wobbly on his feet Jeremy would have kissed the ground as he vowed never to travel by sea again. The voyage gave him a new respect for the men of the Royal Navy.

On the ride to Aldershot for their debriefing Jeremy and his bunk mates peered out of the train windows at the appalling damage the Luftwaffe had inflicted. When he had left Southampton in May 1940 the city and its docks were orderly and relatively prosperous. Now the Blitz had reduced chunks of city and the dockland region to piles of rotting, weed-covered rubble. In addition, in residential areas houses, shops, offices, and even churches had either disappeared or were roofless and boarded up. Jeremy had wondered when trying to sleep in the desert under the North Africa sky if the sacrifice they were making was worth it. Seeing the ruin the Nazis had wrought, all he could do was mutter under his breath, "The bastards, the bloody bastards."

At last he grasped how vital it had been to stop Rommel's army in its tracks at El Alamein and the huge advantage they had with the Americans shoving hard from the opposite direction following their landing in Morocco. He felt intensely proud to be British but also appreciated that he would probably now be spending the best years of what remained of his life rebuilding this beloved, broken, bankrupt, but stubbornly noble country.

He thanked God for the Prime Minister, visionary and cantankerous as at times only he could be. What had that bull of an old man said in May 1940 while he was being shipped out as that tired old P & O liner headed down the Atlantic, across the Indian Ocean, and eventually to Suez and Egypt? "We shall go on to the end. We shall fight in France, we shall fight on the seas and oceans, we shall fight with growing confidence and growing strength in the air, we shall defend our island, whatever the cost may be. We shall fight on the beaches, we shall fight on the landing grounds, we shall fight in the fields and in the streets, we shall fight in the hills; we shall never surrender…" This is what Mr. Churchill had foreseen when he challenged them to face down the enemy, and he, Jeremy Lisle, although a small cog in a very large Allied wheel, looked forward to the approaching victory.

The next day was Saturday, and after a thorough debriefing he was given permission to begin his leave; after nearly 54 months he was going home. As the crowded troop train approached Waterloo Station in London, Jeremy again witnessed destruction as bad as Southampton, if not worse. On top of the ruins he became aware of the freshly frayed nerves of these tenacious Londoners, now on the receiving end of Hitler's Vengeance Weapons that were being lobbed at regular intervals from hidden launch sites in parts of the Continent that Germany still controlled.

At least Doodlebugs, what the locals called the V-1 flying bombs, gave some warning for people to take cover because their engines would suddenly cut out and the weapon would take a few seconds to glide downward towards its unsuspecting target. V-2 rockets were vicious. Brilliant German scientists had invented the world's first ballistic missiles and then Hitler tested them on London. Aimed from hidden mobile launch sites in the Low Countries and Northern France, radar was not yet sophisticated enough to lock onto them as they sped across the Channel, and then there was no warning where they would come down. All would appear to be perfectly normal until a huge explosion burst right out of the blue, obliterating anything on which it landed. The resulting terror reminded them that Adolf Hitler and his barbaric followers were prepared to fight to the last drop of blood for their boasted thousand-year Reich.

Jeremy was surprised he could find a cab from Waterloo to Liverpool Street Station but would have much preferred not to have to spend the whole overcrowded ride home standing in the train's corridor with all his luggage. Train wheels and brakes squealed, juddering to a stop at every tiny station, yet he comforted himself that each stop brought him one step nearer to Rebecca.

While in Italy, he had managed to send a telegram telling her roughly when to expect him, and then they talked briefly on the phone when he had been at the barracks in Aldershot, but after the call there was a tight, taut, uncomfortable knot in the pit of his stomach. He had lain awake worrying for hours, an anxiety that would not go away as he spent Saturday traveling. Jeremy was puzzled by her offhand responses – the first time they had talked since she had clung to him with tearful goodbyes in May 1940. Why was she so subdued? She sounded so unlike the bubbly overgrown schoolgirl with whom he had never spent any of their anniversaries. He speculated what might await him at Honeypot Hill.

An exhausted Jeremy leaned despondently against the train's window, the wheels clattering beneath him. His bags were at his feet as he absentmindedly puffed his pipe. The smoke added to the foul-smelling fog in the train that masked the even more disagreeable pong of sweaty bodies, bad breath, damp clothes, and stale cigarette smoke. All at once the journey was over, and he found himself standing on the Thorpe Beauchamp station platform. A brisk wind swept off the Fens, and everything felt soggy. One other person got off the train, and she was immediately greeted by another woman who had obviously been waiting for her. There was no one else at the small Victorian train station. Wandering through the station entrance hall he started toward the old red telephone kiosk, intending to call a taxi, but as he did so one miraculously drove up on the off chance looking for a fare.

A few minutes later Jeremy was standing outside his own home paying the fare. The cabbie, an older man, who was remarkably chatty for that time of night. He told Jeremy he had moved to this area when his home in London had been blitzed and was eager to know about the Italian campaign, what Vesuvius looked like, and how much longer the Jerries could hold out. It was a friendly conversation, raising Jeremy's spirits. The driver told him a little about the US airmen he would often bring out to the base, but made an odd sort of face when dropping Jeremy at *Honeypot Hill*.

"Your home, Major?" he asked.

"Uh, hu."

"Nice... er... Well, have a good leave, no doubt you've earned it. I hope you find everything as you want it to be now you are home," the driver said as he backed into the driveway, turned the vehicle around and headed to the tumbledown little cottage he and his family called home. What on earth did he mean by that?

Jeremy stood for a few moments in the darkness looking towards the darkened house about which he had daydreamed so much for so long. He lovingly ran his finger across the little wooden sign on which he had painted the house's name before shipping out, now very much in need of fresh paint. Rebecca had not taken as much care of the garden as he would have hoped, but it was wartime and she was busy. He shivered involuntarily. After years in the Mediterranean it would take a while to adjust to Fenland's chilly dampness; suddenly exhaustion enveloped him and all he wanted to do was get inside.

The knocker gave a hefty thud against the solid oak door and was followed by a long silence after which came the sound of scurrying feet coming downstairs. The door was cautiously unlocked, and silhouetted by a very dim light he found himself staring into his wife's face – every bit as beautiful as he remembered.

"Oh, Jeremy, darling," she said softly as she took his hand and pulled him inside.

With the door closed kisses were exchanged, the blackout rechecked, and lights turned on. Rebecca now held her husband at arm's length to take a good look at him. He was spent, his boyish looks having long since disappeared. Wrinkles replaced smooth skin in places, and while his face was tanned it was also pallid and more angular than she remembered. His hair startled her. It was thinner on the front while graying round the temples. The man wearing Second Lieutenant's insignia whom she had kissed goodbye had been like a schoolboy going off to play soldiers; the man standing in front of her wearing a Major's insignia had more than done his duty for King and Country yet was older, sadder, wiser, and she was to realize would never fully escape the scenes of death and bloody suffering he had witnessed.

Given the state of the trains, she had not really expected him home that night and had hoped the following morning to have soaked in the bath and pampered herself – and damn the regulations that only allowed her five inches of water. Rebecca had intended to do her hair properly and put on her war paint, trying to disguise her anguish in the wake of the ecstasy and agony of Chuck. At least she did not have curlers in; Chuck had always hated those and Jeremy didn't like them much either. Yet now it was Jeremy wrapping his arms around her as she dutifully lay her head on his shoulder. Her husband was home, but what sort of future could the two of them have – and for how long?

Sunday, October 8, 1944 — Honeypot Hill, Thorpe Beauchamp

Rebecca was secretly relieved Jeremy had arrived home so utterly exhausted because she felt awkward, even embarrassed, by his presence. They may be legally married, but, truth be told, she had long since given herself body and soul to Chuck and was not sure she could ever restore her husband to his rightful place in her heart.

Talk was inconsequential while she prepared him something to eat, then Jeremy quickly bathed and fell into bed. Hardly had his head hit the pillow than exhaustion won out. For a long time Rebecca sat cross-legged at the other end of the bed, her arms over her breasts clasping her shoulders; she stared at him, wondering who this stranger might be. Where Chuck had been sleeping until a few weeks ago, where their unborn child had been conceived, now lay her husband, a seasoned soldier. How she wished things were different.

It had been common knowledge that since war broke out sex had hung in the air all over London and other British cities and towns like a fog. When she and Chuck had made their occasional forays to the West End for a show, dancing, or a nice weekend at a lovely hotel it was blindingly obvious how fashionable fornication and adultery were. She knew of clandestine clinics where unwanted pregnancies could be dealt with for a price, but these came with horror stories. With Chuck's death, since she had been aware of her pregnancy she had been tempted to get rid of the baby, but, try as she might, she couldn't bring herself to do it; the child was the final precious reminder of Chuck.

The last time she had set eyes on her sleeping husband she felt little more than a baby herself, and being a wife was still an exciting fresh experience. Rebecca had thought then that her love for Jeremy could never die, that absence would make her heart grow fonder; but being alone, young, and attractive came loaded with far too many temptations. Since they were last together amid the mayhem of war she had grown up, become an independent woman, and gradually modified naïve notions about the sanctity of marriage. What if Chuck had come back from his ultimate mission, where would she be now? Certainly not here.

As she gazed at Jeremy's exhausted body, listening to his steady breathing, she was in turmoil. It wasn't that Rebecca could not bear him touching her, but she wondered if all that had happened since they were last together now meant she had somehow grown out of him. It seemed more like a former boyfriend walking back into her life than this being the man with whom she had made vows in the presence of God. A dim ray of light from the hallway accentuated troublesome wrinkles on his face and graying stubble on his chin. The young man with whom she had fallen in love, dynamic and hungry for life, was now someone who appeared to have aged well beyond his thirty-three years.

Those eyes that had once so mesmerized her had lost their sparkle and were now like those of a tired but faithful old dog, full of pain, wistful, sad. Her husband was no longer the wet-behind-the-ears soldier boy wearing a handsome uniform but a creature who had aided and abetted killing, maybe had actually been in the position where he had to put a bullet through another man's heart. How many had he watched die, how many had he maimed, and could such a caring man as Jeremy Lisle ever recover from the inner scars that such actions surely left?

The place in the bed where he lay was rightly his, but her whole being ached for the other man to whom she had yielded herself. Two months ago Chuck had been so vibrant and alive, and the future was full of promise. Despite his stressful role in the air war even on the last day of his life he had a vivacity that fifty-four grueling months had stolen from Jeremy.

Jeremy had returned home and could only sleep, yet however late it had been when Chuck came in they would kiss, cuddle, make love, and as they lay in each other's arms make plans about their life together and the children they would raise. He would tease her about needing to alter her accent when she got Stateside. All this was now a mirage. The body that had been so eager for hers lay smashed and rotting somewhere at the bottom of the North Sea – all that was left were memories and nightmares. She had spent hours poring over Jeremy's old school atlas with its map of the North Sea and English Channel, craving to know just where Chuck had gone down.

Since receiving news of his death she had wept copiously, but she had reached the point where grief had become anger which, for reasons she did not understand, her mind now turned against Chuck. He had thought more about aiding his crew to escape than about her. What use was a posthumous medal, and why hadn't he considered their happiness in those last minutes? No one would have blamed him if that old kite had sunk when he had jumped to safety – but until the very end he *had* to be the hero. It was his last mission, for God's sake, a weary old B-17 was of far less value than the living beings who flew it. But he had to show off, be the big man on campus. More tears. When she had blamed him in the most terrible, hateful way, then guilt came creeping in and started to eat her up.

Chuck was dead and nothing could bring him back. Fresh springs of guilt bubbled to the surface, for her love for Chuck ought now to be transferred back to this good man she was watching as he slumbered for the first time in well over four years in his own bed; but the question emerged again, what sort of person had he become?

Chuck she had known in every way imaginable – every mole on his back, every hair on his chin, each of the playful little wrinkles around his eyes, that scar on his thigh that he got when he fell off his bike when a kid, the patterns of hairs on his chest. They had talked and loved and dreamed in a way that faithful old Jeremy could never understand. In her bedroom drawers and wardrobe were clothes and other gifts Chuck had showered upon her, little pieces of jewelry and the most fabulous engagement ring. This symbol of their love now had its own special secret compartment in her jewel box, but as she sat she knew she could never wear it again. In the future there would be times when she would take it out, try it on and admire it and all it had meant, and deep inside she would mourn for what might have been. She ached all over that she would never go to America, and nor would she be Mrs. Vanderhoven.

She had hardly started to digest the fact that the unimaginable had happened to Chuck, than hot on its heels came the news that Jeremy was coming home. Rebecca's whole being seemed to be tearing itself apart, especially when she could no longer deny the mysterious things happening inside her. She found herself hoping her period had perhaps been delayed by the shock of Chuck's death, hoping each morning she would wake up to that familiar discomfort. Surely the topsy-turviness of her emotions had scrambled her body's natural cycle, yet deep inside she knew better. The only solution she could come up with was having Jeremy to make love to her as soon as he returned, then pass off Chuck's baby as his, but the very idea was sickeningly repugnant.

It was past midnight when, utterly exhausted, Rebecca finally undressed, cleaned her teeth, and slipped into bed beside her husband.

She turned the light out, her insides heaving with apprehension about what tomorrow might bring. Hardly had she drifted into a fitful sleep than the man beside her was fighting both 'ghosts' and the bedclothes. Jeremy writhed, groaned, and then came a petrifying shout of "No, no, no... God, man, don't walk there." His legs and arms thrashed in agony. Barely awake she instinctively reached out to hold him, assuring him he was safe.

Chuck had nightmares, too, but they were not in this league. Chuck would cry and whimper, especially after a particularly alarming mission during which enemy flak might have finished them off or the sky had swarmed with Luftwaffe fighters and he had watched helplessly as one of their band of brothers had been blown out of the air and no parachutes appeared. What Rebecca witnessed now was the outcome of watching Allied soldiers being blown to smithereens as they advanced through a minefield that you thought your own unit had successfully cleared.

Jeremy seemed to writhe and moan forever before eventually calming down. Sweat pouring from his entire body, his arms clasped hers, tears soaking the front of her nightgown and dampening her breasts. Not only had time and distance turned him into a stranger, but the manner in which he raved left her wondering how much of the kind, sensitive man for whom she had fallen more than five years earlier might be left. Only as war was ebbing were doctors of mind and brain beginning to plumb the depths of this post-traumatic ailment from which both Chuck and Jeremy suffered.

In the Great War it had been called 'Shell Shock.' And in both this war and the last it was often perceived as a kind of cowardice, its sufferers disdained if they made a fuss about it. Suffice it to say that men in the hundreds of thousands who went off to serve King and County may seemingly have returned with few physical wounds, yet something unseen was uncoiling itself inside them; in the worst cases what remained was the mere husk of who these men had once been.

Years later, on one of her extravagant shopping expeditions to

London, Rebecca was to run into a man with whom she had grown up. He had been the most brilliant member of their little coterie. He won every award imaginable at Oxford, married one of the brainiest women of their time, and had joined the RAF when war broke out, becoming a Lancaster bomber pilot. After being shot down he languished in several prisoner of war camps, finishing up in Colditz castle, the highest security prison for the most ardent escapers. There, it seemed, all that he had once been was scoured from him. Instead of the Edwin of sparkling conversation and incisive wit, all that was now left was a hollow man. Neither university nor City could find any use for him. He found it impossible to hold down a regular job, so here he was sweeping the streets of Knightsbridge grateful that his wife had stuck with him and was cushioning him from a cruel world.

As the sky lightened that first Sunday morning, long before Jeremy stirred, having taken care of her morning sickness in the downstairs toilet, Rebecca fished into her jewel box, fumbling for the never-to-be-worn-again-in-public engagement ring tucked away in its special secret spot, and with tears dribbling down her cheeks she kissed it a fond farewell. She then retrieved her wedding ring, slipping it back on her finger, not sure how she would respond when Jeremy sought to act upon the vows they had made on that faraway day before the guns of war had begun their cannonade: "With this ring I thee wed, with my body I thee worship…"

Rebecca remembered almost bursting with pride when the Vicar had taken their hands in his, wrapped his stole around them, and proclaimed in his sonorous voice, "Those whom God hath joined together let no man put asunder". Rebecca sat pondering as she fidgeted with the wedding band on her finger; what chance did such an ideal have in a world turned upside down and chopped to pieces by the absurdity of war? In different ways the two of them had fought for their lives and sanity thousands of miles apart; how on earth had they ended back in the same place, the same but now very dissimilar people?

Sunday was subdued. It was the middle of the morning before

Jeremy awoke, pottering for a while then dozed in the armchair that Chuck had once commandeered. He was hungry but could do little more than play with his food, and although Rebecca plied him with questions about these last years his replies were distant, even monosyllabic. Like so many of his generation, he could never to tell her or anyone else much about what he had been through. For most of that day he sat slumped in his chair gazing into middle distance as if reliving the nightmares that had troubled him the previous night.

When in bed that night Rebecca was once again awakened by his thrashing and screaming, this time seemingly taking cover from the pounding of incoming artillery. For nights to come, she would cradle her husband's head as he shuddered, babbled, again and again re-running the horror of watching men being blown beyond recognition by anti-personnel devices in the sector that his unit had failed to properly clear. She sincerely hoped that these nighttime episodes were the brain flushing out noxious toxins of war, or was this evidence Jeremy was broken beyond repair?

Her friend Laura's handsome husband has been a Spitfire pilot, burned beyond recognition when his plane had been shot down. She was destined to spend the rest of her life nurturing an utterly broken man. In psychological terms, would this be Rebecca's fate?

Jeremy continued subdued for days. Slowly his appetite improved despite their inadequate diet, but it seemed to be when his mental guard was down after falling asleep that the consequences of the battlefield resurfaced, triggering re-runs of the grisly incidents through which he had lived.

She did not know whether to be appalled or relieved when, about two weeks into his leave, Jeremy's orders came through saying that following the medical appraisal made at his debriefing he was to be granted ten more weeks leave, at which point his condition would be reassessed. He was not expected to report back to barracks until January at the earliest, and in the meantime was seconded to the family engineering business and told to reacquaint himself with the work. The next chapter of his life was being set up because he had a part to play in the country's postwar reconstruction.

"Oh God," she prayed as she lay beside her now-sleeping husband the night after the letter from the War Office had arrived, "the army has given him the rest of 1944 off... by then I will be showing? How on earth am I going to tell Jeremy about the baby?"

Huddled in a fetal position, Rebecca dissolved. She was already sensing Jeremy was quietly piecing together odd scraps about the life she had lived while he was away and particularly her relationship with Chuck – and wondering, perhaps, if there were others. When he knew the whole truth would he want anything more to do with her? Her parents would be equally unsympathetic. Her father, Arthur Johnson, was a good upright man, the son of a strict Baptist deacon, but he had always been irrationally starchy when it came to sex; his response to his youngest and favorite daughter's flightiness would not bear thinking about. She could already see the glee on her sisters' faces as she imagined them daubing on her chest a big red S for Slut. Her panic coupled with Jeremy's nighttime agonies stole sleep away from her.

Saturday Afternoon, October 9, 2004 — Honeypot Hill, Thorpe Beauchamp

"Mumsie, are you sure you're not putting two and two together then making five?" Millie asked with a quizzical frown, talking on behalf of her husband who was tongue-tied, still trying to digest the implications of these new pieces of information. "There must be something you haven't thought of to explain the conundrum?"

Now Amanda cut in. "Perhaps Granddad was sent home earlier, but you have no evidence to prove it at this point?"

I shook my head. "I wish to goodness I wasn't so absolutely certain that I'm right. All the old standards of sexual morality lost their hold as the country wrestled with wartime ferment. Imagine the confusion – men sent off to fight, women coming out of cities and working on farms, people of different classes mixing with one another in ways they may not have done since perhaps the Romans were here. Then there was the Blitz, and everyone in target areas would wonder if this day would be their last, seeking comfort and gratification of the closeness of someone else's body.... then the tide of war started to turn as hundreds of thousands of Americans flooded the country. Strong, healthy, impressionable men, many leaving home and loved ones for the first time, their hormones were passionate, and they came into the midst of a population of women starved of male company. Restraints came off, even in out of the way places like Thorpe Beauchamp...At least four children in the village primary school with me had unknown GI fathers, and maybe there were more."

Amanda looked like a thundercloud, "So?"

Millie sort of responded to her sister-in-law. "I remember Daddy telling us when we were youngsters when he was driving us through the Piccadilly area of the West End that there was a place there, on the corner of Shaftsbury Avenue, I think, that was called the Rainbow Club. I believe he said it had been set up during the war by the Red Cross for lonely GIs as a sort of home away from home. Daddy said it became a magnet for girls – and even not-so-young married women would tart themselves up to see if they could pick up a man."

"Oh, Millie, that proves nothing. Gran would never have gone to a place like that?" Amanda snapped, a submerged puritanical streak in her personality suddenly surfacing.

I smiled at the girls as they locked horns. "Ladies, you both make good points... I believe there were any number of American clubs dotted around, especially in London. Amanda *is* right, Gran would never have gone to a place like that; she would never have needed to. My mother was, as you know, one of those women who, until quite late in life, could walk into a room full of men, and they would swarm around her like bees round a honeypot. As a teenager, I dreaded going out in her company because the male response would cause such embarrassment to a plain little creature like me."

"OK," David growled, emerging from his stupor, "so she could pull guys, that doesn't prove anything."

My children seemed determinedly unwilling to accept the realities. "True, but she didn't need to go to London to find guys, there was a whole airfield of them just down the road... she could hear their voices in the distance as they yelled to one another and could not miss their planes flying over her house day and night... she lived in a small village that in a couple of months went from being an agricultural backwater to one swarming with red-blooded young Yanks. To the transatlantic male, not having a husband around was interpreted as a woman being available."

"But would she have made herself available?" David followed up.

I shook my head. "This is painful enough already, I don't want to go there. There's enough to indicate something was going on, and accumulating evidence points to the incontrovertible likelihood that I'm the end-product of whatever was happening."

I leaned my head back and closed my eyes. I recalled my gawky self being dragged to the tennis club where I had no option but to sit with a bottle of Coca Cola or lemonade and watch Mummy mingling. As a small girl I had wanted to grow up to be like her, but as I got older my inner self dreaded such a possibility. My mother was slender, about 5'5" tall, well-proportioned, the size of female that men would enjoy cuddling, with an attractive personality. No matter what she wore, and she had this magical touch with clothes, she could not help oozing seduction, gently brushing a man's arm with her fingertips, stirring his heart with a smile, and flirting her way around a room like a butterfly. In such settings she took on added color as she flitted from place to place, person to person, enticing, enchanting, staying in a spot just long enough to allure but never get trapped.

She was always one of the best dressed women in the room and intuitively knew how to be noticed and admired. Her lifelong wail was "I don't have anything to wear". Despite her inclination to ditch garments that had outlived their usefulness, every closet and wardrobe in *Honeypot Hill* had always been bursting with skirts, dresses, blouses, evening gowns, robes, underwear, and so forth. In addition,

Mummy, while not exactly Imelda Marcos, accumulated shoes and possessed enough accessories to make most women permanently envious. For his part, Daddy just kept on spoiling her.

Like many middle-class women in those Spartan post-war years she was the faithful client of a skilled seamstress; by means fair and foul she would get hold of some divine piece of fabric that Gina O'Neal would turn into something enchanting, like a dress to attend a wedding that she knew perfectly well was likely to upstage the bride.

When I was at Cambridge I discovered the *hetaerae* of Ancient Greece, a class of females raised to provide stimulating intellectual and sexual company for males, both single and married. I wondered when I read about them if there was not something of the *hetaera* in my mother.

After I married I was surprised to discover just how primitively possessive my own husband could be. All this led me to marvel how calm Daddy could stay in light of some of Mummy's antics. When I finally mentioned this, he shrugged and smiled. "My darling girl, she's operated like that as long as I can remember and I'm told was every bit as bad as a teenager... I've learned to put up with it because I know she loves me and because I've loved her since I set eyes on her." I always wonder why I had not inherited so tolerant a spirit.

"Mother, Mother," I heard David exclaiming as I tuned back into the conversation. "You were a million miles away, weren't you?"

I looked at him sheepishly. "Not so much miles as years. I was remembering things your Granddad said more than forty years ago about Gran... He was such a remarkable man it has grieved me to discover that if Chuck Vanderhoven was my natural parent I have none of Grandad's DNA."

"But how do you know you're not wrong?" my son shot back.

"Sweetheart, I'm not 100% certain of anything, but the evidence has been stacking up; why else would I feel as if my whole life is turned upside down? I thought I was the precious single child of a loving faithful couple, long yearned for but delayed by the outbreak of the twentieth century's second most ghastly war. Instead, I appear to be the accidental outcome of an intense love affair between my mother and an American flyboy, conceived unintentionally not long before he disappeared over the North Sea never to be heard of again."

"What difference does that make?" Amanda asked. "You are still Sarah Charlotte Lisle Quinn, our beloved mother."

I reached out and took the hands of both my children. "Darlings, I'll never stop loving you, ever, ever. But in these last days I've had this falling sensation and have had to come to terms with a very different genetic lineage than I had imagined. I feel like I'm lost in a strange city without a map, there are no street signs, and I don't speak the language. I'm so disoriented I don't have a clue how to extricate myself."

"But that might be fun, mightn't it?" Amanda encouraged.

I grimaced. "Maybe, but I've got to get used to the idea first. In due course I might come to embrace all this with enthusiasm, but right now I feel trapped in what has become a bewildering nightmare. The question uppermost in my mind is whether I am a Lisle or a Vanderhoven. I may have borne the Lisle name, but I'm no longer sure I am part of the Lisle bloodline. But I haven't quite told you everything yet.

David was about to blunder in when his wife glared at him, grabbed his wrist, kicked his shin, gave him a stern look, and shook her head vigorously. I never ceased to be amazed how well this petite young woman could keep my son in order. He made a face and then did as her eyes had told him.

I smiled my thanks to Millie. Since we began talking I had been holding a letter from my father to my mother. "This seems to further corroborate my perception that Granddad was not my natural father. He wrote Gran this letter telling of an extensive hospital stay while in Sicily in late 1943. It seems they were billeted in a small town called Milazzo on the north coast of the island, living cheek-by-jowl with the local population, most of whom were only too happy to be liberated. I'm sure the soldiers, many of whom were big brothers, fathers, or wished they could be fathers, played football with the town's little boys. It would appear there was an epidemic while they were there. Granddad caught whatever was going around, suffering high fever with swollen glands for a good few days. From the little bits and pieces of information in the letter, and from my experience as your mother, and as a result of my poking around the Internet, I suspect the epidemic was mumps. Most kids shake this off with no long term ill-effects but not so adult males. A brush with mumps won't destroy a man's sex drive but it very often destroys his potency."

"So Granddad could well have come home firing blanks," David supposed, finding his tongue again but without looking in Millie's direction.

I sighed. "A rather crude way to put it, Davey, but yes. I've never been to Sicily but, if it is anything like the bits of Italy I do know, people in small towns lived in tight-knit communities. Susceptible people would pick up any and every bug doing the rounds, especially if their diet was poor. All you'd need would be a couple of kids who were carriers coming in close contact with soldiers, who the little boys were bound to hero worship, and hey, presto… Your grandfather had been in the desert and was likely physically and emotionally run down, and, as you know, he always loved kids, and they loved him. His immunity would have been compromised, making him a prime candidate to pick up whatever these children were carrying."

"Could we confirm that in some way?" Amanda asked.

"Knowing what a hoarder your grandfather was, and bearing in mind that there's a lifetime's archive of his documents in the garage, the old summerhouse, and goodness knows where else, someone with patience might easily track more information down."

• • • • • • •

It had been a heavy day, but getting it off my chest had been an emotional relief for me. Now I was no longer carrying this burden alone. As early evening gave way to dusk, with the rain having passed, David and Millie shooed Amanda and myself from the house again to take a short walk while, with Millie in command, David was dragooned into helping her prepare a simple, but adequate, evening meal. By the time wine had been consumed, spaghetti bolognaise devoured, and the dirty things loaded into the dishwasher, conversation was petering out and wholesale exhaustion had set in. Millie excused herself, saying she was going to bed; I was also weary so the two of us went upstairs together.

I had just clambered into bed and was tidying my fingernails when there was a little tap on the door and Millie's face appeared, apparently to say goodnight, but in truth she wanted to curl up and talk babies.

"Mumsie, I want you to be there when our little imp is born," she announced sheepishly.

"But what about your own mother; that should be her privilege?" I suggested, not wanting to ruffle her mother's feathers any more than I had managed already.

"Oh, I have this horrible suspicion that Mummy doesn't care one whit about my baby. I'm still just that perishing little afterthought who spoiled her summer plans when I was born in 1974 – I wish I knew how many times she has told me that her over-sized belly made it impossible for her to enjoy Ascot that year. No, Sarah," she continued, "you've been far more of a mother to me than the Countess ever pretended to be."

By making such a request my daughter-in-law knew she had put me in an awkward position. Of course, I would love to be there when my first grandchild was born and to help during those early days, but Melissa, her mother, was the sort of woman who considered me to be many rungs below her on the social ladder because I was, as she would put it, "in trade." In other words, selling expensive pictures to wealthy clients from all over the world put me in the same category as a costermonger along Petticoat Lane or in Notting Hill Market.

"Sweetheart," I said softly, taking her hand, "I'm touched that you asked, and you can depend on me to be there night and day up to the great event as well as afterwards, but I think it wisest for you to give your mother first refusal on being there with you. If she says no then I can't think of a greater honor you and David could bestow on me." I swallowed hard, feeling my ragged emotions churning but this time for a very different set of reasons.

My daughter-in-law cuddled up, "I thought you'd probably say something like that, and I love you for it, you are so sensitive and caring…" she then knelt on the bed beside me, her hands in her lap. "And I think I know just a teeny bit how you've been feeling since all this stuff about Gran came up. I've never really felt that I quite belong in the family into which I was born. Every extravagance was lavished on my sisters… David *is* wicked but he's very close to the truth when he calls them the Ugly Sisters. I'm Cinderella-ish but your Davey is my Prince Charming. I love him to bits, and I love his family to bits because it's now my family… especially I would do anything for his mother."

"You are very special, Millie, darling," I responded, taking a grip of myself and holding back tears. "And thank you for being so considerate."

We sat in silence for a few moments listening to the rise and fall of Amanda and David's voices as they sat downstairs talking animatedly.

"It isn't often these days that those two have the opportunity to talk like this. I suspect they're still trying to make sense of all I've told them."

"Maybe, but for Amanda details have always been so important that as far as she's concerned all the facts need to be thoroughly verified before she will accept that your birth father was actually that American."

"She's right to be apprehensive … David doesn't seem to understand how this alters the way I look at myself. The man whom

I will always consider my Daddy appears to have adopted me, with additional evidence suggesting that my parents were incapable of having children together… among the friends with whom I grew up I was a rarity as an 'only.' People tended to go for two, three, four or more children in those years following the war, possibly helped along by the welfare state and the arrival of the National Health Service. In some ways if Daddy adopted me rather than helping conceive me, my love for him soars. Nevertheless, that still makes me somebody else's little cuckoo dropped into his nest, but he neither left my mother nor did he tip us out. That's a self-confident, wonderful man."

"And you, Mumsie, darling, are a confident and wonderful woman. I've never told you this, but after you interviewed me for the internship I went and sat in Trafalgar Square, grateful you had offered me the position on the spot, but wondering how different my life would have been if you and not Her Ladyship had been my mother."

"Really?"

"Really. I think one reason I fell for David was that you were his mother and I idolized you, but please don't tell him that. There is so much of you in him. Of course, I'll love him forever and ever for who he is, but he's the jewel in the crown of the most wonderful family in England as far as I'm concerned."

"Sweetheart, if you're not careful you're going to have me bawling my eyes out," I responded, reaching for a tissue.

"Sarah Quinn," she said, now very serious, "You've spent your life under-estimating yourself. You were a wife and mother cruelly robbed of her husband, but who picked up the pieces and went soldiering on. There would be no gallery today if it had not been for you, and David knows this more than any of us. David and Amanda would not have had such wonderful educations and a start in life if you had not worked your fingers to the bone for them. You've scrimped and saved to give them the very best… in my family it was all handed to us on a plate, for our clan privilege was, and has been, taken for granted."

"What are you trying to tell me, darling?"

"That you are not only my wonderful mother-in-law but you're also my role model. I want to be the sort of wife of whom your son is proud, as well as a businesswoman with your integrity. I want to be the sort of mother that you have been to your children. You don't know how content I am being plain old Millie Quinn rather than Lady Millicent Blah-de-Blah Fitzpatrick-Evans. I hope as my kids grow up, and there *will* be more than one, I promise you, that I am known as Jessica and Robbie's mum more than anything else."

"You've agreed on those names?" I asked.

"Not really, but David Quinn will do as he's told when it comes to names, mark my word," she said quite seriously, wagging her finger to emphasize the point before collapsing into hysterical giggles. Yes, she had him right under her thumb, and he seemed content to remain there.

A few minutes later she kissed me goodnight and went to her room, allowing me to turn off the light. Her words had made me feel so much better. I took a sleeping tablet and drifted off listening to my children's muffled voices from the living room below. I had this feeling that they were cooking something up. In a way this pleased me because since David had married Millicent their relationship, which had once of necessity been very close, had cooled. Perhaps the tide was turning.

Sunday Morning, October 10, 2004 – Honeypot Hill, Thorpe Beauchamp

During my childhood, our family was a fixture at the Sunday morning service in little St. Andrew's Church, next door to our home, *Honeypot Hill*. Those were the days when people got togged up in their Sunday best for church, and, even though the congregation was fairly small, Daddy would always wear a dark suit and his regimental or old school tie. For almost as long as I could remember he was one of the churchwardens, which made him the confidante to the procession of Vicars who came and went over the years.

Mummy was not an enthusiastic churchgoer, but she could never pass up the opportunity to dress up and would almost always appear to be a beautiful butterfly in the midst of a congregation of dowdy moths. As the bleak years of clothing rationing and making do faded, and as Daddy's business emerged from the lean war years, beginning to prosper again, she took full advantage of changing circumstances, becoming stylishly striking. When she was old, several times she confessed what a relief Christian Dior's New Look was in the wake of the threadbare grayness of the war years. When we went to church she dressed me up in one of the dozens of little outfits she bought or had made for me, determining that I would grow up to be as much as a clothes horse as herself.

Some of my most precious childhood moments were spent in that church, which was more than nine hundred years old, despite my mind forever wandering when the sermon was being preached. I seldom listened long enough to work out what was being said, but there was something reassuring about what was preached from the pulpit as I sat with Mummy and Daddy, one on either side, Daddy often with his arm wrapped around my shoulders. That wonderful old building helped cultivate my aesthetic sense, triggering an interest in paintings, sculpture, and magnificent buildings.

My teens coincided with the mid-Sixties, the soundtrack of my short but energetic youthful rebellion being the Beatles, followed on closely by the Rolling Stones. After a series of ferociously fought battles with my parents, I submitted to going to church with them at Christmas, Easter, and then on special occasions. I never actually stopped believing in God, but until I was well into my middle years I managed to forget the Almighty as if he were tucked away in a file permanently relegated to that nether land at the rear of my mental filing cabinet. After Timothy had died, God had slipped further down my priorities so that I never had to give him any consideration.

It was only when I moved back to *Honeypot Hill*, first taking care of my mother, and then living there on my own, that I picked up the faith that I had left in a bundle at the same church door at which I had left off forty years earlier. With the church virtually in my backyard, and Mummy, despite her half-heartedness, never having broken the churchgoing habit as an opportunity to dress up, I could go and sit in exactly the same pew our family had occupied when I was a child and quietly slip back into the faith. Only now what happened there had a far richer meaning for me. As the months had passed I had found myself becoming so much of a pillar at St. Andrew's Church that I was elected to the Parochial Church Council and regularly took my turn arranging the flowers! What had stunned me on my first Sunday back was that the vicar was no longer a crusty old man but a vivacious blonde, wearing elegant three-inch black patent heels, a clergy shirt in pastel blue with ruffles down the front, and the brightest shade of red lipstick. At last, the ordination of women caught up with me!

The Reverend Antonia Fry was young and ambitious for something more exciting than our sleepy little village, so that, not many months later, she became chaplain of a university college in London. We kept in touch and occasionally would lunch together when I was in town, Antonia regaling me with stories of the students, musicians, and academic eccentrics who now peopled her busy life. Several years after she had left Thorpe Beauchamp she invited me to her wedding to a rising star in the field of public relations. Following Antonia at St. Andrew's was a married couple, middle-aged and both recently ordained. They shared the vicaring of seven small Fenland parishes, as well as parenting their three lively offspring. Instantly I fell in love with both of them.

The Reverend Jackie was magnificent as Mummy ailed, coming by regularly to bring her Holy Communion, and then she took her funeral when we finally laid my mother to rest in the same grave as Daddy. Daddy was a starchy old traditionalist when it came to church things, which makes me wonder what he would have made of Mummy's funeral. Relatively few women had been ordained in the Church of England when he had died, and he had insisted on the traditional 1662 *Book of Common Prayer* service. Mummy's service was conducted by Jackie and the whole style was far more contemporary. I confess that at heart I am old-fashioned so much preferred the traditional!

• • • • • • •

I awoke that Sunday morning when the children were with me and followed my usual pattern of slipping out to the eight o'clock Communion service. I was also in the habit each week of taking something from the garden to lay on my parents' grave. Coming downstairs I found Millie waiting for me. She was a picture in a smart mid-length pink coat, complete with black velvet collar that I had never seen before. She sat at the kitchen table drinking herbal tea, but there were dark shadows under her eyes that her makeup had not entirely disguised.

"That husband of mine and his sister didn't come up to bed until goodness knows what hour," she complained. "I think David must have emptied every liquor bottle in the house because as soon as his head hit the pillow he was snoring like a bear," she said wearily.

"How do you feel now?" I asked, with concern.

"I'm OK, a bit tired. I suppose I got four or five hours, not really enough for the baby. But I was restless until David appeared, then sleepless because of his snoring. Besides, these days I feel awful first thing...," she sighed.

"Why are you all dressed up?" I asked, knowing the answer already.

"Because I knew you'd be going to church this morning, Sarah, and I'm coming with you. I've always liked church. As you know I'm a great admirer of Her Majesty, who is such a fine churchwoman. Contrary to the snide criticism of my family I have always thought that if she believes it then so can I... and I wanted to be with my adorable mother-in-law."

She had heard me fussing around upstairs so had already brewed a strong pot of Yorkshire breakfast tea. Looking sheepishly at her I admitted, "I've gone and sat in the church quite often these last few weeks. It's a pity the place has to be kept locked so much of the time, but vandals, copper and lead thieves, have become such a menace even in a little place like this. However, the Reverend Jackie allowed me to hold onto our family church key... Daddy used to go every morning of his life, unlock the building, then sit in the church to pray, however cold it was. He began this habit when he was in the

Western Desert in the army. Then he would lock the church up every night."

A few minutes later we stood arm-in-arm before my parents' grave. I was still desperately trying to make sense of all that had happened when Millie reached around my shoulders and said, "She was a good woman, Mumsie, you know that. She deserves to be there. The challenge now is to see if we can identify how the trail wound its way to this point."

I leaned across and kissed her cheek. "How good it is to be blessed by such a wise daughter-in-law."

She smiled serenely. "I had a good mentor… her name is Sarah Charlotte Quinn, daughter of this Rebecca Lisle for whom we thank God and whose memory we now honor."

The service was serene, short and sweet, and there were only seven of us in that chilly nine hundred year old building. I then introduced Millie to the Reverend Jackie whose immediate response was to give her a huge hug and tell her she had to look after me – then holding Millie at arm's length, she exclaimed, "What a pretty coat. I have been secretly coveting it all through the service."

"I didn't think priests were supposed to notice such things when celebrating Holy Communion," Millie laughed.

"Oh, I don't expect the boys do, but well, as you know, we girls are much better at multitasking! I was thinking how much you looked like Jacqueline Kennedy actually."

"My mother told me that… then decided it didn't suit me because she thought that Mrs. Kennedy was an awful, common woman," Millie said, a haunted look in her eyes as she spoke of her mother. "Mummy also thought it was entirely inappropriate for a pregnant woman."

"Millie, don't take any notice of her. You look divine. Then the priest turned to me, wagged her finger, and demanded, "Why, Sarah Quinn, did you not tell me you were going to be a grandmother?"

"Because I was sworn to secrecy, and I was raised to keep promises."

She made a face. "Phooey… this news should be shouted from

the housetops. When is this great event?"

"Early July by the look of things," Millie told her.

Then looking Millie straight in the eye she said, "Girl, I'll never forgive you if you allow anyone else but me to baptize this little mite."

It was a mild autumn morning so we walked the long way home rather than climbing over the church wall at the back of the house. David and Amanda were unlikely to emerge for hours. We chatted amiably. Millie suddenly stopped, turned to me, and took both my hands in hers. "Mumsie, David and I had a terrible row the other night about having the mini-Quinn christened. I'd already made up my mind my baby should be baptized here in Thorpe Beauchamp where David and you, too, were baptized. My mother insisted a long time ago that all the children in our family, if they were done at all, should be baptized at the Chapel Royal. The row erupted when I told him what was on my mind. He said christening didn't do him much good, so he was damned if any child of his would have ceremonial water slopped over it by some simpering priest."

I sighed. "That sounds like David at his most obnoxious; I expect he had been at the wine bar with his pals before coming home. Don't worry, we'll work on him."

"But if I can't make him do it, I don't know you will succeed," she groaned sadly.

I squeezed her hand. "Sweetie, you forget that I'm his mother... He also so reveres the memory of his grandfather that, when I tell him how upset Granddad would be, he would find an excuse to save face and change his mind."

"Jeremy Lisle was a really religious man, wasn't he?" Millie asked, astonished.

After a long pause I told her, "There were things that happened in the war that profoundly impacted him. At the end of his life his bad knees forced him to literally drag himself up the hill to services, but he refused to miss Holy Communion each Sunday morning – and nine times out of ten Gran went with him."

"What happened in the war?" she inquired.

"I'm not entirely sure, but if what your husband and sister-in-law were gabbing about during the night bears any fruit, I suspect they could have hatched a plan to uncover a lot more about Granddad Lisle's war and so, by default, Gran Lisle's war as well."

Monday, October 9, 1944 – Honeypot Hill, Thorpe Beauchamp

Rebecca Lisle awoke with a start much earlier than usual. She shot out of bed in a flash, threw up in the downstairs toilet, then bathed, dressed, and ate breakfast. After greeting Jeremy and drawing the curtains, she was on her bike and going. While the first night with him had been frightening, the second he had been calmer, but Rebecca still had little idea what to expect – or when to expect it. She felt utterly wrung out even before the working week began, having spent the night catnapping rather than properly sleeping.

It was still dark, the wind lashing rain against the bedroom windows, and in the distance B-17s were being readied for their wartime job over Occupied Europe or Germany. Rebecca's emotions somersaulted. How many mornings had she listened to these same sounds and worried about Chuck as he began his day's work fighting the enemy? If they left on their mission particularly early she sometimes could recognize the sound of his plane, *The Rebecca Anne*, as it climbed into the sky right over her home.

Her home? How much longer would *Honeypot Hill* be her home? While Jeremy was far too much of a gentleman to force himself on her before she was ready or immediately throw her out when she told him the truth about Chuck's baby now firmly implanted inside her, how much longer would she be able to stay here with the man who was her husband but not the father of her child? She tried unsuccessfully to eliminate such thoughts from her mind.

Rebecca's morning rituals were changing and usually began with her kneeling in front of the toilet fielding waves of pregnancy-induced nausea. She would tiptoe to the toilet downstairs, quietly closing the door, hoping her husband would not hear her retching. It was also a new routine for her to wander the house while boiling the kettle for her cup of tea, making sure she had not missed overlooked signs of Chuck which Jeremy would be able to pick up on.

Despite her every effort Rebecca was on the edge of panic, knowing the whole of the rest of her life hung in the balance. She would have liked to have thought things were in God's hands, but she felt the Almighty was thoroughly disappointed by the way she had been living during the years Jeremy had been away. She regretted, too, that Chuck was not the first man she had been unfaithful with, but neither had she been the pure virgin she had claimed when she fell in love with Jeremy. Without doubt, Chuck was the great romance of her life, but, now that her husband and she were living together again, pangs of regret mingled with the warm, sad memories she had of her American flyer.

She would never forget that Saturday afternoon shortly after the Americans had built their airfield in the middle of her precious view; the Commanding Officer of Bomb Group 599(H) drove up in a jeep and, with his hat at a jaunty angle, had rung the doorbell at *Honeypot Hill*. She worked Saturday mornings and had just arrived home, windblown from the bike ride. It had been a chilly day with a gale blowing straight from Scandinavia off the Fens, so she invited him in, but there was no warmth in her invitation. This was her first direct contact with those 'bloody Yanks' who had so spoiled her outlook, whose planes made the windows rattle whenever they took off or landed, and she hated the way her sleep was being disturbed when they were warming up their engines in the small hours as they prepared for the coming day's raid.

The Colonel had learned about her attitude and wanted to apologize for what he called "the inconvenience of this damned war". He even invited her to drinks and dinner at the Officers Club. She accepted the invitation, not because she wanted to spend a whole evening in the company of these asinine Americans, but because they had the sort of food that had not been seen in England for years. The evening she accepted their invitation she ate steak for the first time in as long as she could remember, and, by hook or by crook, a more cordial relationship gradually evolved.

Little by little, she became an occasional guest at the airfield and vaguely remembered Chuck as a new face in the crowd when he first arrived. With men starved for female company always pushing themselves forward, Chuck's perfect Southern manners made him hang back. The first time they talked he had told her a little about his B-17 flight training in Arizona and then in Dyersburg, in his home state of Tennessee. Danny, his co-pilot, who was listening in on the conversation, then took up the story of how their crew had flown their plane across the Atlantic. There was a nervous eagerness on both their faces as they spoke, making them seem like a pair of naughty little boys on their first day at school. It was not until later, on one of her routine volunteer visits at the cottage hospital, that she and Chuck met properly, after which the sparks began to fly.

Before she really got to know Chuck there had been a few harmless flirtations with other airmen, and she was shameless about her ulterior motives – American men had access to an endless supply of stockings! She would sometimes have boys, as she called them, around for dinner in pairs. The deal was that they brought the food and she cooked it, except for the fresh vegetables which she grew in her garden.

For a while there was a young man named Milton Gates, a tail gunner homesick for the family farm in rural Illinois. He hardly seemed old enough for a driver's license, let alone flying off to war, but he took enormous pleasure digging and weeding her vegetable plot. He died when the *Lady Bountiful* was hit by flak as they attacked a ball bearing factory, and he had been unable to extricate himself from his cold, cramped space at the rear of the plane. Rebecca had nightmares about that terrifying death. He was not the only airman she had been getting to know who ended up in a German grave or as the guest of the Nazis in a *Stalag Luft*, an air force prisoner of war camp.

But after Chuck had endeared himself to her, interest in any others died. This, of course, was now history; Captain Vanderhoven's disappearance over the North Sea put paid to her dreams of escaping dreary old England and making a new life in America. She had been intoxicated by what he had told her about Tennessee and Nashville, his home town, and found herself aching to get there, live with him, be his wife, bear his children, and live happily ever after – the only thing that made her cringe was what he said about the intense humidity of the summer months, which he told her she would get used to.

"But we have a place up in the mountains," he said one night as they lay in bed in each other's arms. "It's over 2000 feet up on the Cumberland Plateau, surrounded by thousands of acres of woodland nearby. I went to college on the Plateau in a place called Sewanee, which is like a miniature Oxford set amid those forested hills; even when days are hot, at night it cools down, and as it gets dark the air is filled with the chatter of cicadas and other insects who live in the trees. The women and children tend to migrate there toward the end of May... I think you'll love that."

Rebecca had smiled as he had held her more tightly. If Chuck said she would love it, then that was enough. After hating the Americans for coming to Thorpe Beauchamp with their beastly planes and their naïve enthusiasm and envying them for their occasional chance to eat decent food, their men rigged out in impeccable uniforms, she now found herself falling for all things American. She started living for the time when she would be there and could become an American. She practiced what her married signature would be on odd scraps of paper until she was satisfied: *Rebecca Vanderhoven*.

On August 28th the dream had turned into a nightmare. Chuck was gone, but now Jeremy was here, and all that remained of her lover was the tiny creature nestled in her womb and already making huge demands on her body. Why did she crave baked potatoes? That Monday she had sat at the breakfast table sipping tea, sobbing for what might have been. Then, gathering her wits, she went upstairs with a cup for her husband, still sound asleep in bed. Rebecca's stomach was jumpy, but she was thankful he had not heard her bout of morning sickness.

Dawn was just breaking as she drew back the curtains, put the cup and saucer on the bedside table, kissing his forehead, and sat down on the edge of the bed. "Wake up, sleepy head," she said as gently as she could. "I have to go to work."

Jeremy's eyes flickered open, he smiled slightly, and, turning over, looked her in the face and whispered sleepily, "Good morning, my wife… Mmm, that sounds so good to say after so many years."

"Did you sleep alright?" she asked, ignoring his comment.

He hitched himself up, plumped the pillow, and after taking a sip replied, "Did I disturb you with another nightmare?"

She shook her head. "Not so much, but I wish there was some way you could give me forewarning," she replied, watching him intently while feeling awkward in his presence. His face was furrowed by years of stress, although she thought he was starting to look a little less haggard. "Do the nightmares happen often?"

He shrugged and was silent, then answered, "I don't always remember, but I'm told most nights… The men I shared a cabin with on the way home told me I was at it every night, but then, I wasn't the only one."

"What causes it?" she asked curiously.

He smiled wanly. "As I told you in my letters, after leaving England and ending up in Cairo and Alexandria, the first year or so wasn't too bad. There was pleasant weather, the food was good and plentiful, it was like an overseas posting in some quieter station of the colonial service. But when Rommel and his German friends came to stiffen Italian resolve everything changed; there was tension, anxiety, discomfort, thirst, hunger, bloodshed, endless deaths, and I'm sure most of us have some kind of inner wound."

"How do you mean?" she asked, at that moment noticing a scar on his neck she had never seen before; she would learn later that this was the memento of a small wound he received when his Jeep came under fire in an ambush as they moved westward through Libya after leaving El Alamein. His injury had been trifling, but his driver would never walk again. Jeremy hadn't written her about it, not wanting to frighten her, colluding with the doctor to make sure no report should be made of something he felt was negligible.

"That's when it became a real war – the fear was palpable, the country club atmosphere long gone, and for what seemed like an eternity we were fighting not just the Germans but were struggling to survive in the desert amidst the heat. We sweated, sand got everywhere, there were flies, disease, not enough food, and never enough water – and all the time death seemed to be just over the horizon. I learned more about bloody landmines in those months than I thought possible… God, I hate those atrocious things." His voice was starting to crack. "… and what they do to people."

"Go on," she prompted.

He gathered his thoughts, then continued. "Merely talking about anti-personnel devices, and what they do to a man who accidentally steps on one, makes me feel physically sick. At the best, a bloke might lose toes or his foot, but he could have his legs blown off, or it might erupt into his groin thus turning him into a eunuch... the lucky ones are the bastards who don't survive ... good friends and fine soldiers among them," Jeremy added as an afterthought. There was anger, sadness, and grief in his voice.

"At Alamein and then all the way across North Africa I watched fine men being blown sky high – sometimes because my own mine clearance squads, despite every effort, had missed something ghastly that Jerry had buried... The Krauts are ingenious, but with every passing month they became more cunning, designing devilish tricks into their mechanisms. I have a close friend who is in a rehab place down in Hampshire now. He has no face or hands... In the quiet of the night when I'm asleep all this comes creeping back, and there's no way I can hold it at bay. I had hoped being away from the battlefield these horrors would diminish, so I'm sorry to bring them back with me, my darling."

As Rebecca cycled to work it felt as if she was carrying the woes of the world on her shoulders. She had listened to Chuck agonize over the deaths he had seen in the air: men covered in flames leaping from mutilated planes as they tumbled from the sky, frostbite due to the bitter cold at 20,000 feet, his navigator suffocating to death when something went wrong with the oxygen line, shrapnel piercing the ship's hull and leaving men without legs and genitals. Now she was Jeremy's confessor as he regurgitated the war in the desert, but she had nowhere to take it all. How much more could she and the other women of Britain stand?

Yet, inexorably, inside her an embryonic life was maturing, a tiny human being who in due course would inherit this generation's mess. For weeks she had wept for Chuck as she pedaled to work, but now her tears were also for Jeremy and her baby. What would she do if she had to raise her child alone, her little boy or girl the target of the opprobrium of illegitimacy? Who would have her? How had she turned her life into such a tangle?

After finding a sheltered spot outside the food office to leave her bike, she slipped into the Ladies, dried her eyes, repaired her face using the little mirror of her compact, freshened her lipstick, plastered on a smile and walked into the office – she was just getting too good at pretending. As she opened the door her colleague, face ashen, was putting down the telephone receiver. She watched from the doorway as Daphne collapsed across her desk. The phone call had been to tell her that a V-2 had exploded in their street in Ilford, Essex, the previous evening, killing her mother and younger sister. Her father was a few minutes late getting in from work so by chance his life was saved.

As she tried to comfort her friend, Rebecca could only grit her teeth and hiss ferociously again and again, "God, if you exist and if you can hear me, I want to scream and curse as I tell you how much I hate this bloody filthy war."

Feeling like a lemon being squeezed from every direction (oh, when had they last seen lemons?), she wondered how she would find her way through the coming months. The wind had been sown, now came the whirlwind – that was a saying she had a strong feeling might have come from the Bible somewhere.

••••••••

Those first days Jeremy and Rebecca were back together they circled one another gingerly, two wary creatures, each with wounds to lick and far from certain of the other's intentions. For Rebecca this had been her home for five years. Jeremy's absence meant the whole house bore the imprint of her style, taste, and lifestyle – not that there had been much available when it came to smartening up home furnishings. Yet there were the pictures, ornaments, and eye-catching feminine touches such as vases of wildflowers or throws over chairs that told whoever came through the door that a sensational woman by the name of Rebecca Anne Lisle lived here.

That small snap of herself and Chuck beside *The Rebecca Anne*, which had been pinned over the kitchen sink so she could think of him when she was working in the kitchen, was now safely hidden away. No longer in that accustomed spot as a reminder for her prayers, she still sensed that the B-17 and Chuck's body had not been separated by the wild waters of the North Sea, but, having gone down together, they were now interred together on a piece of the seabed between Holland and England. A few months later the band leader, Glenn Miller, was to disappear one foggy winter night over roughly that spot where the North Sea and the English Channel merged, and Rebecca would find herself mentally reaching out to his wife, Helen, understanding precisely what she was going through.

Rebecca sometimes found the house so claustrophobic that she would cycle off to work well before Jeremy was awake. Each day he got up slowly, wandered round doing a bit of cleaning, or sometimes just spent the bulk of the day dozing on the sofa, wrapped in a blanket. But by the time she returned in the evening the house would be as snug as he could get it, another corner of the vegetable patch might be freshly dug, or the back door that had been sticking in its frame for several years would at last be square on its hinges, lubricated, and insulated to keep out as many draughts as possible. While he was not the world's greatest cook Jeremy had learned a few tricks, so the sweet smell of cooking hung in the air – and within a couple of minutes of getting home a cup of hot tea would be placed in her hands as she sat by the fire roaring in the fireplace.

Little by little the male face that greeted her each evening began to relax and meaning began to return to the brief kiss they exchanged. That is not to say everything was fine and dandy (a phrase she had learned from Chuck), but they were finding ways to be together. It was as she pedaled the half dozen miles to and from work each day that she gave herself permission to wallow in misery.

Wishful thinking encouraged her to speculate that there might be an outside chance Chuck had been blown off course, parachuting down behind enemy lines, or was safely locked away in some prisoner of war camp, but her heart of hearts knew this was preposterous. She imagined him escaping the Germans, getting back to Allied lines, and maybe one day he would come ambling into the food office to tell her everything was arranged for them to leave for Tennessee, the place she had begun to consider her future home. Sometimes as she cycled she was blinded by tears, forcing her to stop at the roadside for a few moments.

Rebecca felt she was successfully keeping her unhappiness to herself, but she had underestimated Jeremy. One of the reasons she had married Jeremy was his sensitivity, and that side of him was still very much alive, perhaps more so after all he had gone through. Maybe it was because he was a single brother with five sisters that he had a better grasp of how women act, think, and respond than most males. For his part, he had married Rebecca because of her vivacity and generosity, her good looks, her many abilities, and not least the sexuality that sometimes simmered just beneath the surface. He would have been surprised if she had not been an attraction while he was overseas fighting.

On his own for a good part of the day Jeremy not only had time to nap, mull over the past, contemplate the future, or wander round the house finding maintenance jobs he could do but also to identify plumbing, rewiring, and the like that required a professional pair of hands. His name may have been on the deeds of the house alongside Rebecca's, but during those first days back he felt an interloper. Initially he was looking for obvious things like paint and plaster that needed sprucing up, yet as he did so he became aware other things. Rebecca's home in his absence bore telltale signs of the very different kind of life she had been living.

Beside the traces of the various women who had at one time or another rented a room from her, the evidence told him that he was, for the moment, a mere stand-in for another man – or men. It hurt, but it was not entirely surprising. He felt guilty at his own misbehaviors in Africa and Italy when his guard had been down or was feeling particularly homesick but quickly became aware that what had been going on here was more than a few drunken gropes.

Rebecca thought her regular sweeps through the house had successfully removed all hints of another male's presence, but she was always a bit slapdash. She had never smoked, for example, yet Jeremy found a half-smoked pack of Camel cigarettes that had slipped under an easy chair he moved to check a creaking floorboard. At first, he thought nothing of it – there was an American base close by, friendships were inevitable, and it was easy for cigarettes, American or otherwise, to slip out of a pocket.

Yet as the days passed he stumbled on evidence that pointed inexorably towards a special male someone in Rebecca's life. Why was a men's bicycle not very well hidden under a tatty old blanket in the garage? What should he make of several empty Bourbon bottles tucked behind cleaning supplies in the small outside store room? Then there were several men's handkerchiefs in the drawers that were too high a quality to be his own and a pair of slippers about three sizes too big for him pushed under the bed.

One day, while tracing the course of the hot water pipe from the boiler to the airing cupboard, he discovered a stash of American nylons carelessly tucked under some sheets, as well as a pair of pajamas that must have belonged to someone significantly taller than himself. The final straw was the scrap of paper pushed casually into the address book that served as their personal telephone directory on which had been scribbled, in an obviously male hand, 'Honey, see you later. Marty has loaned me his Jeep so I've gone over to Sammy's to get more firewood. Love and kisses, Chuck'.

Shaken, Jeremy poured himself a glass of gin to think through all of this. He quickly concluded that Chuck, whoever he was, must be the reason Rebecca had been so coy in bed. Knowing her nature of old he would have expected her to be all over him, but, apart from a couple of cuddles and a short session that went nowhere, their life since he returned would have honored a monastery or convent rather than a marriage. He had traveled home with fantasies of sex anywhere and everywhere but had been sadly disappointed.

On his second Thursday back, seemingly endless drizzly rain keeping him indoors, Jeremy again went through the letters he had received from Rebecca while overseas. This was not the first time he had re-read them, but now he looked for specific clues that would help him understand what had been going on. Her correspondence had been as regular as clockwork for more than three years, but then, just as communication with home started getting easier, her epistles became less substantial and more infrequent. By his repatriation from Italy he had been writing three letters to every one reply he received from her. While in earlier years she had shared news and gossip from back home, the village and the family, by the time her last letter arrived it was more like a duty thank you note kids are compelled to write when receiving a birthday present, rather than the outpourings of a loving wife anxious to see again her husband who had been fighting for King and Country.

Jeremy concluded sadly that, towards the end, Rebecca had been self-censoring huge chunks of the life she was living. Also, which was strange given their proximity, she barely mentioned the Americans, yet from the packaged food in the pantry to the US-manufactured dresses in her wardrobe it was obvious damned Yanks were an integral part of her life. It didn't take rocket science to deduce why she was keeping this from him. Jeremy reckoned that there was just one American, this character with the ridiculously transatlantic nickname of Chuck, who had taken center stage in his wife's heart.

He was more than puzzled because this was the woman who only a couple of years earlier was railing against 'bloody Americans' whose base was an eyesore spoiling her view, keeping her awake at night with their 'darned bombers' whose flight path came over her home. She had, it seems, with a characteristically Rebecca-esque flourish, swung 180 degrees from *hating* all things American to loving, fraternizing, and perhaps sleeping with them. Yet it would hardly have been surprising that an attractive woman like Rebecca, with a healthy appetite for pretty things and physical pleasure, would catch the eye of some of the hundreds of charming men all away from home, hearth, wives, and girlfriends. This was what he had dreaded most when he was given orders to go home.

Jeremy was in inner agony, feeling betrayed but having to admit that despite his self-proclaimed high moral standards he, too, had stumbled. There had been that Egyptian diplomat's wife he and his friends had come to know in Cairo, and then the woman who presided over that café in Sicily in whose bed he had woken one morning after being primed with cheap wine that had the kick of a mule. He had been terrified for weeks she had passed on to him some nasty venereal bug.

Rebecca always looked gorgeous and had a magnetic personality. Given the way she sparkled when in male company, perhaps he should have been surprised she was still here when he got home. In glummer moments during the years away he had wondered why she had married such an ordinary fellow as himself; there had been many more eligible candidates. Regretting and feeling guilt-ridden by his own mishaps amid the uncertainties of war, it seemed obvious that Rebecca's infidelities were in an entirely different league.

Getting out and about in the community – visits to the pub, picking up groceries at the village store, chance conversations with Americans in the street – the accumulating evidence pointed clearly towards his wife's romantic involvements. He was particularly taken aback by a cheery conversation one morning with Mrs. Aitchison at the village shop. She was wearing one of her old faded floral housecoats. At that moment he was the only customer, and Ada Aitchison, overweight and usually morose, was in one of her chattier moods.

"Major Lisle," she said, her pudgy face shining and pink cheeks alive with a broad grin, "it is so nice to have you back home again, you were away too long."

Jeremy laughed. "You can say that again, Ada, no one was gladder than me when the government mandated that those of us who had borne the heat of the African and Italian sun the longest should be given some home leave… we deserved it."

She asked him about the places he had been and people he had met but steered clear of the revolting business of warfare itself. Jeremy was happy to give her a glimpse of the local color of distant lands, sharing a couple of funny stories like getting lost in his Jeep in the desert one dark night so that she understood that, although it had been demanding, it had not been without its lighter moments.

Sighing, as the conversation drew to a close, she said, "I envy you in one thing… you got to see the Pyramids. I doubt an old village woman like me will ever see Paris, let alone Egypt. When I was a girl I loved pictures of the River Nile and them there Pyramids… couldn't read enough stories about Egypt." Giggling, she put her hand over her mouth in embarrassment. "I would pretend I was Cleopatra… imagine that, me as Cleopatra."

Jeremy, gathering their meager supplies, paid his bill and handed over the necessary ration coupons. Ada welcomed him home again, then said, "Well, it is wonderful to see you and Rebecca together, so much better than…" She stopped in mid-sentence, her face becoming even ruddier, and he grasped the reason for her embarrassment over what she had intended to say. Intuition told him that had she continued this line of thought it would have been about his wife spending far too much time with a certain American airman.

When Jeremy and his unit had arrived in Naples earlier in the year, they had been greeted by the spectacular display of Mount Vesuvius erupting. It had been smoldering precariously when they got there and then a few days later had roared into action. He had been taught about volcanoes at school, but as there were none in Britain he hadn't taken a lot of notice because he never thought he would witness such geological fireworks. But now he had front row seats, and he and his men tried to help as villages and farms on the slopes of Vesuvius were devastated.

Now, wandering amid the volatile ruins of his own domestic circumstances, it seemed his precious wife had turned herself into someone he could hardly recognize. Inwardly he seethed, and part of him yearned to respond with all the explosive savagery of that Italian mountain. He imagined himself putting her over his knee and thrashing her, but it did not take much intelligence to grasp that would alienate her forever – besides, he knew he could never forgive himself if he did such a heinous thing.

It made him furious and queasy to contemplate her romping in *his* bed with some over-sexed Yank, generously yielding to Chuck all that she had promised would be his in their marriage vows. His heart was close to breaking over this woman who had been his inspiration on dangerous days and nights on the battlefield. He wished he had not seen the charred bodies of good men in ruined tanks or have had to order his unit to dig mass graves in which Allied and Axis soldiers could be hurriedly buried together with the barest of funeral rites so that disease could be kept at bay from both sides. He had gone to war convinced he was fighting to protect Rebecca – and their future family. Now he wondered if it might not have been better to have been blown up by a landmine or shot in the head by that soldier of the Wehrmacht he had accidentally run into and had been incapable of bringing himself to kill, instead knocking him out with the butt of his service revolver.

Sleeping in holes in the desert he was either nearly frozen or eaten alive by a menagerie of insects, yet here she was back in England running around the place like a bitch in heat with interlopers from the USA, always happy to share her bed and body. The Americans might have helped save Britain's bacon, but, at the same time, they were stealing the very women who were precious to the men who were putting their lives on the line to protect their kith and kin from the Nazi marauders.

He would work out his anger with shovel and fork in the garden, by taking long walks, and throwing himself even more furiously into the necessary household repairs; besides, when he left Rebecca and started afresh without her, she was going to need a solid roof over her head and vegetables on her table. Perhaps she would go off with one of these rapacious Americans, maybe she was already making such plans. His emotions were in turmoil, and as he catastrophized his imagination was becoming ever more lurid. He was amazed how successfully he managed to hide his feelings from her, but then she was utterly wrapped up in herself, and one of the things he had learned during these last years was how to keep inner malevolence under lock and key. He did not know much psychology but wondered if his nightmares might be an internal safety valve protecting him from the potential excesses of his fissiparous emotions.

Jeremy had sworn off Scotch, gin, and the like since the uproarious goodbye party in the mess, but having finished the last bottle of gin, what helped him stay sober now was the huge shortage of spirits in the place. Thus he turned to a higher power, and each morning after breakfast, and when Rebecca had gone to work, he would jump the low churchyard wall, sauntering through the graves, then spend twenty or thirty minutes in the hallowed silence of the old village church, pouring his heart out to God. Small though the building was, he came to love this ancient place of worship – he would miss it dreadfully when he moved off on his own. It wasn't just the age of the building that was impressive, but there was this deep sense of peace, as if getting on for a millennium of prayers had somehow soaked into the grizzled walls which were now somehow releasing their essence back into the atmosphere that surrounded him.

Friday, October 13, 1944 — Honeypot Hill, Thorpe Beauchamp

The phone rang as Jeremy was drinking a cup of the oddly flavored brown slurry that these days the British passed off as coffee. It was mid-morning. He had just finished cleaning the grate in the living room, putting in place dry and old newspapers to light the fire later in the day to warm the house up before Rebecca came home. In a few minutes he intended to do some work outside before it started raining again, digging what he intended as Rebecca's next year potato patch. Filling, starchy foods were going to continue to be of paramount importance given the reality that years were likely to pass before rationing finally disappeared.

Answering with a casual hello, he immediately picked up the crackle of a long distance line, then a male voice asked, "Chuck?"

"No, you have the wrong number."

"I'm sorry, I could have sworn Chuck Vanderhoven was still living at…" and an obviously American voice told him the number.

"No," Jeremy answered, trying to sound unthreatened. There was an embarrassed silence, then the caller muttering something about being sorry for troubling him; there was a click, then the line went dead. Jeremy sat staring into the distance. His coffee was getting cold and his innards were churning; the quarter-acre potato patch was forgotten. At least he was now certain of the name of the man who had been Rebecca's American companion.

In the last few days his sleep patterns had gradually begun returning to normal as bone-wearying exhaustion gave way to a healthier tiredness. He was no longer sleeping ten or eleven hours each night, and while there were still nightmares they seemed slightly less frequently. For several mornings in a row he had been aware of Rebecca slipping out of bed early, pattering downstairs, then shutting herself into the little toilet beside the kitchen. Straining his ears he would hear the sounds of her coughing, spluttering, and occasionally throwing up. This added to his anxiety, but she was so fragile when around him that he did not know how to approach it.

The morning of the phone caller asking for Chuck, having abandoned all thought of preparing the ground for potatoes, he needed to do something more energetic to take the edge off his ire. Instead, he finished cutting several large dead branches from an old elm tree with saw and axe, physically exhausting himself while, at the same time, adding valuable logs to the woodpile. The exertion did take the edge off his torment, but his mind would not stop turning over and over in anguish.

During his fighting years, church parades had become increasingly important to Jeremy Lisle. He befriended a succession of chaplains, and as the fighting intensified in North Africa he learned the habit of prayer, fervently asking God that he might be spared from this living hell and be returned home to Thorpe Beauchamp, to his beloved wife and to his much-loved home overlooking the Fens. He knew there would be readjustment problems, but only in his worst nightmares did he imagine that the circumstances accompanying his homecoming might be so distressing.

The chaplain he had appreciated most was Peter Maynard, a man of about his own age and from a similar sort of background. A note from a friend had informed him that this padre was now back in England, too, and preparing to return to Civvy Street. It sounded as if he would soon become vicar of a couple of small communities somewhere in the middle of the country. Peter was originally from Worcester where his father was headmaster of a boys' grammar school, and his mother had returned to nursing when hostilities broke out. The following morning, after a restless night, Jeremy found himself wrestling as he wrote a letter in which as frankly as possible he poured out his soul, seeking guidance.

Several days passed, and then when he came in from gardening to scavenge bread and cheese for lunch, he saw the day's mail lying on the mat. Having washed the dirt of the potato patch from his hands and face, he pounced on a letter that was obviously from his chaplain friend. Before opening it he constructed a sandwich, opened a small bottle of beer, then settled at the kitchen table to read it through several times. It seemed he wasn't the only returning soldier with this kind of dilemma. Chaplain Maynard had received several such *cris de coeur* from men of various ranks who, on coming home, discover family circumstances not dissimilar to his own.

The advice the padre gave Jeremy was eminently sound, just what he would have expected from such a kind and thoughtful man. He included his phone number. Having finished his meal and washed the dishes Jeremy settled down at the always immaculately tidy desk in his small study and, with his heart pounding, connected to the long-distance operator. He did not care how expensive a trunk call would be; what they needed to discuss was worth far more than the few shillings it would cost. He thought he would find himself leaving a message with the army receptionist, but actually reached the priest at his desk.

"Goodness, Padre, am I glad to be able to talk to you."

There was a gentle chuckle. "Jeremy, old man, if it's any comfort you're not the only one. War has been playing havoc with families and marriages... A lot of marital best intentions have come unraveled in the hostilities. I'm just wondering what I'm going to discover when I get out of uniform, back into parish ministry, and living for the first time for years with my own wife and family."

After pleasantries they discussed the situation, Peter helping Jeremy tease out a strategy. The longer they talked, the more grateful Jeremy was that he had not exploded all over Rebecca like a tetchy landmine. The advice he received was difficult but sound, and it was a relief to know that Peter would be at the other end of the telephone line should he need him.

"I can't tell you how grateful I am, Padre," Jeremy said as they rounded off the conversation.

"And I can't tell you how grateful I am that you entrusted me with what must be a frightfully painful and embarrassing situation for you," replied Peter Maynard. "You're in my prayers, old chap, and please stay in touch – even bring Rebecca to see me... I'd love to meet her. I'll be finished with the army in a few weeks, but my bishop has something up his sleeve that I can't talk about at the moment. However, I promise I'll send my new address and phone number as soon as I have them.

After the call had ended, Jeremy covered his face with his hands and wept for the first time since a close friend had been killed in Tunisia in the months following the Battle of El Alamein. Those had been tears of grief, now it was relief that set him crying.

Sunday Lunchtime, October 10, 2004 — Honeypot Hill, Thorpe Beauchamp

Millie and I had just about finished preparing lunch, a fresh chicken soup with all sorts of veggies slung in for good measure, when first David appeared, followed about twenty minutes later by his bleary-eyed sister.

"Don't ask what time Davey and I made it to bed last night," Amanda warned as she entered the kitchen. Having brewed a fresh pot of coffee when she had heard David moving around, Millie was immediately able to wave a mug of extra strong undiluted caffeine under her sister-in-law's nose. "Oh, Millie, you are an angel of mercy," Amanda responded, flopping down in a chair and immediately raising the steaming liquid to her lips.

"What were you both doing through the night when wise grownups should have been in their beds and sound asleep?" I asked as casually as I could, while bursting with curiosity.

David yawned. "You may not believe this, but never before have I spent almost a whole night in a garage with my sister."

"What on earth were you up to?"

"Amanda won't be *compos mentis* until the middle of the afternoon at the earliest, but I need at least one more strong mug of coffee before my little grey cells are alert enough to put two lucid thoughts together," he replied with a fake glare at his wife. Millie smiled indulgently, then grabbing the already empty mug, pouring in more caffeine and giggling, she stuck out her tongue.

When my two children and daughter-in-law left later that afternoon the sun was setting, but I was in so much better shape than when they had arrived. We had also hatched a plan to see how much more we could uncover about my parents' lives during and in the wake of the war, also how it was that Jeremy Lisle had come to terms with his wife's pregnancy.

Daddy's archives were extensive, and with all the compulsive fidgety orderliness of his engineer's mind he hung onto every invoice, receipt, piece of paper or picture, filing them in impeccable order. He seemed to have kept virtually every sheet of paper that had ever passed through his hands, every single letter received, carbon copies of his responses, bank accounts, legal documents, pocket diaries, and a few personal journals – journaling being something he did not seem to have started until around the time the war was winding down.

Amidst this treasure trove were my mother's letters to him during the war and, surprisingly, several letters between himself and the commander of the US Air Base in Thorpe Beauchamp during the time that the whole operation was being decommissioned and returned to farmland. There were photos galore that I had never seen, medals, old passports, military IDs, and on and on. No wonder it had been impossible for as long as I could remember to get even the smallest car into our garage!

During the night, David and Amanda had put their heads together, agreed tactics, and then, after a drink or two, adjourned to the garage. They had not been able to find all the keys, but using skills at lock picking which Amanda seems to have perfected as a teenager, they had managed to find their way into most of the filing cabinets, which at least gave them an idea where relevant data might be stored. For Amanda, an addictive researcher, this new project was like having died and gone to heaven!

"We didn't want to start scrabbling through everything until we'd talked to you, Mumsie," Amanda revealed excitedly over the lunch table, "but we have pulled up a few interesting documents for you to try to make sense of… they're on the dining room table alongside the stuff from Gran's attic boxes."

"What's going to happen, Mother," broke in my son, "is that Amanda has a long paper to write for some research project at work…"

"…. So I'm going to attempt to talk my way into being able to come down here," his sister interrupted, "probably on Wednesday or Thursday. Then I can spend ten days working on my paper and will take leave still due to me for this year so that I can go on a magical mystery tour through Grandad's archives in the garage."

Millie's eyes were alight with excitement. Amanda saw it and smiled. "You want to come as well, don't you, sister-in-law?" Millie nodded enthusiastically. Did this mean that the cold war-like relationship between these two women was starting to thaw? I would suspend my judgment until I had more evidence to work with.

David laughed, "I knew it. Sis, I told you last night you wouldn't be able to keep Millie away, even if she is *meant* to be cozying up to wealthy clients at the gallery."

Amanda stuck her tongue out and wiggled her fingers on the end of her nose, then, following Millie's lead, she also dissolved into girlish giggles. It was like a flashback as I caught a brief glimpse of my once mischievous baby; there apparently was some kind of détente developing between the two girls.

"Do I have permission, my lord and master?" Millie asked in the pleading little girl voice that she knew would wrap him round her little finger.

"I will miss you, darling, but of course you do. However, I don't want you scrambling through all those papers and things in your condition."

Millie instantly shed the little girl act and turned into his cavewoman wife. "Oh, for God's sake, Quinn, this is the twenty-first century, the Queen's name happens to be Elizabeth II not Victoria, and I'm far from a fragile little flower who needs to be hustled into seclusion and wrapped in pink tissue. What was it that the first Elizabeth said when the Armada threatened?" She thought for a moment then jumped up, put her hand on her chest and quoted, "'I know I have the body of a weak and feeble woman, but I have the heart and stomach of a king, and a king of England too.' You forget, Quinn, that my middle name just happens to be Elizabeth…"

Amanda laughed, "Good for you, girl." Then looking at her brother she said, "Back off, big brother – she's in charge!"

"But I'm concerned about our baby," the poor man gasped, only to be laughed at by three women who could hardly believe what a relic he was from the past. My son would have made a wonderful Victorian *pater familias*, and it was not hard to imagine him in a high starched collar, frock coat, and mutton chop whiskers.

Sleeping a little better each night, I gradually began taking an interest in both life and food again. On several brisk sunny days, I took long walks drinking in the countryside as autumn advanced or snuggled in my comfortable chair, a shawl around my shoulders, immersed in Daddy's journals and diaries, loving him more with each passing day. When the girls came back I had found at least a dozen new ways to appreciate the man who had in every way except conception been my father, although the sketchy jottings in his diaries were tantalizing rather than descriptive. While it was interesting to shadow him through his wartime service, appointments and meetings, I particularly treasured words written in October sixty years almost to the day earlier: "And finally I am home."

Wednesday, October 20, 2004 — Honeypot Hill, Thorpe Beauchamp

Amanda reappeared at *Honeypot Hill* first. Millie followed her a few days later having put David on a plane at Heathrow for a quick business trip to Geneva. I then had the pleasure of eating my daughter-in-law's cooking, both girls being determined to put a bit more flesh on my bones, and, at the same time, watching my daughter maneuvering her way through her grandfather's papers like a cat on the trail of a mouse or a barn owl quartering a winter's field in search of prey! Her experience in endless archives gave her a nose for this kind of thing; halfway through the morning of her second day on the job she scampered into the house and laid before me a letter from an army chaplain.

"Mumsie," she said, her voiced high-pitched with excitement, "I've found this letter that Granddad had carefully salted away; I think it sheds light on how he spent those weeks following his arrival home in 1944. He'd obviously cried on the shoulder of this army chaplain, someone I suspect he knew in North Africa. If there were more priests around like Peter Maynard I might start occasionally going to church again... No, let me say that again, I might even go every Sunday!"

The watery ink was fading and the low quality wartime paper had yellowed, but by the time I had read it I was convinced I owed the blessed life I had lived to this man, Major the Reverend Peter Maynard. Later we were to discover that this humble clergyman spent almost all the rest of his ministry in three different rural parishes not too far away from us in the countryside around Peterborough.

---

31 October, 1944

Jeremy, Old Man,

It was superb to receive your letter the other morning, although I was so terribly sorry to hear about the confusing situation you discovered on getting home from Naples. From the conversations we had in Italy before I left for home and before you got your orders I know you were anxious, but neither of us could have had any idea your wife might fall so hopelessly in love with another man.

If I understand you correctly, my dear fellow, you have done some Sherlock Holmes-ing and have discovered that she had been living quite openly in your house with an American Air Force officer for some months. Given the comments and looks you have received you have determined that this was common knowledge – like the taxi driver's face when he dropped you off, and the half-finished sentence of the woman in the village shop.

You know, when I got back to England, my wife and I found ourselves very much strangers to one another, although we had not been apart anywhere near as long as you and Rebecca. We had married when I was a curate with a brand new clerical collar and fresh out of theological college. Like you and your wife, we did not have much time together before the call came to serve King and Country. In my illusions I imagined myself returning home and picking up very much from where we left off. I realize now that would have been impossible. Recognizing how each of us has changed in the many months apart, Philippa and I have deliberately set about exploring new shapes for our relationship, taking into account our commitment to one another but not discounting what might have happened in the intervening years – and what has made us the people we are now, not who we were when we kissed goodbye. It is, I confess, like climbing a sheer rock face and not knowing where the footholds are. These first few weeks have proved a challenge, but things are getting a little less stressed; we are, I think, rounding a corner. That is certainly something you and Rebecca might consider.

Then there's the thorny issue that Rebecca is possibly pregnant – your description of her episodes first thing would, as you guessed, suggest morning sickness. All I can say, old man, is that there's a lot of this going round. I don't mean to trivialize your plight, but there are, I suspect, tens of thousands of little ones up and down our land who are the unexpected byproduct of all the trauma and disruption. Getting angry and accusing her of being slattern will only make matters worse – besides, you are a better man than that. Where else did she have to turn when the anxiety became too much?

This will obviously need gentle handling, for you will be putting your whole future on the line, as well as that of your wife and the unborn child. You should find the right moment to sit down with her, having carefully rehearsed in your mind what you want to say, and don't for God's sake allow anger to divert from your mental script. Be careful not to respond crossly when she comes up with something that upsets you because, remember, she's probably as edgy about this as you, if not more so – she is thinking not only of her future but will be impossibly worried about the baby.

As you know, men in my walk of life are not enthusiasts of divorce, but you cannot hold her against her will – especially if she is carrying another man's child. Like you, I have no idea of the state of play in that relationship – maybe she is being kind by staying but wants to leave, be with him, marry him, and maybe make a new life for herself and their child in America.

If the two of you find some way of staying together, then joyfully accept this little boy or little girl as your own, love the child and cherish it, and I suspect the love you lavish upon it will be returned thirty, sixty, and a hundredfold, as Jesus might have put it.

Be assured of my prayers for you both as this moves forward. I am sure you have poured all this out to God in your prayers. You are a good man Jeremy Lisle, you have been a faithful soldier, I'm sure you are a loving husband, and you have always been one of those officers who tries to do the right thing no matter what; I am sure that is how you will behave in these gnawingly difficult circumstances.

God bless you,

Peter

MAJOR. PETER M. MAYNARD

By the time I had finished reading the letter Amanda had slipped a large box of soft white tissues onto my lap so I could deal with the tears dribbling down my cheeks.

Amanda knelt at my knees and whispered, "Mumsie, I think this tells you that Granddad loved you ever so much."

A moment later Millie was also kneeling alongside her and the two of them had their heads on my lap. At that moment I felt utterly overwhelmed, but, as the padre had said, I was blessed thirty, sixty, and a hundredfold.

Sunday, November 5, 1944 — Honeypot Hill, Thorpe Beauchamp

It was very early on Sunday morning when Jeremy, who had been lying half-awake for hours, felt Rebecca, unaware that he was conscious, delicately slide from beneath the sheets and stumble from the room. Today she did not go downstairs but the bathroom slammed shut as she went. There followed the now familiar sounds of maternal morning sickness, and she hoped to goodness she was not disturbing Jeremy. She had looked utterly exhausted when she arrived home from work the previous afternoon, had eaten little, and then had curled up on the sofa by the roaring fire and fallen sound asleep.

Her swift exit from bed was Jeremy's cue to get up and put on his shabby old dressing gown. By the time she had gathered herself and come downstairs looking pale and gaunt, he was sitting in the living room with a freshly made cup of tea.

"I thought you might need this, my darling," he said. The fireplace had been cleared of embers and a new one had been lit. In addition to tea, on a small tray was a plate with a few slices of toast to entice her.

She smiled, allowed him to kiss her forehead, and answered sheepishly, "I must have eaten something that didn't agree with me." In reality she had eaten next to nothing the previous day.

Wrapping her long pink robe around herself and perching on the edge of her chair she folded the fingers of both her hands around the big old chipped cup and sipped tea while staring blankly into the flames, watching as they enveloped a gnarled old log Jeremy had cut from the dead tree. Then her husband spoke softly and as lovingly as he could. "Rebecca, darling, that is not the first time you have been sick in the morning."

"Oh, you know, sweetie, time of the month, a little bug, and all that," she answered, looking down at her knees but knowing full well he was onto her deception. Time was running out to make a clean breast of things.

"Is there something you want to tell me?" he asked softly with all the gentleness he could muster.

She winced, then fibbed again, "No. These days almost everyone, even the fittest among us, picks up little bugs because our diet has been so deficient for so long. The bugs aren't bad enough to bring us to a grinding halt, but, at the same time, they keep us from being able to function at our best."

He was quiet. "Well, my dear, I'm not going to press you, but when you are ready to talk about it I'll be ready to listen."

She was silent for a moment.

"Did you treat your men like this in Africa and Sicily?" There was astonishment in her voice as she deliberately changed the subject.

"Like what?"

"Trying to sneak information out of them indirectly, by being nice, just like you did with me just now."

He laughed as he felt around in his pocket for his pipe. "I suppose I did, and it usually worked even if it took longer to get to the bottom of whatever might be going on."

There was a long silence, then she murmured, "When did you get to be so wise, Jeremy Lisle?" Her tired blue eyes looked directly at him over the rim of the cup. Oh, how he loved her. He couldn't help himself, neither could he bear the thought of ever having to let her go to someone else – or even that she had already been with that man.

He shrugged. "I discovered before the war that I could get more out of our blokes at the works by coaxing kindly rather than barking ferociously. Dad always barked, which regularly created huge storms over issues that were relatively insignificant. He never grew out of being the drill sergeant he was at the end of the Great War. I'd never been a hugely military person, so I just carried on in the army the way I did in the business. When you are responsible for the lives of several dozen men thousands of miles from home, most of them scared out of their wits and trying not to show it, walloping them over the head with a cricket bat never wins their trust – like donkeys they'll just dig in their heels."

He sat looking into the fire as Rebecca tucked her legs beneath her, settling into her comfortable chair like a pussycat.

"Go on," she whispered.

He shrugged. "This was especially so when none of us knew quite how the whole damned shooting match was going to work out. When the evacuations at Dunkirk were happening, we were on our way to Cairo by way of the Cape of Good Hope, India, and the Red Sea. I was frightened that if I ever got back I would return in chains… and never see you again. I think I prayed harder then than at any time of my life."

Rebecca said nothing, but deep inside she could feel a rising tide of panic as she tried to gauge how much longer she could keep up her act, whether she wanted to go on deceiving him, and as she gazed into the fire she found herself imagining the furious scene when he found out.

• • • • • • •

As November progressed, the weather deteriorated, and Rebecca was permanently exhausted. Being pregnant was fatiguing, especially when you had to cycle several miles to and from work each day. She did not dare go to see the doctor to confirm her pregnancy and as a result receive a more appropriate food ration; her secret would then be out. She knew Jeremy was worried but found it impossible to find the right way to address the issue with him, despite her certainty that he knew all about her condition.

One evening she arrived home drenched, shivering, and grateful her husband was home, that the house was relatively warm, and he was ready to set a lovely cup of tea in front of her within minutes of her walking through the door. He would then help her with her sopping wet clothes. It was as she unwound in front of the fire that she felt something: her innards were churning, and she knew something inside was going wrong. A minute or two later Jeremy, who was in the kitchen preparing their evening meal, heard her gasp, groan, and then let out a little yelp. Rebecca jumped up, dashed upstairs to the bathroom, then locked the door.

Jeremy followed her, knocking on the door and asked, "Rebecca, what's wrong?"

There was whimpering, silence, then moaning followed by floods of tears.

"Darling, what's wrong?"

She gasped, "I think I'm having a miscarriage."

He was quiet and then said, "OK, sweetheart, get yourself ready and I'm going to take you straight to the doctor."

"How?"

"You'll see," came the enigmatic reply.

Five minutes later an ashen, distraught woman came down the stairs. He wrapped her up as if she was a small girl in an old fur coat that had once belonged to his mother. Then putting his arm around his wife, he ushered her out of the house and into his old car now sitting in the driveway, its engine turning over.

"But, how…" she asked in astonishment.

"Oh, I've been talking to the War Office and they don't want me to get back into uniform until we begin to make the final advance on Berlin. Meanwhile, they want me to start lifting the load off the Old Man's shoulders at the factory. Pops is a canny old devil and has managed to scrounge extra petrol coupons for me – and then old Herb Adams down at the garage helped for an hour this morning to get the old lady up and running again. I only got it finished today, so maybe there is a God in the heavens when it comes to taking care of us and our baby."

It was getting light the following morning when they dragged back into the house, having seen the doctor then been sent over to the cottage hospital where the crisis was averted. It had been a false alarm, but Rebecca was now under strict instructions to take it easy for several weeks. Given her condition she would soon start getting the food and other benefits for expectant mothers. She went straight to bed, and Jeremy set out to love her, coddle her, and respond to her every whim.

He was calm and loving each morning as he brought her breakfast in bed. Then she would pretend to read a book while listening to the BBC Light Service's *Music While You Work*. Jeremy settled in the easy chair in the bedroom. He was working through documents, ledgers, and financials his father had been sending in batches so he could get up to speed on the state of play in the family business and start thinking through how they would handle the challenges facing them in the approaching post-war years.

One morning around eleven he brought Rebecca some Ovaltine, then sat on the bed, took her hand in his, and asked as lovingly as he could, "My darling, tell me something about Chuck Vanderhoven?"

She looked shocked and then asked, "Who?"

He wanted to bellow, but instead smiled, his stomach tightening as he restrained his temper, then made his own confession as Peter Maynard had coached. "Let me tell you a story. There was once a very green subaltern who arrived in Cairo early August 1940. He was very frightened, unbelievably homesick, and missing dreadfully the wife whom he passionately loved. His country was fighting for its life and she was back home in an England under siege, bombers and fighter planes engaged in desperate air actions overhead, and he was terrified what the outcome might be."

"Me?" she asked in a little voice, and he held up his hand not to interrupt, this was one of the most difficult conversations he had ever initiated.

"Months passed, all the time he hurt inside and was desperately worried. In the midst of his anguish he was befriended by a gracious Egyptian couple. She was some years older than he was, and her husband was older still, a civil servant who worked impossibly long hours. Her children were grown, but she had this knack of turning men into willing slaves… the subaltern was so, so naïve. Several years later, much wiser but no less vulnerable, this same man fell ill in Sicily. It was while he was recovering that news came through of his promotion to major. He wasn't a heavy drinker, but that night his friends insisted on a party in a local restaurant to celebrate. They were determined to dowse him in the local vino. The following morning he awoke tucked up in bed with the lady who kept the café…"

"Why are you telling me this?" Rebecca asked.

Jeremy's face was flushed when he looked up at her, overwhelmed by his own embarrassment. "Because, Rebecca, my darling, neither of us has come through the war without there being a few dents and some nasty scratches in the coachwork of our marriage. I'm right when I say that you and Captain Chuck Vanderhoven have been pretty sweet on each other for a while now."

Rebecca froze. "Who told you that?"

He shook his head. "No one, my darling, I worked it out. It wasn't difficult."

"Why didn't you tell me what you were thinking?" she asked, stunned that despite all her efforts the story was out, and she found herself appreciating just how much she had hurt him. She wondered if she would be turfed out, finding herself without husband or a home for her baby.

"Because I hoped I would hear it from you. But it took me quite a while to understand just how difficult something like that must be."

Rebecca dissolved. She was not shedding tears just because she had been found out; these were tears of deepest regret. She had hurt Jeremy, Chuck was dead and gone, she was unexpectedly pregnant. She had taken huge risks and her life was in a mess. Only by nearly losing the baby had she realized just how much she loved the child nestled inside her. But there was more to these tears than that. They were about their years of separation, the gnawing, corrosive hardship of war, that Jeremy had been so far away, that Chuck had filled the vacuum; now dread took hold of her.

The storm gradually subsided, and through swollen bloodshot eyes she looked up to where Jeremy was sitting beside her. He was crying too. His head was cradled in his arms on the bed, his breathing punctuated by wracking, shuddering gasps. She had never seen him cry before and was terrified how grief was suffusing his whole body. Only then did it dawn upon her just how much she had hurt him by not coming clean sooner.

Crawling to the end of the bed, she lifted his head and laid it in her lap. Then resting her head on his, she started weeping again. This time the sobs were soft and strangely cleansing. An hour later they had together migrated under the covers; their faces tear-stained, their arms holding one another tight, the radio droning in the background, but the pair of them asleep following the exhaustion of this ordeal. Maybe this was when the healing of their love and marriage really began.

Later, when it was almost dark, Jeremy crept downstairs, re-lit the fire in the living room, and carried his wife to the sofa. Having eaten some bread and soup, they lay together on the sofa under cozy blankets, then after a faltering start began talking in earnest. When Jeremy had gone away his wife had been barely a woman, more a somewhat spoiled overgrown schoolgirl playing house. He had come home to a grown worldly-wise woman whose war had been as dislocating as his own. She still had that enthusiasm for life that enchanted him, as well as her stronger than strong will, but the wartime buffeting had driven her to seek shelter in other men's arms.

As the evening progressed Rebecca lay cocooned on the sofa with Jeremy kneeling beside her, his hands holding hers. Finally, he softly spoke to her. "Rebecca, you know that I love you with every fiber of my being, but since arriving home it has been clear to me that you have given your heart to someone else, something confirmed a thousand times over by the fact that you are carrying his baby. Because I adore you so much I want you to be mine forever – till death us do part, but because I love you I don't want to hold onto you against your will. I'm prepared to relinquish all my claims on your life. I'm prepared to let go of you so that you can be with him in America."

She stuttered, almost choking. Then from somewhere deep down inside her bubbled this piercing wail of grief. Jeremy had grasped the intensity of her relationship with Chuck, but she had never told him what had happened, that his remains now lay rotting on the floor of the North Sea.

"Darling, Jeremy," she managed to choke out when the torment moderated enough for her to speak, "Chuck no longer is."

"What do you mean?"

"Let me begin from the beginning," she responded, holding his hands tightly.

So two aching hearts were finally opened to one another. There were long silences, weeping, and encouraging cuddles as Rebecca manage to unburden herself of all the male friendships she had made around the US air base. She half-laughed over how much she had detested the Americans and what they had done to her lovely view across the fields, the crowning glory of their Philistine ways being to track the main flight path right over her home – something Jeremy had discovered for himself since coming home to *Honeypot Hill*. She told him of the invitations, the visit to the cottage hospital, flirting which began as a game to keep herself in nylons, but finding how much Chuck relieved the intensity of her loneliness. She spoke of the unbearable inner agony she experienced as men she knew went off on their missions in the morning, and then spending all day wondering who would and who would not return. She kept coming back to Chuck, and how one thing had led to another, and another, and then another.

Jeremy asked honest questions about what made her fall in love with Chuck and wondered how the relationship had so rapidly advanced from platonic to passionate, leapfrogging any sense of prudence along the way. She told him how Chuck had wanted to marry her and take her home to Tennessee. Jeremy followed Peter Maynard's advice and listened quietly, trying not to disclose to her how this was stripping his every emotion raw. His head was throbbing and his whole body ached as he listened, coaxing her to tell him more.

At last Rebecca got around to talking about the stuff of nightmares. Clasping his fingers more tightly she confided in him, "A few days before getting the telegram saying that you were finally on your way home, Chuck and his crew made their last scheduled mission. When they got back they would have completed their thirty-five, and would be free to go home. He knew he would be reassigned Stateside, becoming an instructor at an Army Air Forces flight school, probably in Arizona. He had also just about managed to wangle a way for me to go back with him…" She gasped, whispered, "but he never came home," then dissolved into tears.

"What?"

It took Rebecca some minutes to get her emotions under control before continuing. "The boys would talk about the flak over targets sometimes being so intense they could walk on it. I gather that was the undoing of *The Rebecca Anne*. They named their new B-17G after me when it was delivered some months ago. Chuck is… was… a gifted artist and spent days painting my likeness on the nose. Flak hit the ship at an awkward angle as it started to turn for home after dropping its load – they were big bombs, thousand pounders."

"Who told you this?" Jeremy asked.

"Marty… Colonel Martin Robinson…" She nodded her head in

the direction of the air base. "He's the commander at the airfield. He came over a few nights before you got back to tell me the details as they knew them."

He was astonished. "Was that wise?"

Her eyes flashed. "Jeremy, it was what I wanted. I *had* to know what had happened, just as I would have had to know the details if something terrible had happened to you." She kissed his forehead and stroked his cheek.

"Go on with your story then, my darling," his voice now a mere croak.

It took Rebecca a moment or two to regroup but then murmur, "I've been told that it was dumb luck, but that without Chuck's brilliant flying it would have been impossible to get a plane with as many holes as a colander across Germany and almost back. He was aiming to bring her all the way to England, but more important to him were the lives of his crew, especially two with shrapnel wounds. When they were over liberated Northern France, friendly territory, he commanded everyone except himself and Danny, his co-pilot, to jump to safety. All are alive today because of Chuck, even the wounded blokes. Then he and Danny dropped to a lower altitude hoping to skim across the North Sea, crash landing on the first field they came to." At this point she completely lost her composure, and, screwing up her tortured face, all she could gasp was, "They almost made it, but no one knows where they crashed."

Jeremy was dumbstruck. This man wasn't some cheap over-sexed wife-stealer who had problems keeping his trousers on but a genuine hero, a leader who as a matter of course put his men before his own safety. When he ordered the crew to parachute to safety he probably had a pretty good idea he could never get such a mortally wounded aircraft back in one piece. At that moment Jeremy hoped and prayed the Americans would do the decent thing and honor him for saving his men's lives, even if the award was posthumous. He had found out a lot about pilots during his deployment and suspected Chuck must have kept the plane stable enough for the boys to parachute out, thereby significantly reducing his own and his co-pilot's chances of getting back alive – so calculated that two deaths would be preferable to all ten.

Standing up ceremoniously, tears stinging his own eyes, he lifted his right hand to his brow, giving a very smart and very British army salute in the direction of the American airfield down the hill. Then choked with emotion he declared, "I pay a soldier's tribute to the courageous man who is the natural father of my eldest child."

"Your eldest child?" Rebecca was astonished, scrambling from the sofa to stand beside her husband. "Aren't you going to throw me out for being such an immoral little hussy?"

He looked at her tenderly and then put his hands on her shoulders. "Rebecca Anne Lisle, that day I first set eyes on you in your father's office, I lost my heart. I was aware then that half the male population of Bedford would have given their eyeteeth to have you, but for some ridiculous reason you chose me. As far as I'm concerned there could never be another woman in my life. It has been thinking of you that has kept me going these last few years. If you were to leave me I don't have it in me to marry again. With you I've tasted the best - how on earth could I settle for less? Just because that horrible little Austro-German bastard with the Charlie Chaplin mustache upset our lives as he tried to rule the world, I could never fall out of love with you, whatever you did. Even if you had sailed to the other side of the sea, divorced me, and married Chuck, I'd still have loved you. Oh, I'm hurt, but then you ought also to be disappointed in me because I have blotted my copybook, too."

Rebecca clung to him in astonishment. "You're prepared to raise another man's child as your own?"

His voice was deep and rumbling. "In this case, it will be a privilege. Another man may have tried to take my wife from me, but he died courageously, serving his country and mine above and beyond the call of duty. He put the lives of his men first – which cost him his own life on his very last mission. He died for his great land… and for ours. I don't have such qualities, but it will be an honor to raise as my own the child he and my wife conceived together. I never met Chuck Vanderhoven, which is probably a good thing, but I am utterly devoted to you and it is enough that he loved you with the same intensity."

And so it was that, with faltering steps, Rebecca and Jeremy Lisle set out on life together once again, no matter how difficult the journey would be. No one would pretend that it was all peaches and cream, but together they made something lasting out of the tribulations of war. The one who cemented them together through thick and thin during the coming years was their daughter, a child who was always the object of her parents' love and adoration.

Thursday, November 11, 2004 – American Cemetery, Madingley, Cambridge

I must have driven past the well-tended boundary that surrounds the American Cemetery on the outskirts of Cambridge hundreds of times, but beautiful as it might have looked with its stately walled entrance and gatehouse, surrounded by mature trees, it had never occurred to me to go in. Set on the brow of a gentle rise near the picturesque, quintessentially English village of Madingley, it has a wonderful panoramic view across the flat Fen country, much as *Honeypot Hill* but a little further around the escarpment.

East Anglia's Fenland has become the Bread Basket of England, but until a few centuries ago much of it was swampy, crisscrossed by creeks and waterways that in the Middle Ages made a rich living for eel fishers, for back then eels were a culinary delicacy. The nearby city of Ely actually gets its name from the eel fisheries of centuries ago. At the heart of the small city of Ely is one of the hugest ancient cathedrals in England, set on what was once an island that had been surrounded by marshland. The cathedral itself was the focus of a monastic community. In bygone times Ely was enriched by the business of catching and marketing those long slithery fish. Then several hundred years ago, Dutch engineers helped local people drain the swamps and unlock some of the most fertile soil in Europe.

When the air war was being ramped up during World War Two, the Fens discovered a new role that was to shape their future. Being flat and relatively close to the Continent, they were the perfect setting for the airfields from which bombing missions could be launched. By the time the war had reached its climax, more than a hundred British and American airfields were operating in the midst of fertile farmland.

It did not take long after the cessation of hostilities for the runways and hangars to disappear and the land to revert to agriculture, those former airfields producing some of the finest grain, vegetables, and fruit. This happened in Thorpe Beauchamp, although a handful of American bases remain. I can sit quietly reading in my back garden at *Honeypot Hill* and am occasionally treated to the spectacle of US F-15s flying fast and low out of their base in nearby Lakenheath; at other times an enormous lumbering air transport or mid-air refueler will leave its base at Mildenhall for some transoceanic mission. An American friend of mine who worked for a few years at one of the high-tech companies in Cambridge would chuckle whenever he saw these planes and say, "It's good to see my tax dollars working so hard."

When these airfields were set up in the 1940s tens of thousands of cocky, attractive, terrified, enthusiastic young American males, many of whom had never set foot outside the United States, descended on what had until then been a deserted backwater. They managed to change the vicinity forever, but it must also be acknowledged that East Anglia, for its part, changed many of them. As they waged war from these airfields, the possibility of death was so immediate that many just lived for the day, their 'eat, drink, and be merry' attitude profoundly influencing local communities.

Their generals arrived convinced that daylight bombing was the only way to go, yet in early months, with the Luftwaffe still strong and Allied fighter cover over Europe far from adequate, unseemly numbers of B-17 Flying Fortresses and B-24 Liberators and their crews were lost in action. Who would have thought that a farm boy from Iowa would suffer a horrific death, burning alive when the plane in which he was tail gunner plummeted to the ground in flames or was lost at sea, or, if he was lucky, he might survive only to spend the remainder of hostilities languishing in a prisoner of war camp in a sandy pine forest along what is today the German-Polish border? One night would see them chugging pints of ale with locals in a village pub, the next they would have a bullet in their leg with burns over a large part of their body as they lay heavily guarded in a German hospital.

Thousands were robbed of years of their lives as they moldered in prisoner-of-war camps, thousands more lost legs, arms, eyes, and other parts of their bodies, and well over six thousand, the population of a fair-sized town, never came back. Often lives were terminated, like those of Chuck Vanderhoven and his copilot, as they ditched in the unforgiving waters of the North Sea or were burned to a crisp as the plane fell in a fireball from the sky. These brave men will never be forgotten: their names are engraved on a long, stately wall of remembrance that stands alongside the American Cemetery chapel on that Madingley hillside. This spectacular memorial overlooks a now peaceful hillside dotted with white gravestones marking the place where three thousand men and woman have been laid to rest.

That bleak November afternoon, the sight of the wall and the serenity of the burial ground was breathtaking. Amanda, Millie, and myself had not come for the graves, but my eye constantly strayed across the hillside as I wondered how many mothers had over the years come to weep beside their son or daughter's burial place, leaving perhaps a rose or a small wreath or a small bag of crumbled earth from their home in America.

The lofty chapel stands on the crest of the hill, the remembrance wall stretching outward like an arm and overlooking a reflecting pool. Nearly two hundred yards away, beyond the end of the wall, is a mound on which stands a huge flagstaff from which flies the most enormous American flag, reminding all who can see it from miles distant that the United States still cares for these young citizens who gave their all.

I had not realized until we got there that November 11th had not just been Armistice Day in Europe but was also the United States' Veterans' Day, although I was not entirely sure of the relationship between the two remembrances. There had been a ceremony at the Cemetery that morning, but everything had been straightened out by the time Millie drove into the nearly empty car park. We sat for a long moment, all of us uncharacteristically speechless. We had been chattering away like sparrows all the way from Thorpe Beauchamp and then during lunch at a favorite pub along the way, but now we were hushed having entered somewhere sacred. My heart thudded as I fidgeted with the red woolen muffler round my neck. Millie fumbled with her car keys as she burrowed in her handbag looking for goodness knows what; meanwhile, Amanda was laboriously coating and recoating her lips with lipstick, the cosmetic she had since childhood loved the most, and something of a security blanket for her.

We had intended to come to Cambridge the day before, following a bowl of soup for lunch, but these plans were shelved when torrential rain began lashing the windowpanes while we were finishing our meal. We postponed our trip for twenty-four hours hoping for the improved weather the BBC forecasters were tentatively promising.

It surprised me that Millie and Amanda had been able to get into a car together and not squabble. For two women who for so long had been at daggers drawn, they were in the process of becoming surprisingly chummy, and I found myself wondering how much all these new revelations might had improved the atmosphere between them. Knowing how much Millie enjoyed driving, and wondering whether I would be in a fit state after visiting the cemetery to drive us home, I happily accepted her offer to get us to the cemetery.

It may not have been raining but was turning into one of those windy, bleak, dreary afternoons that November does so well in East Anglia! However, the weather forecasters, with glee, had told us that there was much more in the way of rain and storms coming. Why is it that these folk seem to adore nasty weather so much?

Getting out of the car I became acutely conscious that, while Mummy and Daddy's remains lay buried in an ancient churchyard, this wall was the only place where my natural father was memorialized, his bones probably having long since been lost in the grubby tangle of the seabed. I wondered if there might be any evidence of him left where his plane had crashed, quickly dismissing the idea as ridiculous. However, there was something majestically appropriate and military about this graveyard, but whichever way I tried to turn the wall of remembrance was like a magnet that inexorably drew me. The girls strolled arm-in-arm a few steps behind me, communicating in discreet whispers. We ambled along the wall not knowing how the names were organized with Amanda gradually falling further and further behind. Then suddenly there was a little yelp and a shout of "Here it is!" which brought Millie and myself back to where she was standing, pointing eagerly to a name quite high above us on the wall.

To make sure Amanda had it right I pulled my reading glasses out of my shoulder bag, and there etched into the stone was my birth father's name. I gasped involuntarily and tears came to my eyes; instinctively, my hand covered my mouth. For a moment my imagination began to churn as I half-visualized two young bodies, those of my mother and this lanky American airman, tangled together in the old oak bedstead that I remembered from my childhood dominating my parents' bedroom. Sometime in the late 1950s Mummy swept it away in favor of something a bit more contemporary. I should imagine Daddy was relieved to see it go.

There was the name of the man who was my natural father on the stone wall:

Capt. C. A. Vanderhoven - Tennessee

I rummaged in my bag for a pencil and scrap of paper that I tore from the notebook I habitually carried. Amanda was the tallest, so standing on tiptoe she traced the good captain's name onto the paper. When she finished I felt so breathless that I sat down on the stone ledge where wreaths and flowers were occasionally laid, looking up at the name and then glancing down at the paper my daughter had placed in my hand. My stomach churned as I tried to grasp what this meant, about who I truly was, and where I came from. I was blood of this man's blood, flesh of his flesh, yet the cruel sea had swallowed his remains. I did not know what to think or feel, but I knew there and then that my personal journey with Chuck Vanderhoven had barely begun.

I had been raised as a Lisle, I had married a Quinn, but now somewhere behind those two surnames sat a third, Vanderhoven. I wondered if the Vanderhoven family name still continued. I needed to find out if there were still Vanderhovens in Tennessee. I would not truly know myself until I had more answers to all the questions; yet I was aware that once I knew these another cascade of questions would be sitting there demanding an answer.

While I was silently lost in thought the girls had wandered off among the graves. It was a bleak dark day, and as I pondered my own identity one of the Cemetery officials came over and asked, "Is there anything I can do to help, ma'am?"

I shook my head then showed him the paper. "I'm OK, just more than a little confused…"

The uniformed man sat down on the ledge beside me. "You aren't the first person to come here who ends up feeling confused."

I looked at the man, tall with gray thinning hair and a friendly smile, so confided in him my conundrum. "I'm in this strange position of being nearly sixty and have just discovered that the man I always knew as Daddy was not my natural father." I waved the paper at him. "This man, Chuck Vanderhoven, who flew from the airbase that used to be in Thorpe Beauchamp was in fact my natural parent."

He shook his head. "Utterly disorienting. I can understand that."

I smiled wanly as I looked at his name tag. "That, Mr. Schilling, is putting it mildly. During the last few weeks I have been emotionally all over the place... I've shed buckets of tears, lost a lot of weight, and if I don't keep a tight rein on myself you might find yourself with a hysterical woman on your hands."

He laughed a deep bass laugh. "You would not be the first... Miz..."

"Quinn, Sarah Quinn."

We shook hands and then I briefly filled him in on what had happened and how I had discovered all this; he nodded and then asked, "What are you going to do about it?"

"I don't know, but one of the items fast rising up my personal agenda is to find out what has happened to the Vanderhovens in the United States."

"Which part?"

"Tennessee, probably the Nashville area."

He laughed. "Ma'am, I'm from Tennessee, born and raised in a place called Murfreesboro, bang in the middle of the state, not too far from Nashville. While I don't know much about them, I've seen the Vanderhoven name occasionally in our local newspaper, *The Tennessean*. They are quite prominent people as far as I can recall, but I admit that I had not noticed a Vanderhoven from the Volunteer State on this wall until you just mentioned it."

By now Amanda and Millie had reappeared and were standing beside me listening. Elliott Schilling stood up and I introduced him. "This, Mr. Schilling, is my daughter, Amanda Quinn, and this is my daughter-in-law and soon to be mother of my first grandchild, Millicent Quinn."

Millie was feeling cold, but as she and I walked back to the car to get out of the wind Amanda started picking the officer's brains about how she might research Chuck Vanderhoven and his family. We drove home in silence to Thorpe Beauchamp, each lost in her own thoughts about this new step we had taken.

In the weeks following I found myself constantly being drawn back to the cemetery just to look again at Chuck Vanderhoven's name etched on the wall. There was something compelling about the place, tugging at me and making me feel closer to him, perhaps in some way trying to bond with a man who had been dead soon after my conception. Each time I visited I left a little posy beneath his name on the wall. In the windy dampness that is very much part of a Fenland winter I would wander among the graves wondering what each of these men and women might have contributed to their country and the world had their lives not been so cruelly cut off. Some may have changed the world for the better, but others if they had survived could well have been out-and-out scoundrels.

David was upset not to have been part of our little pilgrimage, so I made sure to take him with me when next he came up to see me and talk about the business. It was into December now, and I was surprised how deeply he had been moved. I picked him up at the train station in Cambridge and he was his usual extroverted, talkative self, but as the afternoon proceeded his garrulousness diminished until he was speechless, tears dribbled down his cheeks. The last time I remembered seeing him cry was following his father's death, and when we got back to the car after visiting the wall he wept copiously, burying his head in my chest as he had as a child. This discovery had disoriented us all.

As Christmas approached I cut yew, holly, and sprigs from some of the shrubs at *Honeypot Hill* I knew were there when Chuck had spent those months there with my mother. I made them into a little bouquet tied with red ribbon, then went to the cemetery on Christmas Eve and laid these tokens from our home beneath Chuck's name. I had written a card to go with it.

To Chuck Vanderhoven
Remembering you for the first time this Christmas.
Love from Sarah Charlotte Quinn,
the English daughter you never knew

It would be foolish to say that my issues were now magically resolved – far from it. But as I got on with my life as Sarah Quinn, mother, grandmother-in-waiting, former gallery director, and widow of Timothy Quinn, my mind and heart did their work of adjusting to this new genealogical landscape, giving birth to an audacious plan as far as a woman my age was concerned.

As I talked everything through with my children, close friends, and the Reverend Jackie, I was better coming to terms with the lid having been taken off Pandora's box; the task now was to understand and become comfortable with whatever else might be lurking. I found myself coming to terms with the fact that I could get no peace until I knew more about the man whose final gift to my mother had been me. Maybe I was the consequence of a night when animal passions robbed two intelligent people of good sense. There seemed to be a never-ending flow of questions about this man for whom my mother had been preparing to abandon her marriage vows and everything she had cherished to follow him to a new life in Tennessee.

I wondered, too, whether this emotional turmoil had further roiled my parents' already shaky relationship. How would I have responded as a young wife if Tim had come home one day and told me he had fathered a child by another woman? Assiduously, I worked my way through all the relevant papers, diaries, and documents Amanda kept unearthing from her grandfather's archive – but apart from occasional guarded suggestion, the existence of a Charles Vanderhoven was not something Granddad ever deigned put into writing. However, being haunted by this ghost must surely have set in motion an interminable chain of ambiguities.

Adolf Hitler's evil fantasies had resulted in millions of deaths dislocating hundreds of millions, and I was one of the unexpected products of that disruption. Had there not been a war Mummy and Daddy would perhaps have lived a boringly ordinary middle-class life, but then again the agony and dislocation had been the making of them.

• • • • • • •

Amanda was now coming down at *Honeypot Hill* as often as she could in order to ferret her way through her grandfather's filing cabinets, and in the process she began uncovering all sorts of scraps of information that were helping me to understand Daddy. I was probably the typical only child, spoiled and doted upon, yet he was an intensely private man, and this was especially so when it came to his own heroisms. I suspect Mummy was the only person to whom he ever really opened his heart, telling her things about himself that no one else would ever hear. During that year's long Christmas and New Year break, Amanda was with me and uncovering a steady trickle of the unexpected.

While Mummy could fritter her way through a mountain of money on a typical afternoon grazing through the shops, Daddy was a canny manager of funds as a perusal of his meticulously managed ledgers showed, revealing how over the years he had discovered ways to keep Mummy's spendthrift habits within manageable bounds. He was such a compulsive money manager that Amanda even succeeded in turning up little notebooks he used to record all his income and expenditures while away in the army. At the same time, there were notes of exasperation when Mummy found ways to dodge his frugality. Daddy and Mummy seemed to spend years playing this cat-and-mouse game over pounds, shillings, and pence until the arrival of the credit card, which stymied him however low he tried to set the limit on the balance!

When I was growing up Daddy's passions were his family, business, the village church, and in the summers playing cricket. He was not a great sportsman, but he loved it, often playing Saturday afternoons and the occasional Sunday, and Amanda found pictures of him with the Second XI team for which he was an opening batsman. There were a few pictures of me growing up as I was taken to his games; I would sit on the verandah of the old thatched cricket pavilion on the village green drinking fizzy orange that stained my lips and becoming increasingly obnoxious the more bored I became. Sometimes I would help my mother serve sandwiches and teas, and *that* was a lot more fun. Side-by-side in his filing cabinets were decades of minutes from management meetings of the cricket club together with magazines and minutes from the church throughout his many years as churchwarden. Amanda and I were doubled up laughing at some of the correspondence between him and the assorted collection of vicars.

More fascinating were the years following his sale of the family business in the late 1960s. Through the postwar years the company had experienced steady growth. Some years after my grandfather died a project came along that would require the sort of capital they were unable to raise, making them a juicy target for a friendly buy out. A larger organization came up with a very attractive offer, releasing him to devote the remainder of his active years to refugees and refugee resettlement. He had dabbled in this as Europe struggled with millions of refugees and displaced persons following the war, but was freed up by the early seventies to throw himself into the crisis created by Idi Amin's expulsion of Asians from Uganda, stripping them of all their assets.

I had always been rather vague about my father's passion for refugees until Amanda started digging around in his papers. Like so many old soldiers he told us little about his war, except the occasional funny story – like his pals getting him paralytically drunk at that goodbye party in Naples. Early in 1945, he reported back for military duty. Leaving behind a now obviously pregnant wife, he found himself drafted to accompany invading troops as they crossed the Rhine and thrust into Germany. Daddy was ostensibly there to assess what it would take to put German infrastructure back together after six years of total war.

With the Allies demanding unconditional surrender, they were concerned to avoid the mistake of 1919 when the victors insisted on reparations that humiliated Germany, setting up the climate that would eventually make it possible for Hitler to grab power. Daddy's job was to inspect the damage done to German bridges, roads, and public buildings, as well as the engineering industry that would enable the victors to create a plan that would coax a devastated Europe back into some kind of working order.

Daddy was one of the most sensitive men, and from the journal he was now keeping it became obvious just how much the tragic trails of millions shuffling along ruined roads or squatting in derelict houses pained him. Some were made homeless by war and Allied bombing, while others had been conscripted from all over Occupied Europe to serve the Führer's war machine, often as little more than slave labor. These masses were made up of children and women, as well as men who had deserted or escaped from something horrific. They were starving, their clothes were threadbare, fleas and lice infested their bodies, but with the approaching end of hostilities they now treasured a smidgeon of hope. As the driver of his Jeep dodged these shambling columns of refugees, Major Jeremy Lisle agonized over what he might do to ease their lot.

He and the unit to which he was attached found themselves in Lower Saxony in April 1945, just a couple of weeks before Berlin fell, the guns were at last silent, and the hostilities mercifully ended. We know now, of course, that these days merely paved the way for the Cold War. On April 15th, they left Hanover and drove toward the town of Bergen, to the south of which they watched in horror as the hideous Bergen-Belsen concentration camp was liberated. He never spoke of the sights he saw that day or the former inmates he spoke to, but if accepting me had been one of the defining moments of his life, this was another.

My father wrote reams in the little black-bound journal that he always carried in his pack, and there also were his copies of official documents he had filed. He was at a loss to find words to describe the ghastliness he had witnessed, and in some way it was as if that day a part of his soul died. Even as they drove through the camp's now wide open gates inmates were continuing to die; these saw liberation but never experienced its benefits. Most were little more than skin and bone, stripped of dignity and identity; they had been turned into parodies of what it means to be a man or a woman.

Most wore filthy black and white striped pajama suits with badges of various colors on their chests denoting them as Jews, gypsies, homosexuals, or traitors. The stench was unbearable and wafted out into the surrounding countryside.

In the infirmary at Bergen-Belsen, Daddy met an educated Dutch Jew of about his own age who was dying. The man spoke perfect English, having studied at Oxford in the early 1930s; he had been unable to escape when the Nazis came storming through. Daddy helped him eat some food and take sips of clean, fresh water from a glass. The next day when he came to visit him again, Simeon had died during the night and his body was in the process of being buried with thousands of others in a communal grave. Daddy found a quiet corner in which he cried his eyes out.

Reading and re-reading what he wrote told me how pivotal this was in his thinking. He arrived back from Germany just a few weeks after I had been born and never wore the uniform again. Amanda found the carbon of the letter he had written to Chaplain Maynard in which he said,

---

Dear Padre,

This evening I arrived home from Germany. Rebecca was glowing. Motherhood suits her: she looks tired, but stunning. She placed into my arms our firstborn, Sarah Charlotte Lisle. She is beautiful... (then he goes on to describe me in detail right the way down to my tiny fingernails) *...In many ways life could not be more perfect at the moment. My wife is **my** wife again, **our** daughter has been born, and we look forward to a houseful of children.*

Yet, Peter, I cannot erase from my mind the sights I saw in Germany and wept over. Those poor, poor people. I wondered

as we drove around, visited bombed-out engineering plants, observed countless ruined homes, and saw tens of thousands of lost souls wandering the streets with blank stares and wearing nothing but the rags whether as we stood up to Germany's bullying we have not overdone it.

Then I saw Bergen-Belsen. Worse, I smelled it long before getting there, and met men and women whose hell made our war in North Africa look like a luxury holiday. It was then that I became utterly convinced of Hitler's demonic evil, and as nasty as our response has been, I suspect much of what we did was necessary to stop dead in its tracks such rampant wickedness.

*Now it is our responsibility to treat Germany in such a way that she and her people can be welcomed back to the family of civilized nations and to help young Germans to grow up so they **never** repeat the mistakes of their elders. As I knelt beside a mass grave in Belsen I promised God that I will do what I can to help rehouse the homeless in Europe and give aid to the plight of refugees all over the world...*

After getting home he became involved with the practicalities of bringing relief to displaced persons and refugees. He began by providing aid and assistance to Free Poles now stranded in England by the Soviet annexation of their country. There had been a little displaced persons camp close by and he enabled them to find homes and work, employing some himself while giving time and money to the work of the Red Cross.

When, in 1964, the takeover bid was made for the family business, he explained in his journal how wonderful it was to have been set free to pursue his passion. Suddenly, he had a secure income and time to devote to his enduring concern. Besides my mother, alleviating the plight of refugees became the passion of his life, and in later years he circled the world on this mission, Mummy sometimes accompanying him.

One day toward the end of her life, when she and I were sitting in the conservatory drinking a hot cup of tea and gossiping, Mummy suddenly said, "You know, darling, if I had not married your Daddy my life might have been more comfortable, but it would not have been anywhere near as interesting and adventurous."

These words came back to my mind, enabling me now to see that, while Chuck may have been the great love of her life, Jeremy Lisle was her tower of strength, always there for her and others through thick and thin.

Thursday, February 2, 2005 – Nashville, Tennessee, USA

"Here's another one of these letters from that strange woman in England," the young PA said as she sorted the mail in the offices of the Vanderhoven Memorial Foundation. A middle-aged woman, smartly dressed in a teal green woolen suit, her long light brown hair put up in a French twist, was leaning over her shoulder.

She glanced at the letter and said, "Oh, I don't think we need to bother her with that, Aimee. Just sling it into the recycle bin."

At that moment a stentorian, cultured Southern female voice rang out from the direction of the doorway, "I'm assuming I am the 'her' to whom you are referring; what is it that you intend to throw away without me seeing, Jennifer?"

Sensing that the two older women were about to begin circling in preparation to locking horns, Aimee, the young PA rose from her seat, smiled sweetly at the small lady with perfectly coiffured white-haired standing at the entrance and said as she walked toward the kitchen, "Good morning, Miz Emily, I'll get your coffee – black, one sugar, just as you like it."

When Aimee had sidled out, Emily Vanderhoven McAllister strutted across the room, helped herself to the letter that was still in the hands of Jennifer, the widow of her nephew, settled into the high-backed wing chair which was her favorite perch when she came into the office, placed her Margaret Thatcher-esque handbag in its usual spot on the floor by her feet, and set about reading this missive that, had she not arrived at that precise moment, would have disappeared into the wastepaper bin. She hated other people making decisions for her, and Jennifer had an irritating habit of doing just that.

HONEYPOT HILL
THORPE BEAUCHAMP,
CAMBRIDGESHIRE
ENGLAND
+44 (0) 1935 5551212

12 January 2005

Dear Sir/Madam,

I wrote several weeks ago but suspect with Christmas and the New Year intervening the letter has been mislaid or accidentally sent to America by way of a slow boat! So I write again concerning a possible link between our families that was made during the latter part of the Second World War. That link seems to have been one Charles Andrew Vanderhoven, Captain in the US Army Air Forces, who lost his life over the North Sea while flying his final mission in August 1944. He was stationed at the local airbase near our family home in Thorpe Beauchamp.

Let me introduce myself by saying that I am merely seeking information of a personal nature, an opportunity to 'lay a ghost,' if you will. I had the sad task of going through my late mother's things when we were astonished to uncover the possibility of a close relationship between the Lisle family here in Thorpe Beauchamp, near Cambridge, and Captain Vanderhoven, then a B-17 pilot with the 599th Bomb Group (H) that flew from the airfield.

My name is Sarah Quinn, and I am the daughter of Rebecca Anne Lisle after whom, I believe, Captain Vanderhoven and his crew named their plane. My mother died some months ago and my daughter and I have been sorting her papers and memorabilia. Captain Vanderhoven figures prominently. My mother's papers suggest that Captain Vanderhoven came from Nashville, and after the US entered the war he volunteered and was trained as a bomber pilot. My mother's papers hint that before becoming a flyer he was part of a family law firm.

Research undertaken by my daughter, Dr. Amanda Quinn, an Art Historian affiliated with London University, led us to deduce that the Malcolm, Russell, Klum, Goldstein, Vanderhoven, and Drew partnership may be successor to Vanderhoven and Drew, the firm of which Charles Vanderhoven appears to have been part. As the Vanderhoven Memorial Foundation shares the same address, I am writing on the off chance that this is the case.

Among my mother's possessions we found Captain Vanderhoven's uniform, several of his medals, gifts he made to my mother, and other items that may be of interest to you. I believe it appropriate to restore these items because they rightfully belong to your family and not mine. Let me assure you that we are seeking nothing of your family or your foundation except assistance in dealing with this matter. This letter is prompted by curiosity and a desire to find answers about what was clearly a tumultuous period in my mother's life.

I am recently retired. I spent most of my professional life running The Quinn Galleries, an art business in London, founded by my late husband's grandfather. The Managing Director is now my son, David. I am a widow, soon to be a grandmother, and living in what was my mother's old home, the house where Captain Vanderhoven spent time in 1943-1944. This house is precious to me for this is where I grew up.

Thank you for taking the time to read this.

I remain yours very sincerely,

Sarah Quinn (née Lisle)

Miz Emily, as everyone knew her, scanned the letter, then read it through a second time with greater care. She took a sip from the delicate china coffee cup that Aimee had placed on the occasional table beside her. She had glanced up at that moment, smiling a thank you. There was a soft, strange look on her face as she gazed out of the plate glass windows with their panoramic view of Nashville – vehicles on Franklin Road looked like tiny toys in the distance. The law firm that had once been headquartered in an old red-brick house on Church Street now occupied the top half-dozen floors of one of the taller buildings that had sprung up in the downtown business district north of Broadway.

From where she sat she could see the roofs of Vanderbilt University where both she and her brother had studied. The city had changed beyond recognition during her lifetime but the Belle Meade area where she and Chuck had grown up had altered little, its capacious homes situated further out beyond the university. She had continued to live there until the 1980s, but then, preferring to be a little further out, had built her new home on the family's farm between Brentwood and Franklin.

"Poor Rebecca has died. God bless her soul," Emily whispered, absent-mindedly reaching for her coffee and taking what was now a lukewarm sip.

"You know this woman?" Jennifer asked querulously.

Emily gave her a weary smile. "Of course I did, you silly child. If things had turned out just a tiny bit differently Sarah's mother would have been my sister-in-law. This woman, as you call her, was writing to tell me that Rebecca has passed. Thank God I got the letter before you in your short-sighted stupidity destroyed it... Kindly in the future do *not* make decisions for me about which letters I should or should not read. Jennifer, you can be unnecessarily officious."

"But Captain Charles Vanderhoven?" There was a puzzled look on Jennifer's face.

"You will have heard the name a hundred times. My elder brother. I know I'm the only Vanderhoven left from that generation, but you should by now have absorbed enough family history to remember that I had two brothers. Fitz, the younger, was your late father-in-law, but the elder was Charles... and this letter pertains to him."

Jennifer Campbell Vanderhoven half-sat and half-leaned forward, attentively watching Emily Vanderhoven McAllister gather her thoughts. The content of the letter had obviously come as a shock to her. This tiny white-haired woman always made Jennifer feel miniscule without needing to say anything. Emily, petite and perfectly coiffured, was every inch the well-groomed Southern matriarch, a stainless steel magnolia, but as she stared into the distance her mind was a million miles away.

Emily was remembering the house on Belle Meade Boulevard that would have been Charles's, not far from the country club. If Charles has survived the war Rebecca would have presided over that home, a vivacious woman, determined, very English, who would probably have been the mother of an uncivilized tribe of children – every single one a loveable tearaway.

She had no doubt Chuck and Rebecca would have been ferociously fertile, so goodness knows how many kids there would have been before they learned to discipline their sex life and realized there was such a thing as birth control. Emily had no doubt that she and Rebecca would have been best friends and confidantes. Sighing, she shook her head: so many what ifs. What if her brother had decided to play it safe and not acted the hero on his last mission? She would have preferred her brother to have lived a full and fruitful life than being able to boast of that Silver Star awarded posthumously.

Emily spoke again, this time almost to herself. "It's been a rather bad habit of this family to shed some of its finest blood on battlefields across the world since the War between the States."

She was an old-fashioned Southerner, a Daughter of the Confederacy and never even considered referring to that particular unpleasantness as the Civil War. "We lost men at Sharpsburg, then on the Western Front, then in World War Two, Korea, and most recently Vietnam." She was obviously not in the mood to be interrupted. "My great-grandfather died being heroic at a damned bridge hardly worth bothering about over Antietam Creek in Maryland; my foolhardy uncle managed to get himself shot in the heart while being heroic in one of the very last US actions before the Armistice in November 1918... My cousin was an army doctor in Korea and picked up something ghastly from a patient, while my own son, Charles, named for my dead brother, was wounded then captured by the Viet Cong and died in squalor at their cruel hands."

The years may ameliorate such hurts but never chase them away. Emily continued gazing across the city in which she, like her mother and grandmother before her, had been born, grown up, and lived her whole life. Jennifer watched the old lady purse her lips, her face perfectly made up but wrinkled by the passage of the years, especially as her mind dwelt on this procession of wars in which these sacrifices had been made.

It had been on her twentieth birthday, just as they were making plans for her favorite brother's return from Europe, that news arrived of *The Rebecca Anne's* demise with both her pilot and co-pilot lost beneath the unforgiving waves of that narrow band of water that separated Britain from the Continent. Since that time she had never wanted to make a fuss about her birthdays, and the time had just rolled on.

Only days before the news broke she had received the most recent letter of her burgeoning correspondence with the woman her brother was determined to marry, despite the fact that she was already the wife of a British soldier serving in Italy. From the letters already exchanged Emily realized Rebecca was just the sort of friend for which she had always longed. Now the potential of that friendship died together with her brother. Never again would Emily come across another woman with whom she sensed such oneness. Perhaps that was when she began developing the reputation of being aloof, taking life far more seriously than most of her female contemporaries, determined to be a lawyer, despising the notion of being a debutante.

Emily's wandering mind returned to the present and she looked up, smiled wanly at Jennifer's worried face, and said with a heavy heart, "Then there was Charles... Charles would probably have become the senior partner of this firm, despite his desire to become a professional pilot... I worshipped my brother and was so proud when on Pearl Harbor Day, December 7, 1941, he announced that he would join the newly renamed Army Air Forces. He had always wanted to fly, and Adolf Hitler now provided him with the opportunity. In so doing he became the next in the Vanderhoven line to sacrifice his life on the altar of liberty."

"This letter is about him?" Jennifer said quietly, beginning to feel ashamed of herself for being so dismissive. However she tried, she thought, when it came to Emily Vanderhoven McAllister she always managed to do or say the wrong thing. It had always been that way.

Miz Emily seemed not to hear. Indeed, she was not listening. Her mind had meandered off and was now remembering the excited first letter she had received from Rebecca Lisle in the spring of 1944. Charles had asked Emily to write Rebecca, the woman he loved, telling her what life would be like if she agreed to marry him and come home with him to Nashville as his bride. It wasn't until later that Emily discovered that she was actually still married to an officer who had been away for years serving in the British army. She was initially disgusted that her brother should even think of doing such a thing, but the forcefulness of Rebecca's letters won her over despite her disapproval.

So began a correspondence that long outlasted Charles's death, through the birth of her daughter, the arrival of her grandchildren, and now, after a long pause, news of great-grandchildren – although Rebecca would never see them. Passionate letters had been exchanged frequently, especially when Emily was coming to terms with the loss of her own son, commander of those Swift boats on the Mekong River that were ambushed by the Viet Cong. Then after Jeremy's death the letters gradually trailed off as dementia tore apart Rebecca's mind.

"Losing my brother, Charles, was every bit as painful as losing Charles Cameron McAllister, my son," the old woman sighed. She swallowed hard before going on. "Now this letter has arrived from a past that has always haunted me. If I appear to be withdrawing a little, honey, it is because this has reawakened dashed hopes, a friendship that was only ever half-born, and a reminder that there is still another member of our family who should have been raised and nurtured here in Nashville, and, had things worked out differently, would have been part of our family circle today."

"What do you mean?" Jennifer was mystified and a little irritated.

Emily waved the letter at her. "I suspect you've already consigned the first letter from Sarah Charlotte Quinn…"

"How do you know her middle name is Charlotte?"

"Sweet girl," Emily said with a resigned sigh, "Sarah Charlotte Lisle Quinn, you see I know all her names, carries the name Charlotte in honor of her natural father." Jennifer sat there feeling stupid, exasperated that Emily was once again trying to belittle her. She watched the older woman rise from the chair and walk slowly across the room to the window. "Come here, girl," she commanded.

Jennifer hated being called 'girl,' it was demeaning, but seething inside she did as she was told. Then Emily pointed in a southwesterly direction. "Beyond the buildings of Vanderbilt is Belle Meade."

"Yes, I know that."

Belle Meade had once been a prosperous horse farm, before the Civil War breeding some of the finest race horses in America. But when the economy experienced an almost catastrophic downturn in the 1890s the property fell into debt. It staggered on for a few years then its 2600 acres were sold for the development of what has become the most prestigious community in Tennessee. The Vanderhovens had built their first home in Belle Meade before World War One, and this was where Miz Emily grew up.

"You also know the old Vanderhoven home is on the 500 block of Belle Meade Boulevard," Emily stated rhetorically, and Jennifer nodded. She was not quite sure where Emily McAllister was going with this. "This woman, Sarah Charlotte Quinn, should have been raised in that house."

"You mean..."

Emily turned and frowned at her, a deep sadness in her eyes. "Charlotte is her middle name because Charles Andrew Vanderhoven, my wonderful elder brother, a *bona fide* war hero, holder of the Silver Star, who died in the North Sea while trying to save his Flying Fortress on his last mission over Europe in 1944, is her natural father."

With that Emily sighed, turned, picked up her purse from beside her chair and still holding the letter in her hand marched out of the office of the Vanderhoven Memorial Foundation without saying another word. Jennifer Vanderhoven was dumbstruck. Emily had chosen the foundation's name. Ostensibly it was to honor the memory of all the Vanderhovens who had died on the battlefield, but as far as she was concerned it was more about her brother first and then her own son, the other Charles.

Tuesday, April 19, 2005 — Nashville International Airport, Nashville, Tennessee

After what had seemed an endless flight with impossible delays in Atlanta caused by spring thunderstorms and torrential rain, the bumpy landing on a windy night told us that we had finally arrived in Tennessee.

This stage of our journey had been set up on a filthy Cambridgeshire evening in early February. The wind was whistling round *Honeypot Hill*, lashing colossal drops of rain against the windows when the phone rang. I had just finished scrambling eggs for my evening meal and was feeling glad not to be out on a night like this. The rain had not abated since the previous afternoon, the wind was merciless, and I had hardly strayed out of doors all day. The weather had added to my listlessness; besides, I was just starting to recover from a disgusting winter cold.

"Is that Sarah Quinn?" said the cultivated female American voice.

"This is she," I answered, wondering who on earth the caller was.

"You will not know me but I'm responding to the letters you wrote to the Vanderhoven Memorial Foundation."

With those words I dropped everything, propped my bottom on a kitchen stool, and was all ears.

"Who is this?" I asked.

She did not answer my question immediately, going on to say, "I suspect you have finally found out about Charles Vanderhoven. Is that so?"

"Yes," I responded tentatively. Was this woman trying to wind me up? I was frustrated at her for maintaining her anonymity.

"Honey," she answered after a short pause, "You sound suspicious – if I was in your position I'd probably feel the same."

"But who are you?" I asked, scared this might be some new telephone scam.

"I'm sorry, I've been so nervous about talking to you that I forgot my manners... I'm Emily Vanderhoven McAllister from Nashville, Tennessee. My elder brother was Captain Charles Andrew Vanderhoven, of 599 Heavy Bomb Group, and who was posted to Thorpe Beauchamp during World War Two."

I was speechless. Had writing to the Vanderhoven Memorial Foundation been a dreadful error?

Telephone silences can be embarrassing and this one must have stretched on for several seconds before Emily McAllister continued, "I'm sorry I have not been in touch sooner than this, but my niece, who helps me run the Foundation, thought your first letter was a con, so it went into the recycle before Christmas."

"That's alright," I tried to giggle, "Letters out of the blue like that need to be treated with caution – I sort of suspected something like that might have happened."

"You are too kind, my dear, far too kind, but then I wouldn't have expected anything less from Rebecca's lovely daughter."

With that the ice was broken and we began talking. Several times she tried to persuade me to come and visit the Vanderhovens in Nashville. In my Englishness I had no intention of accepting. Surely her offer came from some misguided sense of obligation, and I managed for at least an hour to hold her insistence at bay. It was only as she persevered that I realized the invitation was heartfelt, so I finally accepted, making Emily's day.

After talking things through with David, Millie, and Amanda, I decided to go in April – far enough away to be able to make careful plans and plenty of time before David and Millie's little one made her grand arrival. By this time we knew from the ultrasounds that the first of a new generation of Quinns was a little girl – Millie's intuition about the baby had been absolutely right!

Life with Amanda was also getting rather interesting. She and Millie, having been at daggers drawn for so long, were now becoming as thick as thieves. It was only when everything was a *fait accompli* that the pair of them, aided and abetted by David, laid out their plan for my approval – although I knew perfectly well they would go ahead with what they intended however much I protested. But it was nice to be brought into the picture. While parts of the proposal needed modification, after a barrage of searching questions I gave my blessing.

Millie had recently inherited a respectable sum of money from an elderly aunt who doted upon her when her parents did not. Amanda, while her interests had been shaped by being part of a family whose livelihood was in the world of art, had never given much thought to the business side of The Quinn Galleries. Together they had hatched a plan for Millie to buy Amanda's shares, and she was now making plans to put her London flat on the market.

"What do you plan to do?" I asked my daughter after it had all been agreed a few days before Christmas.

"If you will have me, Mumsie, I want to either leave the Courtauld or get an extended unpaid leave of absence, move to *Honeypot Hill*, finish researching Granddad's archives, and, making use of the

University Library in Cambridge and the facilities at the Fitzwilliam Museum in Cambridge, finish writing the book of my dreams. With all these other distractions, I haven't had time or space to dig more deeply into how the Virgin and Child have been depicted in the last thousand years as religious attitudes, culture, and painting styles have developed."

I sat back and gasped, "Wow. Will you have enough money from the business and your flat to do that?"

"If you don't ask too big a rent, and if I learn to be frugal, then I might be able to cope for several years before this particular nest egg gives out."

She was a sly thing, knowing full well that I would love the idea of her coming home to me and would refuse her offer of rent; she also knew that I was in a comfortable enough position to spoil her in all sorts of ways, something for which she had yearned since divulging to me her abortion. I said nothing but nodded my agreement and said, "Well, darling, it's your life. I'm not sure I would have made that decision, but then I'm not you… but why do you want to give so much time delving into all your grandfather's musty old documents?"

Amanda grinned the grin she knew could melt her mother's heart. "Because I want you to know precisely where you came from and how Davey and I fit into this puzzle… and because I'm certain this a fascinating story of World War Two that properly written up could be the basis for an intriguing publication illustrating the way that world crisis dislocated stable relationships."

"You mean write a book about it?" I said, in horror that my secrets would be splashed across the red-top daily tabloid newspapers.

"Yes, but not a dry historical piece – perhaps a novel based around the facts where, as the old television programs used to put it, the names have been changed to protect the innocent."

I was not sure I liked this idea but hoped during the next couple of years I could talk her out of it.

Driven by Amanda's persistence and enthusiasm, I tentatively asked Emily McAllister if it would be stretching her hospitality to have my daughter come to hold my hand. Emily was over the moon; the thought of getting to know her brother's granddaughter as well as me led to an outpouring down the telephone that I sensed was somewhat out of character for this well-bred and somewhat restrained American dowager. Amanda, for her part, reckoned that if things got awkward she could excuse herself and get buried in galleries, museums, libraries, or art galleries in New York or Washington, DC.

"And we must go well before Millie's baby is due. She wants me with her when that wee mite comes into the world as the Countess has already declared that watching babies being born isn't her thing any longer." I made a quiet aside. "I doubt whether they ever were; the more I continue to discover about that woman, the more I abhor her."

"And so do I," my own daughter answered ferociously.

Thus the date was set for late April and early May.

• • • • • • • •

The Quinn Galleries was a modest sized business that did not pretend to contend with those internationally known galleries and art vendors, but, with London an ever more global city, we had an approach to the collection and sale of art that had gained us a loyal following not only throughout Britain but in both Europe and North America. This was something David had accelerated since taking over the business. He was never happier than when he was jumping on an international flight to advance the gallery's cause; when I directed the gallery my travel budget was more spartan. I would occasionally fly to New York or Geneva but would usually stick to the parts of Europe that were close at hand, getting myself an economy ticket to get through the Channel Tunnel by train.

Most of the United States was close to being a mystery to me. On the few trips I had made, I had never strayed beyond the art appreciators living in Boston, New York City, and Washington DC;

by accepting Emily Vanderhoven McAllister's invitation I was moving way out of my comfort zone. As soon as I had accepted I felt on edge, wondering what the Vanderhovens were like and whether I had done the right thing. What would they make of me? Would they consider me some kind of imposter or a long-lost relative come home to the fold? I would lie awake at night worrying.

Amanda was determined she was going to come with me and was convinced the Vanderhovens would treat me better than royalty! Like so many grown children, especially daughters, as we prepared for our trip she slipped into her 'taking care of Mumsie' nursemaid mode. The closer the trip got, the more relieved I was that she was coming. I may have grown up as the beloved daughter of Rebecca and Jeremy Lisle as far as the UK was concerned, but in the USA I would be Chuck Vanderhoven's little bastard – some Vanderhovens might not be pleased to see me.

We stayed overnight in the Hilton Hotel at Heathrow Airport, not wanting to fight the rush hour traffic the following morning. By midmorning we were in the air on our way to Atlanta with a planned connection that would get us into Nashville by late afternoon.

The best laid plans of mice and men can be readily scuttled by the uncertainties of spring weather in the American South. Several hours spent kicking our heels on the concourse in Atlanta was our introduction to the danger of tornadoes. I did not like this one little bit as we were not used to tornadoes in England. I was increasingly nervous and utterly wrung out when our flight finally touched down in Nashville, despite having managed to doze for a few minutes during the forty minutes we spent in the air.

It still surprised me that I had had the audacity to come at all, and felt like an interloper when the wheels touched the runway. Amanda had not only urged me to come but had bullied me by buying a non-refundable ticket for each of us so I could not chicken out and cancel at the last minute – she knew how frugal I was when it came to wasting money! I was being browbeaten, but, discerning my misgivings, she knew full well that I might try to dodge the trip. It felt strange wandering around Atlanta Airport thinking that this was the country from which my natural father came and that, in a way, I half-belonged here. Nashville felt even more odd.

Millie had driven us to Heathrow Airport the previous afternoon. She was blooming, was finding sitting for any length of time in one position increasingly uncomfortable, and would soon have a baby bump that could very well impede the steering wheel. David had survived the shock that he had fathered a daughter and not a son and was overly anxious for his wife's health. He had worked hard to turn their tiny second bedroom into a nursery, and, although he had baulked at pink and frills, Millie made sure there were plenty of little girl touches. Disagreements over décor were resolved when Millie made me the final arbiter, knowing full well my preferences!

Even as we kissed goodbye Millie pleaded for me to be available when the baby was born. I would not have missed it for anything, even if it meant sprouting wings to fly back under my own power if necessary. Amanda had booked tickets that would give me plenty of leeway before our little girl made her way into the big bad world.

●●●●●●●●

Why is sitting all day on a plane and waiting on an airport doing nothing so exhausting? The pair of us literally dragged ourselves through the near-deserted concourse at Nashville Airport, beset with cheerful announcements which I was later to discover were made by country music stars welcoming us to "Music City USA". I had never heard of any of them. As we came down an escalator into the baggage claim there was hubbub. At carousels, I always dread my bag not arriving and no one being there to meet us – despite the fact that Emily had reassured us this was under control.

We had hardly stepped from the escalator when a tallish blond-haired man in his mid-thirties, wearing rimless glasses and a conservative dark blue business suit with a striped silk tie, stepped forward and introduced himself. I smiled inwardly because all the time he addressed me he was looking at Amanda.

"Ma'am," he asked, "would you be Sarah Quinn?"

"Guilty as charged," I answered smilingly as I shook his proffered hand. "And this is my daughter, Dr. Amanda Quinn."

He grinned. "As soon as I saw Dr. Amanda I knew I was looking at the right people… and you have had such a difficult journey what with the weather and all. I'm so sorry the United States has been so unwelcoming."

Amanda, a puzzled look on her face, butted in and asked, "How did you know that we were the people you were looking for by looking at me?"

He put his head on one side, his cheeks momentarily flushed, and in embarrassment replied, "Because, Dr. Quinn, your features are strikingly Vanderhoven."

Amanda looked momentarily surprised then shot back, "Who are you?"

"I'm Charles Vanderhoven… er… I guess because of what happened to my uncle in World War Two, Charles has become a bit of a family name," he said in his cultivated Southern accent.

Amanda laughed. She had little patience with what she considered this ridiculous American practice of creating a family dynasty. This was obviously Charles the Second – or maybe even the Third. I could see her supercilious Englishness bubbling to the surface, something shaped by her leftward leaning attitudes of recent years. He noticed her lips curling into a superior grin, a contemptuous look in her eyes. She had pegged him as a naïve, shallow, parochially-minded American, a Southerner no less, and the seed of disdain had been immediately planted, and had taken root. The poor man didn't stand a chance!

Her smugness began to show, and I just hoped she would have manners enough to be respectful in a foreign country. For the moment, however, being American, a Southerner, and Charles the Second (or Third) meant he was guilty. For my part I liked him; he was kind, attentive, and was doing his best to get us to Emily's home before I died of exhaustion.

Satisfied that she had adequately communicated her scorn, Amanda wandered off through the scrum of people looking for an advantageous spot by the baggage claim. Charles's eyes surreptitiously followed her. It had seemed to take forever for her to grow up, but I was glad she had finally stopped dressing like a teenager and, in her thirties, was developing a striking style of her own that at times was breathtaking. Today she wore beautifully fitting blue jeans, a sumptuously tailored ivory silk blouse with a Peter Pan collar, a red linen jacket, and tasseled loafers on her feet. Charles obviously liked what he saw, and Amanda's haughty way of walking made it blatantly obvious to me that she was fully aware his eyes were following her.

I tuned back into what he was saying. "By the way, Miz Emily is my aunt."

I found it hard to listen to what he was saying while trying to digest the name by which he had introduced himself. Looking me in the eye, he gave a reluctant winning smile and went on, "By the way, not many of my friends call me Charles, I guess I'm more comfortable with Charlie or Chaz, even Carlos."

"Let me get this right," I responded. "You're Emily Vanderhoven McAllister's nephew?"

"Great nephew, ma'am," he replied. "It is complicated, but my Daddy and Charles, Junior, were inseparable friends from their first day in elementary school together, so our clan grew up intermingled with the Vanderhovens. My natural father did not even know my mother was pregnant with me when he... er... died."

"I'm sorry. Was it an accident?" I interrupted.

He shook his head. "No, ma'am, Vietnam."

"Oh," I responded, not knowing quite how to digest this piece of information. I prompted him to continue just as the buzzer on the carousel announced the arrival of bags.

"It was a bit of a whirlwind romance, although my mother and my Vanderhoven stepfather had known each other since they were tiny itty-bitty things. They managed to tie the knot days before I was born in 1971... all very messy, I'm afraid. I was named Charles in memory of Captain Charles Vanderhoven, so I'm afraid I'm Vanderhoven more by nurture than by nature."

My mind was whirring as I struggled to make sense of these complex family relationships. The carousel revolved and mountains of bags appeared, setting off a relatively good-mannered free-for-all as travelers lunged for their suitcases. Amanda was in the thick of things, but as yet neither of our cases had reached where she was standing.

"So what do you do, Charles?"

He gave a little grin. "Not very imaginative, ma'am, I joined the family business. I followed the well-trodden Vanderhoven trail through the University of the South in Sewanee, spent a little bit of time overseas... in England actually, then enrolled at Vanderbilt Law School. I don't enjoy the courtroom, preferring the deskwork side of the law; I guess it suits my studious disposition. I tend to do complex research, but I have a little sideline in contracts, property, and wills. I also get a real kick out of the legal side of charitable giving. I guess I try to arrange my life to earn enough so I can pursue my other interests."

"That sounds as if it could be either very boring or rather exciting," I said with a smile. "And your own family?"

He looked downhearted. "I'm sorry, ma'am..."

"Please, Charles, to you I'm Sarah not Ma'am," I told him with a smile and a wink. "I much prefer to be called by my first name. Am I right to assume that you are married and have children?"

He shook his head, blushing slightly. "Alas, no. I suppose I'm a bit of an acquired taste because both the women I have been engaged to pulled the plug on the relationship before we could get anywhere near the altar."

"That must have been hard," I suggested, feeling as if I had strayed from well-mannered curiosity to unhealthy probing. It sounded as if he and Amanda had somewhat similar challenges when it came to relationships.

He made a face. "Miz Sarah, awful. I guess I'm now gun shy when it comes to the matrimonial stakes. I haven't even tried dating for several years. I prefer to stick to my own funny little interests, reading, and playing my fiddle."

I had, it seemed, stumbled upon the root of the reticence I had sensed since he had greeted us at the escalator. Women as a tribe obviously puzzled him. Grasping for something encouraging I said, "Charlie, I expect there is someone really, really special out there waiting for you."

He smiled and his whole rather serious face lit up. "Thank you, Sarah, that's so encouraging. You know, Miz Emily has been talking about you as if you were the Queen. Now I can see what she meant. You are a very lovely lady."

"I'm certainly not royalty, and my daughter-in-law is the only one in our small family with the tiniest drop of aristocratic blood," I laughed, feeling exasperated with Amanda for treating him in such an offhand way after she had hardly met the man.

Amanda's initial impressions of Charles were, as I was soon to discover, resolutely negative. I could sense her pounding exasperation as she sat silently behind me in the back of the car on our way to Emily's house while I sought valiantly to make conversation.

When we got to the house Emily McAllister was the very incarnation of Southern hospitality. She greeted us on the steps of her elegant porticoed home; as I was getting out of the car she came forward and enveloped me in her arms as if we had known each other for a lifetime. Amanda was warm and forthcoming with her while studiously ignoring Charles, who was valiantly lugging our bags to our rooms. Then my conceited little daughter fired off about him to me as soon as the door was closed to the lovely guest suite to which we had been led. Emily wanted us to get settled and prepare for a light late supper. I really didn't want anything to eat, but declining the offer would not be appropriate.

"What a puffed-up ignoramus," she pouted as she sat on my bed, watching as I hung dresses and skirts in what Americans call closets, putting my other clothes into empty drawers. "I suspect he's some kind of right wing looney, one of those frightful fundamentalist Christians who will fight to the death for the right to carry guns and believes gays are the devil's spawn."

I looked over at her, gave her a tired smile, and replied, "Do I get the impression, Dr. Quinn, that you don't particularly like Mr. Vanderhoven?"

"Like him, Mumsie? Please, I have better taste than *that*! He's a stuffed shirt, obviously a well-bred Southern idiot who has probably never poked his stuck-up nose outside what they were once proud to call the Confederacy… who knows, he probably still has a secret yearning to keep slaves!"

I sat down beside her on the bed, refolded a couple of tops, then, looking into her eyes, I said, "Daughter of mine, I don't think I've seen you respond so negatively to anyone for a long time. It is little wonder that men don't want to stay around you for too long. Oh, by the way, he has spent time in England, and has two broken engagements in his past."

She stuck out her tongue. "Well, it's easy to see why women don't stay around too long with this particular Charles Vanderhoven."

I had not seen so visceral a response to someone on Amanda's part since her bitter disdain of the wicked Julian. Was there more going on beneath the surface than she was prepared to admit or even realized herself? As a wise parent with many years' experience I kept my counsel.

By confiding in me about her abortion when I had been in great discomfort about my mother's war and my own origins, circumstances had drawn us closer than we had been for years. Now that she had moved into *Honeypot Hill*, our lives were becoming even more entwined than they had been since that exceedingly awkward teenage chapter of her life. We could now talk more frankly, which helped me grasp just how deep were the scars that had wounded her soul since the time her father was so prematurely taken from us and for her to understand just what the discovery of my actual parentage had done to my inner being.

Some months earlier, on New Year's Eve when she and I had been alone, Amanda had tearfully admitted, "It always seemed when I was growing up that I could never quite grasp what males were about, what it is that makes them tick. They utterly fascinated me, but what they said and how they acted have ever since been utterly baffling. So many of those girls I grew up with at City of London Girls' School had fathers who in some way or another were there and able to steer them through this – that was one of the spheres where I missed out."

She had then nestled up against me on the living room sofa, gazing into the embers of a still warm but once-crackling fire. "You know, Davey and I will always be grateful to you for being both mother and father to us, but I yearned for a Daddy, not just any Daddy, my Daddy. His loss still haunts me. I don't really know what I am looking for in a man, but I have this feeling that, whether I realize it or not, what I am doing is looking for a surrogate Daddy, not a partner and equal. It seems whenever I fall for someone, my expectations are so impossible because I want more than a lover and soulmate, I want more from him than any self-respecting male is ever able to deliver. That's far too much to ask of any man, which is a pretty good reason why they have hot-footed it out of my life with such monotonous regularity."

Now she had confessed her abiding guilt about her unborn child, she seemed to need times when she could revert to childhood and, like a little girl, cuddle up in my arms – often as a prelude to another big confession, oceans of tears, or both. Amanda constantly repeated, "A day does not pass when I don't regret what I did, and the guilt won't go away. I was walking across Russell Square as I was leaving the Senate House a few weeks ago and there was a little girl of three or four playing with her mother. It suddenly hit me that my child would have been about that age and size now… I had to rush across the street to the Russell Hotel and dive into the Ladies because I needed somewhere to hide and cry."

She had been with me at *Honeypot Hill* the early February weekend before Emily had called; in her hurry to catch a train back to London to do several days of research, she forgot the hard copy of the outline of the proposed book on which she was working. Being both nosy and inquisitive, I gathered it up, and, after treating myself to a mug of steaming hot chocolate, curled up by the fire to read it. After surveying art before Giotto and its transition from figurative to representational painting, she carefully unpacked the evolution of the depiction of Virgin and Child, charting the changes in the West as the Middle Ages yielded to the Renaissance and came under the influence of the Reformation. She compared how depiction moved away from something akin to the Eastern church's symbolic iconography, cut off as the Orthodox had been from the new tides of the Renaissance. While Amanda's work was not innovative, her contribution to scholarship had an unanticipated depth, as I saw her intuitively interpreting western art through the indissoluble bond between mother and child that she had grasped due to her own painful experience.

There was an integrity to her analysis that went beyond anything she had ever written before and it took my breath away, unwittingly disclosing her deep yearnings. Mulling over her writing I was heartbroken, and not just for the grandchild whose life had ended before it had a chance to begin. My emotions were so raw because I now knew that when I was conceived I had been unexpected and initially unwanted. Part of me was glad I now knew the truth, but the other side of my personality wished I could have gone through life oblivious to my parents' deception.

Amanda was at this point at *Honeypot Hill* almost all the time as we worked out the Vanderhoven link. She spent hours shivering in the garage as she doggedly plowed her way through her grandfather's archive. She would often work late into the night and would sometimes slip into my bed; I would wake in the morning to find her pretty hair splayed out across the other pillow. She was temporarily escaping the responsibilities of adulthood, and being with me gave her the chance to pretend she was a little girl again. She felt more secure now she had given herself permission to grieve, perhaps hoping that my arms and her tears together would salve her agony. I would hold her, and between the tears she would babble about wishing she could reverse the decision, telling me that her baby would have been a permanent part of our lives. As she churned all this over I was excruciatingly conscious that what she had done to her child could so easily have happened to me.

In my childhood I had been aware that Mummy's and Daddy's marriage was rocky, and there was little doubt that the ghost of Rebecca's unfaithfulness with Chuck Vanderhoven, coupled with the post-traumatic stress her husband brought home from the battlefield and then the concentration camp, had added to the strain. Unwittingly, I as a little girl was piggy in the middle; I hoped with my heart that they would give me a brother or sister who would somehow complete our little family.

Occasionally, when I was small, I would be woken late at night to hear Mummy and Daddy yelling at one another. Mummy's shrieks filled me with terror, while from Daddy came this deep, enraged, threatening growl. He was not a violent man, but my mother knew how to goad him until he teetered on the very edge. She was always volatile, erupting at the drop of a hat. Daddy's temper had a long slow fuse, yet God help anyone in the way when the fuse ran out.

One particularly ferocious night, I remember him shouting something like "Rebecca, I made a couple of mistakes during the war and you know how much I regret them, but why do you keep using them against me? Look at you; I sometimes wonder if while I was cowering in holes in North Africa you were hopping from bed to bed all over the village – and not just with Americans".

"You exaggerating bastard," she screeched back. Then I heard her hand against his face followed by his yelp.

"Your Flying Fortress captain wasn't the only one, was he?" Daddy then snarled.

"That's none of your bloody business, Jeremy Lisle," she bawled. He then said something I did not hear, and she squawked at the top of her voice, "I'm leaving."

I heard him trying to stop her from putting on her coat. She slapped him hard across the face again, there was a muffled response, then the front door slammed; a moment later the car was being backed recklessly out of the gravel driveway and went charging off down the road. Many years later, when she was an old woman, unable to remember what happened five minutes ago, she had perfect recall of half a century earlier. I learned that on those occasions when she flounced out she would go and park in the entrance of what had been the wartime airfield, weep for what might have been, simmer down, return home, and then she and Daddy would often make love hoping for another child.

It was when she was gone that one particularly awful night that I climbed out of bed and tiptoed downstairs clutching my teddy who, having been unearthed in the attic, now sat in pride of place on my dressing table. Peeping around the living room door I saw Daddy sitting, head in hands, struggling with his emotions. The livid shape of my mother's hand was there on each of his reddening cheeks while noises that terrified me came from some awful place far down inside him.

I now find myself wondering how difficult it must have been when my little girl softness nuzzled against him and he opened his eyes to see this tiny little cuckoo who had been planted in his nest through his wife's unfaithfulness. Was I salt in the wound? I will never know because he took me in his arms, cuddling me until I felt safe, despite his knowledge that another man's blood ran through my veins.

After moderating my alarm, Daddy settled me on the sofa, covering me with that warm fluffy blanket, making his lap my pillow. That night he stroked my long hair and comforted me in a gentle, loving voice while I held dear old Teddy in my arms. I obviously dropped off to sleep because when I awoke Mummy and Daddy were standing in the middle of the room in each other's arms, apologies cascading. Together they carried me upstairs to my own little bed, tucked me in, and then I suspect went to their own room to reaffirm their obvious affection for one another.

I'm sure Mummy loved Daddy in her own way, a love that deepened as the years passed, but I am now convinced that Chuck Vanderhoven could never be displaced as the love of her life – and I was the primary exhibit of that union. Now here I was with my own daughter staying with my natural father's sister, Emily Vanderhoven McAllister, having arrived at the place where I would probably have grown up if *The Rebecca Anne* had managed to cross the North Sea on its last flight.

Wednesday, April 20, 2005 – Franklin, Tennessee, USA

My eyes flickered open not long after daybreak. I had been awakened by the raucous chatter of birds outside my slightly opened window. This was not the sweet birdsong of an English spring dawn but harsh squawks from what I would later learn were blue jays. The largish birds with flashes of pale blue were beautiful, but the same could not be said for the abrasive noises that emerged from their throats, something especially disconcerting after a day of transatlantic travel.

Getting up, I quickly showered, did my stretching exercises, then poked my nose around Amanda's door. From the way books and papers were strewn around her bed, she had obviously had a restless night. As was usual when sleep is slow coming she turned to her studies for company; I suspected she might have just been dropping off at about the same time as I was waking up. Her auburn hair framed her face, with one hand lying beside her head on the pillow – just how she had lain when a baby. Asleep she looked lovely and relaxed, something I had not seen much of in her waking self since before her abortion – and maybe longer.

Having dressed and brushed my hair, I creatively daubed makeup on my face to ameliorate the wear and tear of travel; meanwhile, the rich smell of freshly brewed coffee was wafting up the stairs. My nostrils started sending urgent messages to my brain informing my body that without an immediate significant intake of caffeine there could be dire consequences. Slipping on a light cotton frock and soft blue cardigan, I pattered down to the kitchen where I found Emily McAllister. She was wearing a long quilted Chinese housecoat decorated with glorious embroidery and was seated at a large round table in a bay window drinking her morning Cup o'Joe, as she described it, while reading *The Tennessean*.

As I came into the room she looked up, smiled, and said, "Good morning, early riser. I wasn't expecting you or Amanda for a while."

"Oh, Amanda is like almost every academic, an incurable night owl... it could be midday before she appears, probably as temperamental as those storms that delayed our flight for so long in Atlanta. I learned to be an early riser when Timothy, my late husband, died because there was so much for a single mother and businesswoman to do and so few hours in the day."

"When was that, Sugar?" she asked, a concerned twinkle in her eye.

I smiled wanly, memories of that dreadful morning flashing through my mind. "Sometimes it seems like yesterday, but it was getting on for twenty-five years ago," I sighed. "That had to be the very worst day of my life, although I have to confess that learning about Chuck Vanderhoven last October came close to it."

Emily was silent for a few moments then said softly, "My family think I am the nosiest woman in creation, but may I ask what happened to your husband?"

I explained how Timothy had been knocked off his bike on his way to work in London and how the police broke the news to me. Until my dying day the image of his pale dead face as he lay in the hospital mortuary will be imprinted on my mind, eyes closed and lips turning blue. I totally lost it when I was taken by the policewoman and a doctor to identify the body. Then came the afternoon of his funeral, one child on either side holding my hand. Tears furrowed my cheeks accompanied by occasional agonized sobs. I didn't care how I looked, I had lost the love of my life in a senseless accident.

I recounted this to Emily, then tried to lighten the conversation, "I've seen that news footage of Jackie Kennedy with her little ones at JFK's funeral. I suspect I looked a little like that – but without the fashionable chic clothes and natural good taste."

"Honey," Emily replied, taking my hand across the table, "I have an idea that you looked divine. You are very like your mother, but Amanda looks exactly like her grandfather."

"Chuck?" I asked.

"I always called him Charles and sometimes Carlos, but yes, Chuck," she answered softly. "He didn't really become Chuck until the air force. It was perhaps a blessing for poor Jeremy that Vanderhoven looks skipped a generation. Amanda's hair has exactly the same wave in the front as Charles's, and when her face lights up there is a mischievousness that tells me she *has* to be my sweet brother's grandchild – although she was too tired to light up much last night."

I was quiet, then answered, "You're an observant and sensitive woman, aren't you?"

She laughed. "You wouldn't say that if you were on the opposite side of a case in court."

"You're a lawyer?"

She nodded. "When Charles died someone had to take on the family business. I went to law school instead of charm school. I began when there were hardly any female attorneys in Nashville or anywhere else for that matter… When I was still an active member of the firm my male opponents called me the Dragon Lady behind my back… For a few years I was senior partner of the law firm until I retired, but I still go in once or twice a week – old habits are hard to break, but I also need to keep an eye on the foundation."

"And your husband?"

"McAllister?"

"Yes," I answered.

"He was husband number two," she answered. "Number one and I were at college together and should never have married. Let's just say we were young, stupid, and over-sexed; fortunately we discovered how bad we were for each other before we were able to get around to children. My first husband moved to the Low Country of South Carolina. When he retired he settled on Hilton Head Island. Then not too long ago he dropped dead just after putting out on the eighteenth and heading to the clubhouse. A sweet man but impossible to live with, as each of his next three wives were to discover!"

I decided to probe no further, and she was obviously none too eager to dig up what was long since buried. We chattered about this and that, then Emily laughed, winked, and said, "You have such good English manners, Sarah. I suspect you are dying to know about Number Two."

I grinned, feeling my face flush. "Yes, rather."

"Will McAllister had been a friend of Charles during the war. They were in flight school in Arizona and then trained at Dyersburg, Tennessee, together. He was originally from Oklahoma and, like Charles, had grown bored with lawyering at the time of Pearl Harbor. He came to visit us when he'd flown his thirty-five missions and arrived home. Silly little girl that I was, I had just washed my hands of Number One so fell hopelessly in love with him. Daddy liked him so offered him a position in the Vanderhoven law firm. The rest, as they say, is history."

"And family?"

A cloud veiled her face for a moment, and I thought I might have trodden on her toes. Like me, this woman had dark memories, but, after a pause to gather herself, she said softly, "Jeannie was a sweet girl. She was intelligent and the most talented artist at Harpeth Hall, the girls school to which Vanderhoven girls go – and where you would have gone had you grown up here. Alas, she rebelled and went to university out West, got caught up in the stupidity of the Sixties, damaged herself with drugs…"

It was my turn to comfort and encourage her, so reaching across the table I put my hand on hers. "I'm sorry, I didn't intend to raise distressing ghosts."

"No, honey, I need to tell you because it might perhaps explain why I'm so interested in you. Jeannie got a lot of the pieces back together again, but the drugs had left their scars. After this she was martyr to the most terrible depressions. I suspect she deliberately over-dosed one day in the early 1980s just after the umpteenth man had walked out on her. I have never set eyes on my grandchildren."

"I'm so sorry."

"The first time I met you I knew that you and she would have been great pals."

I looked up surprised. "How do you mean?"

"Sarah, you may not remember, but you and I have actually met before."

I was stunned. "I'm sorry, I don't understand."

She looked at me. "You would have been around seven or eight. It was in August, and Rebecca brought you to London to do some shopping before the school year began."

"Mummy could never pass up an excuse for a trip to London and some shopping," I laughed, trying to digest this information.

Emily continued, "You met Will and myself for lunch at a funny little basement restaurant on Maddox Street, not too far from Liberty's. Jeannie would have been a little younger than you, and ever since I have wished we had taken her with us so the two of you could have met. This was our first trip to England. We went over on the *Queen Elizabeth* and visited all sorts of places, including Thorpe

Beauchamp... left a wreath at the gates of what had been the airfield. You were back at school by then and your Daddy was off at work, so we could visit *Honeypot Hill* and not cause any snags ... but I've never forgotten you or your lovely home."

Mummy had loved showing me off. I was her little princess and she took me on any number of occasions to London to meet her friends. My memories were a blur of faces, cooing voices, and women stroking my hair then telling me how pretty I was. She would always meet her girlfriends at that same restaurant just off Regent Street. I suspect it was a favorite place for her and Chuck. I tried to look as if I was listening carefully to what Emily was saying, but my mind was jumping all over the place desperately attempting to remember that particular occasion.

Emily realized my confusion but went on. "London was still disfigured by the scars of war... there were huge swathes around St. Paul's Cathedral where rubble was festooned with those little pink flowers folks called London Pride. Will took some pictures with our very first color camera; when I looked at them the other day the tints had sadly faded to a bluey shade. We stayed at the Ritz overlooking Green Park and not far from Berkeley Square, and in the little hotel shop I found a lovely necklace with a blue kitty cat on it that I bought you..."

"My blue pussycat," I gasped. "I love my blue pussycat – you were the one who gave it to me?"

"You still have it?"

I nodded. "I haven't worn it for ages, but yes, it has pride of place in my jewel box. Sometimes I let Amanda wear it when she was growing up, and, although she pleaded to have it, it was somehow too precious for me to part with it, probably because I had it firmly in my mind that Daddy had given me it."

Emily smiled kindly. "I have a feeling that when I gave it to you I told you this was something to remember your Daddy by... I had Charles in mind."

"You knew?"

She nodded. "I knew."

"Why did no one ever tell me?" I said huffily, and with an edge in my voice.

"Honey, I'm sure it was because no one wanted to alienate you from Jeremy. Your relationship with him was special, and your mother's delight at the way he accepted you knew no bounds. I never met him, but from all Rebecca said in her letters Jeremy utterly adored you. If you had asked him to walk the plank and jump into shark-infested waters, then he would have done so in an instant."

Even as Emily spoke I could almost hear Daddy's voice, remembering some of our special moments from my growing up. There had still been a stretch of concrete where the airfield had been when I was five or six, and this was where he took me for several weekends to teach me to ride my first little bike. He would run around for ages, his hand holding the back of the saddle, until one day I thought he was still there only to discover, when I told him something, that he was standing forty or fifty feet away. Immediately I lost my nerve, tumbled off, and started crying; in a trice he was there holding me tight and telling me what a clever girl I was.

I nodded and sighed. "Yes, Daddy loved me very much, and hardly a day goes by when I don't miss him. This is what made discovering the complexity of my parentage wrenching."

"Sarah, sweetheart," Emily said softly as she took hold of my hands, "if it is any comfort, when finally your Daddy found out about Charles's part in your conception and what Charles had done for his men on that flight back toward England, your mother told me he stood up and saluted a man who he felt duty-bound to honor as a war hero. He told her there and then that it would be a privilege to raise as his own the child of such a brave man. That was when your mother began falling back in love with him, and she loved him to the very end."

Quietly I mumbled, "Daddy was an honorable man himself, great integrity... even deep into old age."

"In this country we are calling these men... and women, the Greatest Generation."

"That was my Daddy... or perhaps I should say my Daddies."

Emily's sitting room was spacious, and she ushered me to it while a fresh pot of coffee was brewing. She wanted to show me her pictures. There were oil paintings displayed on the walls and rich drapes hung at the windows. Exquisite but comfortable, the furniture was set on a dark oak floor with several large warmly decorated maroon Persian and Turkish rugs scattered here and there. On the mantle were delicate items of Dresden china, and the fireplace was surrounded by blue and white Delft tiles, looking appropriately Dutch.

She saw me looking at the tiles, read my mind, and smiled. "With a name like Vanderhoven I had to have something genuinely Dutch in my home. You know, our family claims distant descent from a man who found his way down from New York to South Carolina around the time of the War of Independence, and he was likely a distant descendant of a family of burghers in Amsterdam." She pointed to an early Nineteenth Century portrait and said, "That's William Augustus Vanderhoven, the first member of the family to venture out of the sophistication of Charleston and into what was then the rustic back country of Tennessee."

I laughed. "There isn't much breeding in my family, we're just a group of jumped up peasants – except for my daughter-in-law that is, David's wife Millicent. Her father is an earl, but she has no aristocratic hauteur and has been happily absorbed into the Quinn clan. She's expecting my first grandchild."

"How on earth did David land a blue-blood?" Emily asked in amazement.

I grinned. "She came to work for our business, The Quinn Galleries, after she graduated from university. As a matter of fact, I gave her her first job."

"That's an art gallery, isn't it?"

I nodded. "It was started by my late husband's grandfather, and

David is the fourth generation of proprietors."

"And your grandchild?"

"We would never push the baby into the business," I joked, "but wouldn't it be wonderful if she became the fifth generation?"

"A girl?"

I nodded. "At first they tried to keep the gender a secret, but Millie couldn't help showing me the nursery when they were working on it. The walls were a little too pastel, and there were too many girly touches for a little boy."

Emily smiled back. "Honey, I'm so happy for you."

"And I'm happy for me, too." My contentment showed.

We continued chatting as we wandered back into the kitchen to drink more coffee, too much of which was a bad American habit I had discovered on business trips I had made to New York and Washington, D.C. Finally, Emily stood and began clearing the table. Automatically I rose to help.

"You don't need to do that," she scolded. "You're a guest in my home."

I grinned, shaking my head. "No, Aunt Emily, I do… I'm family, aren't I… there's that Vanderhoven blood flowing through my veins, remember?"

She shook her head and grinned back, then we loaded the dishwasher together as Emily wondered whether to set the table for Amanda. I told her not to worry and that my daughter when tired could sleep for England.

"Perhaps in an hour or two the aroma of mid-morning coffee will coax her out of her nest," Emily suggested. Then taking my hand, she led me across the hallway and into a little room whose patio doors were open. The view was across a small green tree-lined valley with a pond not far from the house. There were a couple of horses grazing contentedly in the field. A comfortable chair over whose back a pretty feminine cotton shawl had been thrown was the place where Emily obviously sat to gaze at the greenery, working and reading. On the small cherry occasional table beside it were several loose leaf files.

"Now, Sarah, these are a gift for you."

I looked puzzled. "What are they.... bills?

Her eyes sparkled as she chuckled. "If you want some of my bills, because you're a member of the family I'd be happy to share them, but no, these are the letters your mother wrote me beginning in the first part of 1944. The last one came just a few weeks after your Daddy died. It was disjointed and confused, and I guessed I might not hear from her again. I've told you that I wished with all my heart she had become my sister-in-law. Then I'd have had a soul mate as well as being able to watch you grow up and flourish; instead, she and I were destined to be pen pals for more than half a century. We'd see each other on my occasional trips to England. I'd hoped she would come and visit me after Jeremy had gone to his eternal reward, but that was not to be... so now I have her daughter and granddaughter here instead, and I can't tell you how glorious that feels."

I was startled. Getting my mother to write a letter to anyone was like getting blood out of a stone. Unlike Daddy she was not an early riser and he always took her breakfast in bed. She would then scan the *Daily Mail* and lie there until the middle of the morning chattering on the phone to her friends – she adored the telephone, as Daddy's phone bills demonstrated. Yet here was a substantial correspondence exchanged with Emily – all of them meticulously filed and preserved. I was eager to get going before my research-addicted daughter grabbed them away from me.

Emily settled me down, brought a cup of tea, made properly, and although weary from travel and a little disoriented I ferreted in my handbag, found my glasses, and flicked through the collection before starting to read.

• • • • • • •

HUNNYPOT HILL
THORPE BEAUCHAMP
ENGLAND

Sunday, 28th May, 1944

Dear Emily,

Chuck is such a dear getting what he calls his 'kid sister' to drop me a line to tell me about a woman's life in Nashville. I love him dearly but am both excited and scared out of my wits by the possibility of moving to America when this dreadful war finally turns up its toes. Right now the rumour mill is over-active, there's lots of military movement all over the place, it could be that something really big is about to happen.

As I consider divorcing, marrying another man, and moving an ocean away I can't think what my parents will say, nor how it will hurt Jeremy, who I married when I was younger and so immature. I was little more than a schoolgirl pretending to be grownup when he left for Africa four years ago. From what I know, the divorce courts will be overflowing when the war ends, but when that happens to me the final alienation from my family will be complete. Jeremy is a good and loving man, but we have been apart for so long that we have little left in common…

And so it went on. Obviously, my mother was eaten alive by guilt about what she and Chuck were planning but unable to help herself. She so wanted it that she was looking for any excuse she could to justify herself. This was always Mummy's way, her heart regularly running far ahead of good sense. For her, if something felt right then there had to be a way to make it right.

This exchange of letters began as two young women getting to know each another. Mummy kept asking questions about everything from what it was like driving on the right hand side of the road to the availability of stockings and what sort of clothes Southern women wear during hot summers. Clothes were never far from Rebecca Lisle's mind. Although I did not have Emily's side of the correspondence in reply, from the way in which Rebecca Lisle responded, it was not difficult to interpret what was going on in this transatlantic conversation between two women drawn together as they lived under the mordant shadow of war.

In late June 1944 were references to the D-Day landings and the fact that Chuck and his new plane, delivered just days before the invasion, had come through the initial actions unscathed.

... and, Emily, can you believe this? After some pretty nasty stuff over somewhere or other the powers-that-be have given Chuck and the boys a brand new plane. They tell me it is called a B-17G, that there are all sorts of new bells and whistles, but best of all is that it carries more fuel, which means that on longer missions they don't have to worry so much about how to cherish a teaspoonful of gasoline in order to get themselves home.

"How like Mummy," I thought to myself. "She was always a bit of a chameleon and was already adopting American vocabulary."

What makes the new plane so special is that, in several days' break in action, Chuck got hold of some paint and put a reasonable likeness of my face on the side under the cockpit. I had no idea he was such a wizard artist. With the agreement of the crew, he used his privileged position as pilot to name it The Rebecca Anne because of me, and while there was no champagne we were able to christen her with a bottle of the best bitter from the local pub that I smashed across its nose! I enclose a little snap of Chuck and me in front of The Rebecca Anne after the ceremony. As my darling man says, it is much nicer piloting The Rebecca Anne than mere plane number 981, or whatever it is.

As I sat there looking across Emily's green valley, she came in with a glass of iced tea, a beverage Southerners seemed to live on. She put it on the occasional table and looked over my shoulder at the picture.

"I always loved that picture – it was the first I ever saw of your mother," she said.

I glanced up at her and answered, "I found a copy of this in the boxes Mummy had in the attic... and in an old suitcase was the frock she's wearing."

She sighed. "I used to keep that picture in my bible so I could pray for Charles and Rebecca each day when I read. When he was gone, then I prayed for your mother as she sought to put back together a life that had been focused on a future in this country."

"When did you find out she was pregnant?"

"It wasn't until toward the end of 1944 that she wrote. I gather that she had spotted and threatened a miscarriage – which was when Jeremy, who had already guessed, was confronted with just how enamored his wife had been with this American airman. As the British used to say, our boys were over-paid, over-sexed, and over there;

maybe Chuck's potency proved this to Jeremy."

"I knew nothing about me nearly being miscarried," I answered in astonishment.

"I'm not sure that's the sort of thing most mothers would share with their daughters in those days," Emily responded, a funny look on her face. Without a word she left the room. I guessed that she might have had miscarriages herself about which she never told her own children.

I flicked over other pages of letters until I reached the autumn and Daddy's return from Africa and Italy.

Oh, Emily, darling, these last weeks have been the very worst. I'm SO, SO sorry I have not written before. The wishful thinking part of me, the fantasy world in which I have been living, wants to believe Chuck is still alive, but I am having the most terrible nightmares about his plane going down in the water, his terror as he drowned, and my heart shatters afresh into a thousand more pieces... then I wake up and find not him but Jeremy sleeping beside me. I want to cuddle up and be comforted, but can't because that feels like disloyalty to Chuck – with whom I had already been disloyal to Jeremy. I'm in such a tangle I don't know where to turn. I cry every morning when cycling to work.

But there is more than that. Emily, I'm expecting. I am pretty certain I conceived near the end of Chuck's life because we spent so much time in bed together. I knew I was going to be with him for the rest of my life and was getting slapdash about birth control, although he was often so demanding that there was no time to get things right. Little did I realize a baby would be his parting gift to me.

In quick succession I lost Chuck, then within days received news that Jeremy was coming home, then before I could put myself back together again the doorbell rang late one night and there was my husband on the doorstep looking thin, tired, and haggard. He has obviously been involved in terrible things. How could I turn him away, especially after the promises I made at the altar?

I feel like a woman on a merry-go-round that's getting faster and faster until it throws me off. During the last weeks I have just kept on keeping on, going to work, coming home again, trying to be a good wife but not really wanting Jeremy to touch me. A few days ago I had to take the train to Ely on something related to work, the old cathedral city not too far from here. After my meeting I went and sat in the cathedral, which is huge, dark, old, cold, and sacred. I was looking up towards the high altar, bawling my eyes out, when I heard a B-17 fly over, probably on its way to the airfield at Mildenhall, quite close by. My heart leapt for a moment as I wondered if it was Chuck coming home – but perhaps it was God telling me that he was gone forever and to pick up the pieces of my life.

I cycled home from the train station in pouring rain. Soaked to the skin when I got to the house, Jeremy wrapped his arms around me, took me in his arms, and just cared for me, but I knew something terribly wrong was happening inside. As he now had petrol coupons, the dear man had been secretly getting the car working again so he took me straight to get medical help. It proved to be a false alarm, but I have been confined to bed for several weeks. So here I sit writing letters.

Jeremy was so sweet and I had to tell him all about Chuck. When I had finished he stood up, saluted, and said it would be an honor to raise a hero's child. Maybe, just maybe if there is a God in the heavens, he is telling me that my call in life is to raise my son or daughter to be a credit to his/her father and Daddy.

After this there is a gap of some months and then came one with a birth announcement card attached to it.

---

*Major and Mrs. Jeremy Lisle
are pleased to announce the birth of their daughter
Sarah Charlotte Lisle
Born at the Mid-Cambridgeshire Cottage Hospital,
Thorpe Beauchamp
Monday, May 21, 1945
Mother and Daughter doing well*

I had never before seen the card announcing my birth. Indeed, I had no idea it was possible to get such a thing printed amidst post-war stringencies – yet here it was, telling the whole world not only that I had come kicking and screaming into it but was being proudly claimed by Daddy as his daughter!

I was so lost in thought that I was unaware that Amanda had crept into the room and was crouching beside me. "What's the matter, Mumsie? You look as if you have seen a ghost announcing you'd just won the lottery."

Saying nothing, I handed her the card. She instantly knew what I was thinking and feeling, so we just hugged.

The rest of the day was taken up with Emily showing us around, pointing out the house in the Belle Meade area where Mummy would have lived if she had married Chuck and introducing us to various members of the family at a dinner at the Belle Meade Country Club. It was a whirl of introductions, faces, and confusion on the part of younger members of the wider family as to where I actually fitted in. I felt drained when I finally flopped into bed that night. I was amazed at how energetic Emily Vanderhoven McAllister could actually be.

Friday, April 22, 2005 — Franklin, Tennessee, USA

The following morning Emily and I breakfasted together again, Amanda having once more slept in. This gave me the time to carry on reading Mummy's letters where I had left off the previous day.

HUNNYPOT HILL
THORPE BEAUCHAMP
ENGLAND

22 September 1945

Dear Emily,

I am late writing this to you, but I wanted you to know that my darling little Sarah came into the world, and Jeremy is every bit as thrilled with her as I. Jeremy always will be an officer and a gentleman (actually he ceases to be an officer at the end of this month when he is officially de-mobbed and then will spend all his time putting the family business back in order after the rigours of war). My husband has been true to his word, treating Chuck's daughter as his own with no ifs, ands, or buts. He spends hours with her asleep on his lap, sitting beside her cot in the nursery, taking her out in her pram for walks, and so forth. The only thing I haven't managed to persuade him to do yet is change nappies – but you know how soppy men are about such things.

Last Sunday, Sarah was christened in the old village church which is right beside our house. Peter, Jeremy's old army chaplain pal, managed to scrounge enough petrol to get here to perform the ceremony, and I was so pleased to meet him. Despite the country still being on a war footing, various members of the family came up with astonishing silver gifts for our little girl, and no one left without us being able to put plenty of good food in their stomachs. I am relieved for Jeremy that Sarah looks so like me. She has my blue eyes and beautiful long fingers. I just hope the poor child does not end up developing a nose like mine.

Alas, I did!

A year has now passed since Chuck died and nearly a year since Jeremy returned home. The army gave him a long leave to recover from the ill effects of so many years away and to get a start on wrapping his mind around the challenges facing the family business. Early in the New Year he was then pulled back into service as part of an engineer unit moved into Germany a little way behind the front line. Their job was to assess what needs to be done to accelerate the victory and start rebuilding a shattered country. He was appalled by the concentration camps, one of which he helped liberate. I suspect his engineering experience getting the Eighth Army across North Africa was the reason they wanted him there. I so hate the Germans that, as far as I'm concerned, they should be left to wallow in their own filth, but my husband is a better person than I.

He came back ashen and silent. For days he was violently ill when he even tried to talk to me about it, often ending up with his head down the toilet. Finally he gave me a small taste of what he had seen, but then told me I did not need to know all the Nazis were responsible for; I accept he will probably carry this additional burden of war for years to come.

What he experienced makes him morose and withdrawn at times. He is not the sort of man who rants or gets on his high horse, but his emotions are raw as he wonders how he might alleviate the suffering – especially that of the women and children. Only when I place his daughter in his arms does he start to relax. He utterly adores her, as do I. Loving her is his gift to Chuck, and she is Chuck's gift to us.

I'm alright, Emily. I am readjusting to being the wife of an Englishman, and while Jeremy and I have our moments I do love him, but never with the passion that I loved your brother. Chuck is forever the love of my life. Thousands of couples in Britain are now watching their marriages come apart for reasons similar to us, but, mercifully, we look as if we might make it. That it will totter and fall terrifies me, because I have nowhere else to go.

My mother did the arithmetic on my pregnancy and was white with anger when she confronted me. I expect others have done the same, too, but with typical English reserve they keep their insights to themselves or, more likely, gossip behind our backs. I doubt Mummy and I will ever again have a close relationship, and perhaps it is her venom that keeps Daddy at arm's length. They did not come to the christening. But Jeremy is protecting me and my child, and he's a magnificent husband and provider.

There are many hard years ahead for this country. The nation is penniless and needs rebuilding from the bottom up. Poor London and many other cities are going to be piles of rubble for years. Having the bloody Labour Party in power doesn't ease our anxieties. How on earth the people had the nerve to tip dear Mr. Churchill out I don't know. Rationing is going to go on into the future as far as the eye can see, and my hopes of finding pretty material for just a few new dresses remain distant dreams. Jeremy's father is putting one foot back into retirement, handing over to his son a business wounded by the war and impossibly short of working capital. This is a huge source of worry, and those worries are unlikely to evaporate for a long time yet, but we will survive! I will keep in touch.

Lots of Love,

Rebecca

And so the correspondence continued along these lines year after year, each woman sharing her own joys and sorrows. I had heard of pen pal friendships going on for decades, but never in my wildest imagination did I suspect my own mother being capable of participating in one that had lasted half a century. I wondered how much Daddy knew of it. I suspected Mummy's letters were written then slipped by her into the small red letterbox outside the village shop when he was off at work.

After I was born Mummy never again worked outside the home. She threw herself into motherhood, adored flowers, took great pleasure in her garden, joined the Women's Institute, played tennis, and had a coterie of girlfriends who shared her somewhat limited interests, as well as her delight in nice clothes, fine wines, and taking care of their families. The house was always spic-and-span, although there was a cleaning lady who came in from the village. When Daddy got home in the evenings she usually put on something attractive and freshened up her lipstick so the pair of them could share a cocktail before we ate dinner. It irritated Mummy, but Daddy would always say grace and say it in the Latin he had learned when he was a boy at Berkhamsted School: *"Benedictus, benedicat, per Iesum Christum Dominum Nostrum. Amen."*

It took several days for me to fully digest Mummy's letters to America recounting the passing of the years but always with special reference to me. She knew full well that Aunt Emily would cherish every tiny detail – and there were usually pictures of me slipped in with each letter. From reading the letters, I learned that I had cried for my mother almost all that first day at primary school, that in the middle of the bitterly cold winter of 1963 central heating was finally installed at *Honeypot Hill*, meaning that with doors open and holes in walls we froze for several weeks. A few years later Mummy had become convinced Daddy was out of his mind when he sold the family business to focus on the needs of refugees.

> "Oh Emily, I don't seem to be able to knock any sense into this man's thick skull when it comes to his passion for refugees. What he saw at the end of the war in Europe had such a lasting impact on him that I sometimes think he's more concerned about them than he is for me and Sarah. By the way, right now Sarah is being a perfect little horror. She is turning out to be one of the bolshiest girls at Newnham, her college at Cambridge University. What is worse is that she has fetched up with Tim, a boy at Selwyn, the men's college that is just across the street, and together they do all the same courses. They are as thick as thieves, but I hope it won't be too long before it breaks up."

Of course, Tim and I did not break up, and over the years my darling husband managed to wheedle his way into my mother's good graces. Rebecca Lisle's hatred of my husband started to dissolve not long after she visited me at the hospital a few days after David was born. Tim placed her grandson in her arms, she smiled this beatific smile, and whispered to no one in particular, "Oh, darlings, he looks just like his grandfather." She was, of course, talking about Chuck, for both my children have seem to possess a Vanderhoven cast of face.

Some weeks after Tim had been killed she wrote despairingly to Emily.

> "Emily, dear, we have been through an awful, awful time and Sarah is now experiencing what I felt when Chuck was killed that horrid August day so long ago. (She went on to describe

the accident and in true Rebecca Lisle style managed to make the whole thing sound far more dramatic than it actually was. You would think that what happened within spitting distance of the steps of All Souls' Church was actually World War Three breaking out). *Sarah is being very courageous, and we have spent a lot of time together during the last few weeks. You would be so proud of her as she works out how to maintain the gallery, earn a living, be mother and father to her children, and keep a roof over their heads. London is so expensive, you know, but she has the guts of her natural father and the tenacity of her beloved Daddy. Thank God for the insurance settlement and that the capital we raised from the sale of the business Jeremy has invested prudently.*

Timothy Quinn was a man in a million. I said nasty things about him when he hooked up with Sarah, but he proved himself more than worthy of her time and again. I wish they could have had a long and fruitful marriage, with both of them able to see their children grow up and their grandchildren come into the world. I hope that somewhere down the road my daughter will find another man who will love her, much as Jeremy has loved and cherished me, but I suspect when she gave her heart to Tim it was forever, and that no one will ever displace him."

I smiled sadly. Oh, how I still missed Tim so much, but Mummy had it right – I was Timothy Quinn's widow and it was highly unlikely I'd find another man to whom I would entrust my life, much as I enjoyed male company.

After my Daddy died the correspondence slowed, finally petering out with a confused and confusing letter. I now remembered going with her to put it into the letterbox at the Village Shop. We walked there together that balmy afternoon, dementia already stripping away distinct elements of her identity. It was sad. This once vibrant woman was turning into a mere shadow of her former self, a little old lady with a funny laugh. Once the life and soul of the party, a feminine creature on whom all eyes rested when she entered a room, she was now being emptied out and was turning into a recluse.

Emily had come in at this point with a fresh cup of coffee and found me staring vacantly into the distance, tears dribbling down my cheeks. The two of us were alone, Amanda having borrowed one of Emily's cars to visit the Frist Center for the Visual Arts in Nashville, where Charlie Vanderhoven had opened a door for her. This would be her third visit in as many days, and she was delighted by the interesting people she was meeting while seeking opportunities for research on her planned book. Having discovered her own sort of people, she was realizing that Nashville could be an exciting place.

"What's wrong, Sugar?" Emily asked. Then without me answering she, looking over my shoulder, saw the last letter in the series. "Oh, sad, isn't it?"

"Emily, I was with her the afternoon she posted this ... If I'd known how confused her mind had actually become I would have intercepted it. It wasn't long after this that I stepped down from my position at the gallery, gathered up all my toys in London, rented out my house, and went back to the Fens."

"Regret it?"

I shook my head vigorously. "At first I did, but not now. Those weren't easy years, I'll grant you, but after all she and Daddy did for me what else could an only daughter do?"

Emily perched on the chair opposite me. "Sarah Charlotte Quinn, having you here has been a tonic for my old soul. I have loved introducing you around. I can't tell you how proud I felt when you came to church with me on Sunday, and you have such a lovely singing voice. But seeing you and getting to know you has been the best gift God has ever given me… And Amanda, goodness that girl's a chip off the Vanderhoven block."

I smiled at her. There was a vibrancy to her voice and a brightness in her face that said something of the young woman she had been when Chuck introduced her to my mother by letter during those climactic years of war.

We were silent, then I smiled again and commented, "Now, Emily, I think I'm getting to know you well enough to realize you are building up to something."

She laughed, "You are far too perceptive for your own good, Sarah, honey."

I laughed back, wiping the last tear with the back of my hand. "I didn't spent all those years selling pictures without ascertaining something about what was going on in the minds of the customers."

For a moment we silently enjoyed the pleasure of each other's company. Then she went on. "Would you do an old woman a great favor?"

"If it's in my power," I replied.

"Tomorrow afternoon we have a meeting of the Vanderhoven Memorial Foundation board of trustees. I'm wondering if you would accompany me to that gathering as my guest?"

While I could hardly say no, I failed to grasp that she was busy spinning a web into which I was about to fly!

Sunday, April 24, 2005 — Old Hillsboro Pike, Franklin, Tennessee, USA

I sat drinking my coffee, wondering how I might broach the subject. That night I had tossed and turned, indignant that Emily had set me up as far as the Vanderhoven Memorial Foundation was concerned. I thought I was going with her as an interested guest so had been sitting there listening, but totally off my guard. Then the invitation was proffered that I become one of them. I had no problem being part of this charitable foundation, especially one with such noble aims, but I resented being put on the spot with a dozen people I did not know looking on while I struggled to make such a significant decision.

After the meeting, Fitz McPharlan and his wife, Dodie, took me out to dinner and then dropped me back quite late at Emily's home. When I came in I discovered my hostess was already in bed. I was glad, in a way, because I did not want to confront her at the end of the day, but not having put to rest my deep disquiet meant that however many sheep I counted, none of them helped me doze off. I appeared at breakfast wan, weary, and exhausted.

I was so quiet that Emily finally said, "Sugar, you're not pleased with me are you?"

Sighing, I made a face and shook my head.

"I'm sorry, honey. Jennifer called when I got home and was rightly livid with me for putting you on the spot. Contrary to her usual opinion of my decisions, she thinks you are a wonderful addition to the board, but she was furious with me for being such a manipulative old woman."

I reached across and put my hand on her forearm. "Emily, I don't know whether that's true or not, but I do know that you made me feel very uncomfortable – and how on earth can I manage to fulfill my obligations from three and a half thousand miles and an ocean away?"

A few tears had already formed in Emily's eyes. "Does that mean you are resigning?"

I shrugged. "I don't know, I've been worrying about it all night."

"So I kept you from your beauty sleep?"

"You certainly did, aunt of mine, although if ever I was beautiful it has long since gone the way of all flesh."

"Nonsense," Emily huffed, pulling a tissue from her sleeve and dabbing her eyes and nose. "I decided not to wait up because I suspected we would get into a row and probably say things we both regretted."

"You didn't sleep much either, did you?"

"Sarah, I didn't sleep at all."

"Oh, Aunt Emily, that's not good.

"No, but here we are now, let's get this sorted out? I know that I can't sit next to you in church this morning without getting this straightened out… the Bible says something about that, but just being a mere Episcopalian I have no idea where I would find such a text. Let me begin. I'm sorry for putting you on the spot. The only excuse I have is that since I was an itty-bitty girl I have been able to get people to do what I want. By the time I was three I had my Daddy wrapped around my little finger, and that brother of mine, your father, was even easier to control than Daddy had been. Since then at home, at work, and in the courtroom I've been pretty good at getting my own way. I'm afraid this must have been a bridge too far, and you, niece, are teaching me a lesson… Do you want to withdraw without losing face?"

"Auntie, I don't know what I want, but I appreciate your apology very much." Leaning across the table I kissed her on the cheek and then spontaneously whispered, "Emily Vanderhoven McAllister, in these last days I really have come to love you."

"I would adore telling you a little about the Foundation, which will probably show why I wanted you on the board. We formally launched it soon after my darling son, Charles McAllister, was killed in one of those dreadful Swift boats on the Mekong Delta in Vietnam. His father and I immediately set aside some of what he would have inherited as the foundation's principal, but this wasn't the first time the family had done something like this."

"What do you mean?"

"Sarah, the Vanderhovens aren't just lawyers, you know. We have been around Nashville quite long enough, in good times as well as bad, and have managed to accumulate a few businesses, quite a lot of farm and development land, a share in a bank or two, that kind of thing. I really don't know how much we are worth as a family, but God has been good to us and we in turn have always believed it our duty to give back in gratitude. As the Bible says somewhere, from those to whom much is given, much will be expected – and we have been given more than we deserve and have had the wit to take good care of it."

"That's laudable, but I can't see where this is going," I replied, pouring another cup of coffee.

"We didn't exactly set up a foundation in 1944 when your natural father was killed over the North Sea, but during the next several years, once peace came again, we worked out what portion of Vanderhoven holdings might have been his if we were to liquidate everything. We then set aside that proportion of the profits each year for charitable and religious work. In 1972 we rolled all that into the foundation and have continued channeling more into it ever since."

Smiling, I squeezed her hand. "I like that."

"If at that time your mother had allowed me to talk about you as Charles's daughter, today you would be a wealthy woman because much of what is behind the income and the work of the foundation would have been yours."

"Auntie, darling," I said assuring her, "I'm not financially a wealthy woman, but our family might best be described as fairly comfortable. Also, in the years after Tim's death, I had to earn every penny to support the three of us; this gave me the most wonderful lesson in both the value of money and how to manage it. I wouldn't have missed that for anything – I suspect I could have become as spendthrift as my mother without my nose having been on the grindstone in this way..." I paused, then continued, "When I look at my daughter-in-law's sisters, who have been cosseted and spoiled, I can see that I gave my children some very healthy financial lessons as they entered adult life."

Emily grinned. "You never cease to amaze me, Sarah – how did you become such a wise woman? Your mother, rightly, I think, made up her mind that it would be better for you and your English Daddy that no Vanderhoven money should come your way... Honey, you may have noticed some gaps in the correspondence I shared with you. I actually held back several of your mother's letters from those you've read because they discussed just this, and she and I had one or two transatlantic phone calls, which were fearfully expensive in those days, in order to thrash this issue out. I may be manipulative, but I didn't want to make life difficult for the Lisles"

"And so you marched me there yesterday to corner me into being part of all this without explaining what was behind it?" I suggested.

She shook her head vigorously. "I suppose it might have been somewhere at the back of my mind, but what I wanted you to see was what had been done in your natural father's memory so that you would yearn to be part of it. I wanted you to put that alongside all the wonderful work for refugees that Jeremy was able to do so that you could be gratified by both of them and also be proud of your American as well as your English heritage."

I smiled softly and said, "But then you got a little bit too enthusiastic with me sitting there beside you so you thrust me into the limelight where I would have looked disagreeable if I refused?"

She shook her head again. "I have fallen in love with you so much, Sarah, that I couldn't help myself. I promise it wasn't my plan, but when you were invited to make comments the insights and ideas you brought to the table were astonishing. Take, for example, that request for funds from the riding stable that works with disabled children. Your suggestions were magnificent, and as their business plan, reputation, and references were excellent, we not only gave them what they asked but a little more to enable them to forward plan for the future. We wouldn't have done that if you hadn't been there."

I shrugged. "It just seemed to make sense. I've guided a business that has struggled through hard times, so I know exactly what it must be like for those good people and their mission."

"Honey, it made good sense to all of us because you pointed it out. Most of us have lived coddled lives so have not experienced much of that."

I felt myself blushing, unsure where all this was leading.

"I have two personal reasons for wanting you to be part of the foundation. The first is foolish and selfish, the other makes perfect sense."

"Go on."

"The one that makes perfect sense is that, as we take on a few more international projects like that donation to the church in South Sudan for medical care, and funding for that high tech project in Cambridge, England, with you we have someone in our midst who has a far less insular view than those of us born, bred, and raised in Middle Tennessee. You can challenge some of our American notions."

"I suppose that makes sense," I responded tentatively.

"The personal reason is that I am an old woman who may not have many years left. It may surprise you, but I have spent my whole life dreaming about you and imagining what it would be like to embrace you as my niece and give you the opportunity to enjoy something of your natural father's family and heritage, our family... Sarah, you stole my heart that time we met when you were a little girl. I have prayed for you regularly ever since, and as you saw from the letters, your mother kept me up-to-date on your doings. When your husband was killed I ached for you, and when you told me the other day about awaiting your first grandchild I rejoiced as if that baby were my own."

I did not know what to say so sat there desperately searching for words. Then she unclasped the locket that she had been wearing around her neck ever since we had arrived. She opened the small silver frame, and there was a picture of my eight-year-old self. "I have worn this most days since I first set eyes on you, Sugar, and knew for certain that you were my darling brother's offspring... I patiently waited for you to contact me rather than barging in like an ugly American, although I had expected that Rebecca would have talked to you about my brother before she died."

"Mummy was always brilliant when it came to denial," I answered. "But to be fair, she hadn't planned to drop into dementia in the way she did, which I suspect short-circuited her intentions."

"I'm glad you aren't a denier," she came back. "The money that has been given away by the foundation would have been yours, which is one of the reasons I wanted you to be involved with its distribution. Besides, I have thought that it would be wonderful to have someone who could introduce us to non-profits in the Thorpe Beauchamp area that might be in the business of looking for money."

"Do you give money to churches?"

"Why?"

"Well, the old parish church in Thorpe Beauchamp is a place where God has been worshipped for at least nine hundred years and possibly several centuries before that. It is a big thing for a congregation of a few dozen people like us to keep such a place spic, span, and standing upright. When I think of church I always think of St. Andrew's, Thorpe Beauchamp, because that is where our family has always worshipped. During the war the GIs worshipped there, too. I was christened in the old Norman font, as were both my children and I hope my grandchildren, too. Millie is determined that is where her little one will be done, despite her mother petitioning for the Chapel Royal in London and my son, David, burbling away about not believing in baptism."

My aunt laughed, "And why so many problems?"

I shook my head. "Poor Millie is the runt of this earl's snooty litter. Her mother has no more breeding than I do, possibly less, but is the biggest aristocratic snob you'll ever encounter. She wants Millie's little one baptized by a royal chaplain in one of the posher places in London so she can crow about it. When I left, my lovely daughter-in-law had not been talking to her mother for several weeks because of the row they have been having."

"The earl's wife sounds like a doozy," Emily muttered.

"If I was not a lady and in respectable company, I would use a far stronger word than that."

Emily erupted with gales of laughter, so much so that she got me chortling too. When the humor had died down she spluttered, "You know, we Americans are absolute suckers for ancient things – a nine hundred year old church would be magnificent."

"Do you think Chuck would have liked that?"

"Your father wasn't much of a churchgoer; after he was confirmed by dear old Bishop Maxon he was strictly a Christmas and Easter man, I'm afraid. I suspect he'd support something like that because it was in Thorpe Beauchamp. That was where he fought and also where he met your mother, the love of his life."

I suddenly had a thought. "Emily, would you like to come to my granddaughter's christening?"

"Do fish like water?"

"You do?"

"Of course, my darling, because I love babies..." We chuckled again when she added, "Besides, I want to see what you have done to *Honeypot Hill*, the house Rebecca built."

• • • • • • •

During the next week, Emily took it upon herself to thoroughly educate me in Vanderhoven family lore, at the same time giving me an exhaustive overview of Vanderhoven holdings and assets. By the time my visit was drawing to a close I finally had a distinct picture of what I had missed growing up as Sarah Lisle from Thorpe Beauchamp rather than Charlotte Vanderhoven of Belle Mead, Nashville. Emily arranged a tour for me around Harpeth Hall school where several generations of the family's girls had been educated; then we strolled through the grounds of Montgomery Bell Academy where Chuck had been a student. Emily made sure that one day we ate lunch together at the Vanderbilt University Faculty Club.

By serendipity we ran into the Episcopal bishop. I was also introduced to a country music composer and afterwards found myself trying hard to remember the names of various bankers and attorneys whom I had met. Then there was Lawrence Macdonald, someone we made an appointment to see. Now an old man and full of years, he had been one of Chuck's closest friends growing up. He regaled us with some of the pranks they got up to and how Chuck and he had used to play a game of chicken on the railroad tracks as they headed westward out of Nashville alongside Highway 100.

"How old were you both then, Mr. Macdonald?" I asked.

"Oh, I would say Charlie was fourteen and I was a little younger." He chuckled. "You should have seen that boy shift once when he realized the train coming toward him as he lay on the track was not the slow freight he'd been expecting. He was a dare devil, so it didn't surprise me that he went off and flew one of those gosh darned Flyin' Fortresses. I spent my war being a military pen pusher. That feller liked everyone to believe he had nerves of steel." He shook his head. "The world lost one wonderful guy when he crashed in the North Sea, but he showed his worth by the way he saved the lives of most of his crew."

Three weeks later I was back home and found myself sitting in the large Memorial Day gathering at the Cambridge American Cemetery in Madingley. It was a moving occasion and I'm glad I had made sure to set myself up with plenty of tissues. What finally broke me up was the fly past with which the ceremony ended – among the planes was a B-17, the *Sally B*, just the sort of plane that my natural father had flown for thirty-five missions over Germany and Occupied Europe. I wished that David, Millie, or Amanda could have been with me, but Millie was too uncomfortably pregnant, David was overly anxious about his wife and soon-to-be-born daughter, while Amanda had yet to come home from Nashville.

Monday, May 30, 2005 — American Cemetery, Madingley, Cambridge

"Ma'am, ma'am."

The voice broke into my reverie. Since the *Sally B* had flown over earlier, a B-17 Flying Fortress like the plane Chuck piloted, I had been lost in a world of my own. I was never aware of having seen one before, but as it came over at about two hundred feet and I heard the deep-throated drone of the engine, my emotions were awash. My birth father had flown a beautiful aeroplane exactly like that and had gone to his death in one. He had named his plane after my mother, painting her likeness on the nose cone, and it was likely his bones and the rotting remains of *The Rebecca Anne* were still close to each other on the bed of the North Sea.

The wind was starting to gust and there were little squalls of rain, but the experience had riveted me to my seat with a feeling of immense privilege that I was there. I had known for years that the Americans had their big Memorial Day commemoration at the American Cemetery, but until now there had been no reason to take any notice of it. Now I was sitting among veterans, their spouses, children, grandchildren, well-wishers, re-enactors, and so forth. I wondered how many beside myself were here because their loved one's name was on the long memorial wall or their remains had been laid to rest in one of the perfectly tended graves on the hillside.

American military pageantry is strikingly different from the Victorian-tinged British approach, but now I had been introduced into my American family, it felt right. A chaplain opened the proceedings with prayer, and the national anthems of the two nations were played by a small US Air Force band. There had been speeches that emphasized the sacrifices that had been made and the lasting bond between our two nations. Then came the intensely moving ceremony of floral tributes being laid by the wall of remembrance – my father being one whose name was engraved there. Up to this point, the American flag had been at half-staff at the far end of the wall, but following a twenty-one gun salute the enormous Stars and Stripes was raised up to the full height of the huge pole. I had felt my eyes prickle when this happened, then I had lost it completely when the B-17 came over.

"Say a prayer for me," Emily had said when I had spoken with her the previous evening, telling her where I planned to go the following day. I would probably have held it all together if Amanda had been with me, but I was alone. Finally, I was the only person left sitting amidst the hundreds of chairs that were now being stacked and cleared away. The cemetery staff and men and women from the US Air Force bases wanted to get the huge patio around the reflecting pool tidy so that they could get home to enjoy the rest of what is also a bank holiday in Britain.

"I'm sorry to get in your way," I apologized with embarrassment, quickly rising to my feet.

"Lady, you have nothing to say sorry for... did you come here because of family?"

I nodded. "My father's name is on the wall."

"His name?"

"Captain Charles Vanderhoven, he was a B-17 pilot…" I paused, but he was waiting for me to go on. "It's silly, but I'm sixty and I only learned about him a few months ago, and the whole thing has been utterly disorienting."

"That sounds fascinating, tell me more."

I shrugged. "There's not a lot to say. Chuck Vanderhoven was lost over the North Sea in September 1944…"

"Same month as the Nazis began lobbing those wretched V2s across the Channel," he muttered.

"Really, I had no idea."

Then he commented, "Ma'am, if I may say so, you don't sound as if you come from the United States."

I shook my head. "No, I was actually born within a few miles of here and was adopted by the man who I always thought to be my natural father. This time last year I had never even heard of the Vanderhovens; now I am here grieving an airman who was my father but whom I knew nothing about."

He stood silent for a moment. "Sounds confusing."

I laughed as I stood up, tucking my Kleenex into my handbag. As I looked around to make sure I had left nothing behind I told my tall gray-haired questioner, "That's putting it mildly. I just wish my parents were still alive so I could talk about it with them."

"Why do you think they shielded you from this?"

I made a face. "Your guess is probably as good as mine…"

"You must have some thoughts." He was obviously fascinated.

"I think they wanted to keep from me what a naughty girl Mummy probably was during the war. I think in the end she lost her nerve and never said anything. Besides, in the last year or two of her life her mind was addled by dementia, I'm afraid."

"She wasn't the only one, you know. We've had various men and women around your age coming through trying in some way to connect with fathers they never met or knew about. I've seen estimates that at least 23,000 and maybe as many as 80,000 kids in the UK had daddies who were GIs. I suspect there are a good few like you who don't even know it. One lady was in here not too long ago saying that without knowing who her natural father was she feels as if a part of her is missing."

I gave a small smile. "I understand her completely. I have been fortunate, I suppose, the man I always knew as Daddy was more than wonderful to me, but this has been a steep learning curve as I've sought to find out something about who I am and what I'm about."

"Ma'am, why don't you come back in the next week or two. I'd love to talk to you some more. Right now I need to make sure everything is put back in order following the gathering this morning, which means keeping these young servicemen and women on their toes! My name's Arnold Dingle. All you need to do is call and ask for me."

I shook his hand and told him who I was. He grinned and flattered me by saying gallantly, "What a pleasure to meet such a lovely lady."

Following this conversation I began visiting the American Cemetery even more, always taking with me a posy of flowers from the garden of *Honeypot Hill* to lay beneath the name of the man I was learning to think of as my father on the Wall of Remembrance – each time feeling a little closer to him because I felt I had done something for him. Every so often, when driving into Cambridge, I would stop by to visit Chuck, as it were, before parking my car nearby and taking the Park and Ride bus into the center of the city to do my shopping, visit the bank, for a dental appointment, or whatever other business I had to deal with.

I found myself developing this unexpected deep need to in some way be near Chuck. One day I slipped into the office to say hello to Arnold, who was becoming more than a nodding acquaintance, and an older man was there, also an American. He had been on the staff of the Cemetery a number of years earlier and tried to get back each summer to visit Cambridge and to see the many friends he and his wife had made while living here.

Arnold introduced him to me as Marvin Elliott, and I was told he was now living in Virginia, not far from the huge naval facility at Newport News. "This is Sarah Quinn," Arnold said as I shook hands with a man who still stood straight and tall despite the fact that he was probably eighty or more.

Marvin's grin was huge. "You must be Rebecca's daughter."

"My mother was Rebecca Lisle," I answered. "Did you know her?"

"Miz Quinn," he laughed, "Your Mom was in here several times a month to visit the wall and to do what I suspect you have just done, leave some flowers under Captain Charles Vanderhoven's name."

"She was?" I was stunned. "I had no idea."

"We got to know each other pretty well, so I know your story."

"You do?"

My children would both rightly accuse me of being an inveterate talker, not easily lost for words, but on this occasion all I could do was drop my bottom onto a conveniently positioned chair in astonishment. I had no idea Mummy had done such a thing. Marvin took me by the arm, almost lifting me from where I was perched, and guided me to an arrangement of armchairs where we sat down together.

"You look taken aback, Ma'am," he commented as I sat down, smoothing my straight fawn skirt over my knees and dropping my shoulder bag on the floor.

"It's Sarah, please," I replied. Then after a pause I continued, "And, yes, I am. How long had Mummy been doing that?"

He smiled. "My predecessor said she was a regular visitor in his time, too, and his predecessor had told him the same. I suspect she'd been coming here since the cemetery complex was completed in the 1950s and maybe before then. You didn't know?"

"Marvin, this time last year I was utterly oblivious of the fact that I was the child of an American GI. It was only when my daughter and I started going through my mother's papers following her death that the circumstantial evidence mounted up. Twelve months ago

Chuck Vanderhoven would have been just one more faceless name among thousands on the wall."

He shook his head. "You aren't the first GI child I've met who had little or no idea of his or her American parentage until well on in life. How do you feel about it now?"

I told him a brief and sanitized version of the discovery and where it had led us. I talked about Aunt Emily and the family's footprint in the Nashville area. He listened intently, asking intelligent questions as my explanation continued.

"So you started bringing flowers to lay by your father's name on the wall spontaneously?"

Nodding, I answered, "Yes, it just seemed to be an appropriate way for a daughter to bond with the father she never knew. I can now think of him as that, while my adoptive father, the man who raised me and whom I loved with a passion, I will always think of as my Daddy."

"Sounds like a good sharing out of the responsibilities," he responded, a big grin breaking across his craggy face.

"Sarah, if I may say so, you are *so* like your mother that it's uncanny. I first met her when she was probably around the same age as you are now. We often chatted, shared a cup of tea, or something like that, and I came to admire her greatly and consider her a friend. I guess she stopped coming around the time her husband's health was deteriorating, which was about when I retired and Arnold took my place."

I shrugged, "Like mother, like daughter."

After a moment of silence he asked, "Do you feel British or American?"

"Oh, British," was my response, "but when the American flag was raised from half-mast and the *Sally B* flow over on Memorial Day there was an unexpected emotional surge I had never experienced before."

"You are a privileged woman," he answered. "One foot planted in the life of one great nation, and one foot planted in the life of the other."

Our conversation drew to a close, we exchanged email addresses, and I returned home to *Honeypot Hill* through the warmth of a perfect summer afternoon, Chuck Vanderhoven never being very far from my mind.

Wednesday, June 29, 2005 — Honeypot Hill, Thorpe Beauchamp

There were three messages on my voicemail when I got home. I left them for a moment to make myself a cup of tea, but no sooner had I switched the electric kettle on than the phone started ringing again.

"Hello, Sarah Quinn," I answered in an offhand way.

"Mumsie, Mumsie," came Amanda's excited voice. "Guess what?"

My mind was still processing my conversation at the American Cemetery, so my mental cogs tussled with changing gear.

"I haven't the slightest idea, my darling, you tell me."

"I think I'm engaged."

I was a little startled, but she had now been in the USA for some weeks and had been very cagey about what she was doing. Research, writing, and learning her way around the Vanderhoven world had been key to her time there, but I found myself wondering what I was not being told. Before she made this announcement I had concluded she was keeping me in the dark about some of the things she was up to.

I sat down on one of the stools at the kitchen counter. "Now, sweetheart, begin from the beginning."

"Well, I've been trying to get you for the last several hours since getting up... You really ought to switch your mobile phone on when you are not at home."

"Are those voicemail messages the ones you left on the machine?" I answered.

"Uh-huh," came her reply. "Two of them are."

"Let me just check the third for a moment, then I can call you back, settle down, and give you my fullest attention. Of course I want to hear all about this, but I have a sense the third message might be just as important."

I made a cup of tea and listened to the breathless Amanda, the breathless Amanda again, and then my son. "Hello, Mumsie, the day has dawned. Millie is just starting contractions, I am taking her to the hospital, please come."

Talk about everything happening at once!

"Sweetie," I said to Amanda as I called back after talking to her brother. "This isn't going to be easy – the other message was from your brother telling me that Millie has gone into labor and they want me there. It doesn't sound like the little mite is going to come in the next five minutes, but they are at the hospital now and Millie is being admitted. So, let me get the details and then you can fill me in on the whole picture a little later."

I could hear her pouting. "You're not interested in me, are you?"

I sighed. "Of course I'm interested in you, but I'm a mother being torn between her daughter's wonderful news and my granddaughter deciding in the last couple of hours that the time has come to launch herself onto an unsuspecting world and, as you know, I promised Millie and David that I would be there for them..."

There was a long pause, then she said, "Sorry, Mumsie, I'm just so excited and am feeling hurt that you don't share my excitement."

"My lovely child, I do share your excitement, more than you could imagine, but can I suggest something?"

"Go ahead."

"In about an hour I am going to be sitting on the train to London preparing myself for the arrival of little Miss Quinn. I will travel First Class so we can get some privacy and we can talk on the mobile phone then. Give me a number and I will call you and we will be able to chat for the best part of an hour if you want…"

There was another pause. "If that's the best you can do."

"Amanda," I said losing my cool. "you are my daughter and I love you with all my heart, but I also love David with all my heart too, and while news can be savored and chatted over, babies wait for no one. Now please don't lay a guilt trip on me or try to manipulate me in the way your Aunt Emily does."

There was a stifled sob on the other end of the line. "I'm sorry, Mumsie, I'm so happy and I just wanted you to share my happiness."

"Darling, I do. Now give me a phone number and I'll call you back in a little while, OK?"

She did as she was told, but I knew from the tone of her goodbye that she was turning morose. I sighed as I put the phone down and went to pack a bag.

• • • • • • •

Ninety minutes later, having spent what felt like a small fortune so I could travel in a quieter part of the train, I spent another small fortune calling my daughter. It had been a rush to get a bag packed, the house shut up, and myself to the train, but, miracle of miracles, I got out of the taxi at Cambridge train station with enough time to buy myself a ticket.

"Hello," came Amanda's voice when she answered. Then before I could continue she went on. "Mumsie, Carlos tells me that I was very rude to you and I should say sorry. It was really, really bad of me to jump at you like that. You're anxious about Millie and the baby, and all I could do is pour my stuff over you. Can you forgive me?"

"My darling, you were forgiven hours ago. I would probably have been a bit stroppy if I had been in your situation."

She sighed. "I don't know how you do it. Here we are, Davey and I are both in our thirties and supposedly grownups, yet we keep leaning back on you as if we were still teenagers or younger."

I smiled. Perhaps my daughter was at long last reaching an appropriate level of maturity that, until now, I thought had eluded her.

"Now, who's Carlos?"

The tone of her voice told me all I needed to know about the grin on her face. "You know Carlos – Charles… Charlie Vanderhoven."

When I had left Tennessee some weeks before I had noted that Amanda was beginning to get over her arrogant British superiority and disdain towards Charlie. They had become sort of friends it seemed, but I had not even sensed a whiff of a romance. I asked Amanda how I had missed it.

She was obviously now grinning from ear to ear. "You missed it, Mummy dearest, because when you left there was no romance. Oh, he'd been very nice and we'd discovered a few interests in common, but you know me – since that bastard, Justin, I have tended to steer clear of becoming entangled with those human beings cursed with XY chromosomes and testosterone poisoning."

"What changed?"

"Oh, darling, how long have you got?"

I chuckled. "Sweet girl, I'm trapped on the train to Kings Cross, there will be no stops and no interruptions, so we have each other as long as my international calling card will allow me. Is Charlie with you?"

"Yes."

"Well, put the phone on speaker so I can talk to you both," I insisted, and instead of arguing as she normally would, she did as she was told.

"Why Carlos?" I asked.

She giggled. "Charlie doesn't pull my chain as a man at all. Do you remember that nasty little man Charlie Gillette who used to work for Granddad?" She needed to say no more: this particular individual had been trusted by Daddy, only to fall foul of him when it became clear that he was stealing thousands from the company. Hardly had I reached this point when I realized Amanda was sailing on with her explanation. "I also think of that silly farce 'Charlie's Aunt' and then those unkind headlines in the tabloids about the Prince of Wales being a proper Charlie, and so on. When at Oxford, some of his friends got to calling him Carlos, which I gather is when this name stuck. Being from a Cambridge family, I might not be a great enthusiast of his Dark Blue flavoring from the Other Place, but this suits him far better as far as I'm concerned."

"I see, and how does he feel about that?"

A male voice broke in. "I'm great with it, ma'am... Amanda can call me what the heck she likes as long as she will always love me and never let me go."

"Ah, Charlie... Carlos, congratulations on taming my wild girl."

"Aw, Miz Sarah, she's not wild, just highly intelligent, strong-minded, and very willful."

"She's willful alright, but then she came by that honestly – her mother has a stubborn streak, her grandmother definitely had, and her Vanderhoven grandfather sounds as if he was the sort of man who also very much liked to get his own way. Grandfather Lisle knew how to get his own way, but he was usually a lot subtler about it... Then she's had to stand up to an older brother for whom the adjective 'domineering' does not adequately describe his personality."

Charlie laughed. "That sounds like she's had good training for our bunch here in Middle Tennessee."

"How long were you at Oxford, Charlie... or should I call you Carlos?"

"You can call me whatever you like, ma'am, but I was at Oxford for two years."

Before I could ask him to tell me what actually took him there, Amanda broke in and announced proudly that her Carlos had graduated Summa Cum Laude from the University of the South in Sewanee and then won a Rhodes Scholarship. He had been at New College and earned himself a First in Politics, Philosophy, and Economics, and while he now did all sorts of lawyering, he spent a lot of his time working with clients who needed economic counsel. "But his passion is the work that he does with non-profits and charitable donors, which," she assured me, "is why he spends so much time at his desk and researching and so little pontificating in courtrooms. He often finds himself looking out of his office window over Nashville while talking to clients in Hong Kong, Dubai, London, Berlin, and New York all in one day."

"But, sweet girl, how did you fall in love with him?"

She sighed, "By totally misjudging him at the outset."

"I'm glad you said that because you were positively damnable to the poor man from the moment he first met us at the airport."

She let out a huge sigh then continued. "I had gone out with so many losers that, alas, I projected onto Carlos all the wicked attitudes I had developed towards his gender. What I didn't know was how modest he is and how many lights he was hiding under his bushel."

At that moment the train slowed down and halted. We were just outside Hitchin; it was rush hour and there came the announcement of a ten-minute delay because it was particularly busy that evening. Thus, I found myself sitting staring out across the train tracks just as it began to rain.

"Well, I had no idea he was not just clever but brilliant. Only brilliant people get Rhodes Scholarships, and I gather that is very special as far as a small college like Sewanee is concerned."

"What other lights had Carlos been hiding?" I asked, trying out Amanda's chosen name for the first time on the man.

She laughed. "You know that nice log cabin-type building that is at the far end of Aunt Emily's field?"

"Yes, what about it?"

"The evening after you went home I was feeling lonesome so decided to go off and do some exploring. I eventually fetched up behind the cabin and could hear a solo violin playing Mozart. I thought perhaps it was a CD or the radio, but when the player effortlessly slid into Bruch and then a few minutes later began sounding more like Django Reinhardt and the Hot Club of France, I knew it was someone playing for their own pleasure."

"Carlos?"

"Carlos... I crept away that evening not wanting to interrupt him. Besides, I had not even known that it was his home. He had told me he lived close to the McAllister house, but he didn't tell me he was that close. I only found out it was his home when I asked Aunt Emily who lived there, telling her about the lovely music however it was made."

"And?"

"She just rolled her eyes and said that it was Carlos's home and then told me that she sometimes wished he had become a concert violinist – his musical talents were wasted among the philistines who worked in the law firm."

The man in question now butted in. "What Emily McAllister forgets is that a man has to earn his living, and there was ample evidence that I was never quite good enough for music at that level."

Amanda cut in and prattled on, "You remember, Mumsie, that first night he told us he played the fiddle, I was under the impression he played Blue Grass or Country fiddle, not the whole classical violin repertoire as well."

"I can play jazz and country, too," Charles Vanderhoven joshed, "and if Miz Amanda wants it I will even give her a bit of Blue Grass."

We talked more and Amanda told me how Carlos had invited her out to a Nashville Symphony concert. I already knew he had smoothed the way for her with the people she had come to know at the Frist Center, but it now seemed that on those days she was there he started dropping in and out to see her and take her to lunch.

Amanda's words kept tumbling out, and it appeared they were becoming inseparable.

"We even go to church together?" my daughter said, astonishing me. "He wanted me to hear the beautiful choir at St. Francis Church. He sings there and is part of it."

"So, my darling, where is all this leading?"

"No, honey, this is my question to answer," Carlos said from the background, shutting her up for a moment. "I know that a transatlantic phone call with you sitting on a train isn't as formal as I would have liked it to be, but yesterday evening I asked Amanda if she would consent to be my wife. I am pleased to say that she answered in the affirmative. But before we can make it official it is appropriate that I ask you if I have your consent to marry your daughter. I promise I will love her till the day I die, I will care for her, and I hope that together we will give you more grandchildren. So, Miz Sarah, will you let me marry Amanda, with whom I fell in love the moment I saw her coming down the escalator at the airport… and was so unladylike in the way she treated me?"

At that moment the train jolted into action again and we creaked our way through Hitchin station before gathering speed as we headed in the direction of London.

"Charlie, Carlos, whatever you want me to call you," I responded, "I don't know you well yet, but in the last few months I've learned a lot about your background. I can't think of anyone else that I would prefer to see marrying my daughter, nor can I think of a worthier person."

There was a pause, Amanda giggled, I heard the pair of them exchange a kiss, and then they said simultaneously, "Thank you."

We talked a little more before the embankments, bridges, and small tunnels made it difficult for my phone to hold its signal, so we ended a conversation that had given me more food for thought than I had imagined. It also gave me much about which to pray and for a little while had ameliorated my anxieties for Millie as she labored to bring her little girl into the world.

Nine hours later, at around one o'clock in the morning, and having vaguely napped in the hospital waiting area, my first grandchild, Charlotte Sarah Quinn, was delivered into my arms by her exceedingly proud father. I then said what every grandmother in history is bound to say when holding her granddaughter for the first time, "Oh, she's the most beautiful baby in the world."

"Ten fingers, ten toes, 8 pounds 7ounces, no apparent problems whatsoever," said the tired but jubilant Millie as she presided over introducing Charlotte to me from her hospital bed.

"Millie, you're a wonderfully clever girl," I said proudly.

David had told me that before I came to the hospital I should go to their house, drop off my suitcase, and bring Millie's own suitcase which was sitting beside the front door, so he was the one who cut in and told me what had happened.

"This morning Millie insisted she was coming to the gallery because of an appointment with this particular client and by lunchtime had pulled off just about the biggest sale in the company's history. I'm not sure the client would have bought the painting if she had not been eased along by my sensitive, patient, well-bred, and impossibly pregnant wife."

"And?"

Millie looked daggers at him as if to say it was her turn to take up the tale. "While we were getting the final details sorted out, all documents signed, that kind of thing, I could feel Charlotte stirring and saying, 'Mummy, Mummy, now you've got all your chores out of the way, I have something else that is likely to take up the rest of your day.'"

"We grabbed a cab and came straight to the hospital because we were not sure Charlotte would wait if we decided to slip by home first. In the event there was plenty of time, but as this is baby number one we didn't want to take any chances," continued David.

I looked up from gazing in adoration at the baby's face and said to Millie, "So you've been a busy girl all day?" My daughter-in-law nodded. I looked back down at my granddaughter and went on,

"Now you are going to be a busy girl for the rest of your life, how do you feel about that?"

She grinned, pointed at David and then said, "After marrying this lump I knew it was what I was made for."

I laughed. "I agree with you, he can be a bit of a lump sometimes."

With introductions over and Charlotte returned to her mother's arms, I told them, "It's my turn now to break family news."

"Oh?"

"I found myself juggling calls all afternoon from both my children."

"Oh God, what's the problem with Amanda now?" her brother groaned as he thrust his hands deep into his pockets.

"Sweet boy, there is no problem with Amanda at all."

"I find that hard to believe. Why did she ring you then?"

"It wasn't just Amanda who spoke to me," I responded, stretching this out so that I could savor the impact the news would eventually have.

"I'm lost," Amanda's sibling replied. "She's usually in some kind of scrape or another."

"David, I won't tell you the news until you are prepared to be a good boy, to sit down, and to listen to what your mother has to say." Turning to Millie I winked and said, "I used to love teasing him like this when he was a little boy, he rose to the bait every time – and still does."

"I think I know what it is," Millie said as David sat on the bed and reached out to the tiny fingers of his daughter. "Amanda and I have been talking quite a lot on the phone during the last couple of weeks, but I was sworn to secrecy."

The relationship between the sisters-in-law had obviously already changed beyond all recognition.

"So?" said David, flopping into the chair.

"Amanda is engaged."

"What?" David yelled, jumping off the bed as if he had found himself sitting on a porcupine.

"Let me repeat it for your benefit... On what is now yesterday afternoon, I consented to the forthcoming marriage between your sister, Amanda Quinn, of *Honeypot Hill*, Thorpe Beauchamp, England, and Charles Vanderhoven of Nashville, Tennessee, United States of America."

He thought for a moment. "She can't do that, they would be close blood relatives."

I shook my head. "Not in this case. It is true that Amanda has 25% Vanderhoven blood running through her veins, but her name is Quinn. Charles Vanderhoven's natural father died before he was born, his mother married her late husband's best friend, Emily's brother, and Charles... or Carlos as Amanda prefers to call him, was immediately adopted into the Vanderhoven family. Odd, isn't it, she is Vanderhoven by birth and he is Vanderhoven by name..."

"And now she'll have them both," Millie mused.

David sighed. "Knowing my sister's prickly feminist ways I can see her voting to remain a Quinn, become a Quinn-Vanderhoven, or something even more outlandish." My son looked over at my little smile and continued, "Mumsie, is there something you know that we don't?"

"I'm not sure," I answered. "Your sister is a strong woman with sturdy views, but she has confided a fair amount in me since she moved back to *Honeypot Hill* during the last few months. I think in the light of this new turn of events she will be quite happy to be known as Dr. Amanda Vanderhoven."

A very tired Millie nodded knowingly. Clearly Amanda had also confided in her, and then a huge penny dropped. "Millie, darling, you knew about Amanda and Charles Vanderhoven all the time, didn't you?"

My daughter-in-law blushed, and her mouth turned into a pert little grin. "Amanda has been talking to me about him since you got back from America, but she wanted to keep it under wraps until she was clear about his intentions. She also thought you might have something to say about the way in which she was so cruel to the man when she first met him."

I was a little upset that Amanda had not kept me in this particular loop, but the other side of the equation was that these two girls were becoming fast friends, sisters in the real sense, something that made me very happy.

I went over to the bed, kissed Millie on the cheek and whispered, "Thank you, darling, for looking after my difficult daughter. Now, you need some rest so that you can properly care for this little girl." Then I kissed my granddaughter on the pate of her almost bald head.

Tuesday, July 12, 2005 – The Quinn Galleries, London

The immediate outcome from the birth of the first of the next generation of Quinns was that when Millie and Charlotte came home from the hospital, I had made an executive decision as Chair of The Quinn Galleries, that David take several weeks of paternity leave so that he could help his wife and spend quality time getting to know his brand new daughter. It took some persuading, but he only yielded to his mother's will when I assured him that, while he was at home, I would be there minding the store.

It was fun to be back in harness for a little while. When word got around that Sarah Quinn was (temporarily) back on her throne old friends started to appear as if by magic; clients of many years standing would emerge unexpectedly, and hardly did a day pass when I was not being taken out at lunchtime or at the end of the day to some wine bar so that my granddaughter's head could be well and truly wetted. If there was no time for this, then friends and I took to catching up over a cup of coffee in the little kitchen-rest area behind the shop that looked out over the untidy back yard that was cluttered with weeds and dustbins.

I had forgotten just how much I enjoyed gallery work, but these few weeks gave me the time to explore at first hand all that David and Millie had been doing with the gallery since I had retired. I realized by stepping back into the fray that the pair of them had been developing a remarkable vision for the business and were in the process of making something very significant out of it. Between them they had all the gifts necessary to move the venture forward in fresh directions, in the process building up a younger clientele.

About a dozen days after Charlotte had been born, I was working on a project near the rear of the gallery, behind a screen that prevented me from keeping an eye on the door. I was so engrossed by what I was doing that when I heard the door open, instead of rushing out, I decided to let one of the two assistants in the gallery attend to the visitors. A minute or two passed and I heard no voices, not even the usual warm greeting with which we tried to welcome all those who came in. My irritation grew I put down what I was doing, ready to do a little on-the-job training on receiving potential customers.

Rounding the screen that had been blocking my view of the front of the gallery, distracted by the sight of our employees giggling, I walked straight into the wide open arms of Amanda. Charles Vanderhoven, the man she was now habitually describing as 'my Carlos,' was standing right behind her, a wide grin on his face and her voluminous bag already in his hands.

"Hello, Mumsie," Amanda whispered as she clamped her arms around my waist and held me close. She then planted kisses on first one cheek, then the other, and finally on my lips. Her face was all smiles as she sighed and said softly, "I do so love you, Mumsie."

"What are you doing here?" I gasped. She had given me no warning that she was intending to come home in the various phone calls we had had.

She shrugged and then grinned. "Aunt Emily told Carlos that in her opinion there was no better place to buy an engagement ring than London, despite the fact that there are some excellent jewelers in Nashville. So we grabbed our passports and hopped a flight that got us in from Atlanta first thing this morning. We went straight to Mortimer's on Regent Street, which Aunt Emily recommended, then when the deed was done decided to stroll around the corner to surprise you."

With that she unclasped her hug, drew back a couple of feet, then waggled her left hand right in front of my nose so that I could see her ring. Her finger sported a beautiful solitaire diamond set in white gold. It was tasteful, neither too big nor too gaudy, and knowing a little about the stock at Mortimer's, the stone was without doubt of the highest quality.

"Congratulations, my darling," I responded with a kiss to her Show and Tell. "I knew one of these days you would find a man worthy of you."

Then I turned to Charles Vanderhoven, gave him a kiss on the cheek, and said proudly, "Welcome to our family. I must confess that I had no idea when you met us at the airport several months ago that you would be the one who would finally entice my headstrong daughter into marriage."

What I kept to myself for quite a long time after that was my thought that a man named Vanderhoven had not just swept my mother off her feet but had now done exactly the same thing for her granddaughter. My, what a tangled web we weave!

After this I handed over responsibility for the galleries to the two members of the staff and took Amanda and Carlos off to lunch at one of my favorite little restaurants on the fifth floor of Waterstone's bookstore in Piccadilly. I have a rule never to drink at lunchtime, but on this occasion the three of us shared a half bottle of sparkling white wine so that I could well and truly congratulate them and express my relief that, at last, this great event had come to pass.

When lunch was over Carlos excused himself to gather their

luggage and find somewhere to take a nap as he had worked a long day before leaving Nashville yesterday. This was when he told me that, as a member of New College, Oxford, he belonged to the Oxford and Cambridge Club on Pall Mall, and he had booked rooms for himself and Amanda there for the next three nights. They had then been planning to come down to Thorpe Beauchamp, and I quickly found myself making mental plans to show him off!

Amanda was still on such a high that it would be hours before she dropped with fatigue; she came back to the gallery with me so that we could have that very important mother-daughter conversation that this new reality demanded. We each got ourselves some iced water and closed the office door behind us for the necessary privacy.

"So, Little Miss Secret-Keeper, I am delighted not only with your news but also to see you, but what on earth has been going on during those months you were in Nashville?"

"How do you mean, Mumsie?" Amanda responded, looking sheepish and obviously playing for time.

"When I left at the end of May, all I had to do was mention the name of this particular Charles Vanderhoven and your answer would be a long face and a big sigh. What on earth has happened to get from that to this…" I said pointing at the diamond ring on her finger.

"Was I *that* nasty to him?" she answered.

"Sweetheart, do you need me to repeat some of the vicious things you said about him?" She shook her head. "So, please enlighten your aging parent as she is delighted but somewhat confused."

"Mumsie, you are hardly an aging parent."

"Ha, ha. When I was trying to get up into the attic at *Honeypot Hill* last autumn you were scared to death that such antics were beyond an old girl like me."

She shrugged, gave me a little grin, and said, "Maybe I was being a bit protective, but when you came unthreaded in the following weeks, that gave me reason to think that the judgments I had made at that point were valid."

"True, but obviously I have since shed twenty years together with the dozen or more pounds that those anxieties about my origins had engendered... and I will have you know, young lady, that I have kept almost all of that weight off."

"I know, Mother, and you look really good. That was something that Aunt Emily kept saying."

"And Aunt Emily was in on your secret budding relationship with her nephew, I should imagine?"

"Uh-huh. I couldn't hide it from her as I was living under her roof, and she was the only person to whom I could turn without racking up huge transatlantic phone bills. She actually read me like a book from the evening that I stumbled across Carlos's house and heard his brilliant violin playing. She made sure the following evening that Carlos came over to dinner, and then she left us alone in the living room to talk... and we gabbed away until about three in the morning. It didn't seem that long, but by the time I got into bed I couldn't sleep due to excitement."

"So?"

"So at about seven o'clock I got up and walked across the dewy field to Carlos's house, where I found him taking intravenous doses of coffee before going off to work. He looked so smart in his dark blue suit, white shirt, and what I immediately recognized as an Oxford University tie."

"And?"

She grinned, "I asked him if he had the right to wear that tie. Then he grinned and asked me if I had ever heard of New College which, of course, I had. Then talk about fools rushing in, because I immediately accused him of just having done some kind of summer course there, but he shook his head and said that he had been awarded a little scholarship and had been there for two years. I didn't pursue this, so it wasn't until I asked Aunt Emily about his scholarship to Oxford that she told me ever so proudly that he was a Rhodes Scholar. I could have died with embarrassment."

I laughed. "Darling, you will never die of embarrassment, you are much too brash for that. You take after your grandmother in that. But I'm sure the discovery helped you see him in a new light. Was that when you started taking him more seriously?"

She nodded. "Yes, that was part of it."

"And what else?"

Amanda looked down at her hands then looked back up at me. "Was I really that awful in the way I treated him when we got to Tennessee?"

I gave her a wry smile and nodded. I had been quite ashamed of her arrogance and the cold-shoulder treatment she had given him despite all his efforts to help her and introduce her to folks around the city who he thought she might appreciate."

"OK, Mummy Dearest, I confess that I was a bit of a bitch."

"A bit?"

"OK, I was a big one, and didn't give him a chance. I had this preconception of Americans being unthinking and unreflective and possessing not one whit of culture. Not only did I discover my preconceptions to be for the most part utterly false but that this man who had fallen for me was brighter and better educated than most of the men I've ever dated, as well as myself. Just being with Carlos is so stimulating."

I decided to change the subject and go back to her morning walk across the field to Carlos's house where she challenged whether it was legitimate for him to wear an Oxford University tie. "How did Carlos take to you arriving as he was getting up to go to work and checking up on his attire?"

"Oh, he was darling. He hadn't slept very much either, so we each had a bagel and several cups of strong coffee while we sat on the porch and listened to the birds in the trees. He wasn't mad at me at all, in fact he seemed very pleased to see me. We talked about this and that, he told me what he was going to be working on that day while I told him that I would probably try to make use of Vanderbilt University Library or go to the Frist."

"And…"

"And he said he would drive me down to the Frist and then come and take me to lunch somewhere nice."

"Was that the only time this happened?" I said slyly.

She shook her head and grinned. "After that I started going over the field first thing every morning and having coffee with him, then going down into Nashville in his car, and most days we were able to have lunch together. He even took me into his office and introduced me to some of his colleagues. Everyone was very sweet, but all the women seemed to jump to the right conclusion and had that female knowing look in their eyes."

"How often did you go to church with him?" Now I really was curious.

"Oh, Mumsie, haven't I been so silly about church? I went every Sunday with him. The church is like a cathedral, with wonderful music and a fabulous choir in which Carlos sings. He has a lovely tenor voice. I would sit with Aunt Emily, and she introduced me to the Rector – who seemed very interested in the study I am doing for my book."

"So my militantly agnostic daughter is changing her tune?"

She blushed. "Your daughter is changing her tune... partly because Carlos is such an intelligent man and helped me understand that when you go to church you don't have to leave your brain at the door. He could not figure out why I was working on the Mother and Child theme with such passion when I had been so dubious about the Christian faith."

I finished my glass of water and then answered, "Sweetheart, having read a little of what you are writing I must say I share some of his perceptions."

"But you must realize, Mumsie, that my poor little baby has something to do with that."

"Yes, I'm not quite in my dotage, I had no problems working that one out." The time had come to probe a little deeper. "Now, have you told Carlos all about the baby?"

There was a woeful look on her face as she nodded, let out a long sigh, and her eyes teared up. "That was the hardest thing to do..." She slid from her chair and knelt before me, laying her head in my lap so she could sob. Finally, she looked up at me and repeated what she had said before. "I am so, so ashamed of what I did and the reason I did it. I still find it very hard to forgive myself and had a real meltdown when I told Carlos. From some things he said I had suspected this was not something with which he would be sympathetic – and I was right."

"And so?"

Her eyes were now red and swollen, with mascara running down her cheeks. She looked wan and weary, which was not surprising given she had hardly slept on the plane the night before.

"Carlos asked me if I would marry him when we were sitting on his porch drinking our coffee three Saturday mornings ago. His asking came as a surprise, but for several weeks it had been what I had wanted more than anything else in the whole wide world. I felt my insides heave when he told me that he wanted me to be his wife and for us to have babies together because I knew at that moment, before we went any further, that I had to tell him the whole truth about myself.

As she spoke her description was so vivid that I could almost see their conversation.

She had told him, "Are you sure you want to marry me?... because there's a lot you don't know about me."

He was on his knees in front of her proposing in a very traditional and old-fashioned way, just as I would have expected of a Southern gentleman like him.

"Oh, I don't suppose there is anything that would shock me," he answered light-heartedly.

"But there is, and I want you to know the whole story first. After I have told you this you may want to change your mind."

She was weeping by this point, but she talked to him about her rebelliousness at university and how often she had compromised her values. Then she talked about the various men who had been through her life since then and ended by telling him about Julian, getting pregnant, her delight after getting over the immediate shock, then how he had weaseled his way out of any responsibility for the child, in effect blackmailing her to have an abortion.

"… And I hate myself every day for what I did" were her final words as she got up, ran into the house, went straight to the bathroom and locked herself in. Carlos spent the next hour pleading through the door for her to come out so they could talk more about it. She didn't want to talk about it, fearful that he was going to condemn her for what she did and expel her from his life forever. Amanda has always been prone to catastrophize and come up with worst case scenarios when in difficult circumstances.

Finally, the house was quiet and she thought it now safe for her to come out and escape. Instead she found Carlos sitting in a chair about ten feet away from the bathroom patiently waiting for her.

"What was all that about?" he asked.

"Oh, Carlos, I'm sorry, I should have told you about this a long time ago. But I am so ashamed of what I did and thought that you would be horrified that you should have even considered that a woman like me is suitable wife material for a Vanderhoven."

"Honey," he replied, wrapping his arms around her, "Let's get a few things straight here. While I don't condone your actions, I fully understand why you did it. I have often wondered what it must be like for a woman to find herself in that position – and how I would respond to it if she were me."

"Oh," she sniffled.

He smiled down at her and taking a tissue from a nearby box wiped her eyes and nose. Then he continued. "Secondly, you have to remember that you are the Vanderhoven in this partnership, I just happened to get the name by accident. If my Dad had not been killed in Vietnam then I would have been a Schlenkel, for goodness sakes."

"Oh," she sniffled again.

There was quite a long silence before he continued. "I am

profoundly grateful that you told me what had happened. I have to confess that I have wondered what was wrong with British men that so lovely a woman as you with such a love for life should not have been snapped up by some lovesick swain a long time ago. Now I understand that you have been holding them at arm's length for several years. Right?"

She nodded. "Yes, right. And not just men but everyone, my family included. By and large, I was not a nice person to be around – I buried myself in my work, and I gave up babysitting for friends because I could not bear to be around children who might be about the same age that my son or daughter would have been."

"You have been flagellating yourself haven't you?"

"Oh, Carlos, far worse than that."

"What we have got to do is to help God, myself, and you to work this through so that it is not there to mar the rest of our lives. What's been done cannot be undone, but let's see if we can help you get it into a different perspective as we begin our life together."

She was astounded. "You still want to stay with me?"

He took both her hands and held her a little back from himself so he could look into her eyes. "Sweet woman, I have wanted something like that since the moment I set eyes on you at the airport. You, being the feisty lady that you are, made sure that what I wanted would be challenging for me to get, so let me ask you again. Dr. Amanda Quinn, would you do me the honor of becoming my wife? I have been waiting for you for the whole of my life, I don't want to lose you, and honestly, I can't live without you."

Ten Years Later, Wednesday, September 15, 2015 — Video Conferencing, GPDS Partners, London

At the time that it surfaced, I had no idea how the upsetting but seemingly insignificant business of finding that old letter from my mother's former lover would have such life-altering consequences for both myself and my family. Never were these more apparent than on a balmy early autumn evening in London almost exactly ten years later.

Most of the investment partnership's employees had left for the day when I found myself sitting in a lavish video conferencing facility that overlooked the gardens of Buckingham Palace and calling a transatlantic conference meeting to order. Something unexpected and extraordinary had happened during early August, and it had become necessary for me as the Chair of the Vanderhoven Memorial

Foundation to report details to our trustees and then try to guide the conversation as we teased out the action we should take as a result of this discovery.

Never having done anything like this before, I felt rightly nervous but was encouraged that to my right sat David, my son, his temples greying a little and his face grown slightly more pudgy; despite the nagging of his wife he was less than willing to take enough exercise. To my left sat my son-in-law, Charles Alexander Vanderhoven, or as his wife always called him, "my Carlos." Staring at us from the curved array of video screens at the other side of the table were almost all the Nashville-based trustees of the foundation; although thousands of miles and six time zones away, their life-sized images made it seem as if they were almost in the room with us. My family now spread across the two continents, so I had long since become familiar with Skype, but this was Skype on a grand scale – about as close to virtual reality as you could get at this point.

Early in the summer months, routine Royal Naval sonar exercises had stumbled across the almost intact remains of a B-17 now covered by little more than a dusting of sand. Closer inspection revealed *The Rebecca Anne*. Divers had been able to more closely examine what sonar and underwater cameras had identified, affirming that the now pitiful remains of pilot and co-pilot were in the cockpit and that the aircraft was probably recoverable. It would appear that they had attempted to land their Flying Fortress on what must then have been a sandbar as they flew low over the water with the tide out; squelchy sand was obviously unable to take its weight.

David had excused himself from The Quinn Galleries that afternoon while Amanda had sent Charles Vanderhoven, her husband of nearly ten years, to use his legal mind to help sift through the data and confer with experts about the nature of the wreck and the possibility of recovery. More than seventy years after their disappearance, this had been a spectacular find, suggesting that, hoping for a gentle landing, the crew of two had to the very end thought this would be safe and they would be rescued.

Media from around the world had picked up on the story, happy for a few days to be sidetracked from the sight of tens of thousands of Syrian refugees fleeing across the Mediterranean into Greece and seeking refuge in western Europe. Suddenly, our family was bombarded by everyone from the *Wall Street Journal* and *The Times* to the BBC, Sky News, Aljazeera, CBS, MSNBC, and CNN for interviews. What made this so disconcerting was the manner in which these journalists had characterized me as this very proper white-haired English widow who had actually been a cuckoo's egg laid in the nest of a British soldier, engineer, churchman, and, later in life, a much respected champion for the world's refugees. They kept bugging me about the torrid wartime affair between Rebecca and this feckless American flyer rather than considering the patriotic service of both my birth father and my adoptive father. It added spice to the story that the Lisles and Vanderhovens were now intermarried to the extent that Amanda and her children had found it necessary to go into temporary hiding until the fuss died down. I tried when journalists interviewed me to correct this impression, but so many minds were already made up. I concluded, sadly, that facts seemed no longer important – what they wanted was to sell more newspapers, magazines, or online advertising.

It was when the media had been scrambling over each other to get their own take on this story that they had begun doing calculations like those I had done in 2005: it did not take a great deal of education to work out on the back of an envelope that I might well have been conceived not long before Chuck Vanderhoven flew that last mission. Rather than denying this, I had been upfront both about my father and my Daddy, about my mother as well as my American family in Nashville. Denial would have just led to an even more unseemly feeding frenzy – although it was bad enough as it was.

The byproduct of this was bundles of letters being delivered almost every day to *Honeypot Hill*, and countless emails from women, men, their sons and daughters, mostly from Britain, but some from other parts of the world, telling their own stories of GI fathers who they never knew. I was surprised how many, like myself, had not found out the identity of their American parent until quite late in life or still did not have any idea who he might have been. My forthright honesty unwittingly turned me into the champion for an embarrassed group of individuals, American eggs laid in British nests, by both responsible and irresponsible American GI fathers, men who were lonely and thousands of miles from home.

Given my druthers (a descriptive American word I have learned and enjoy using), I would prefer to have left Chuck's remains at rest where they had lain for seventy years, washed by the tides and currents of the North Sea close to where it flows into the English Channel on its way to the vast Atlantic Ocean, eventually reaching the shores of my father's homeland. However, *The Rebecca Anne* appeared to be one of the few remaining B-17Gs still in existence, and the impetus to raise her rapidly gathered momentum. If the plane could be raised, and a million dollars had already been offered toward its recovery and refurbishment, it would have pride of place in some museum or other – why not try to get it to Nashville? The question that was most troubling was where would be the final resting place for Chuck and Danny, the two pilots?

Aunt Emily's health, which had seemed so robust when we had met a decade earlier, began to steadily decline in Spring 2010, soon after torrential rains and devastating floods had done so much damage in the Nashville area. She lost close friends, a couple whose car was washed away in a flash flood, and irreparable damage was done to several places that had been the landmarks of her life. It was as if after that she lost heart, and her body was weakened by one little infection after another, yet her mind remained razor sharp until the very end.

This was when I at last fathomed out how much over the previous several years she had been playing a long game at cornering me. I had neither sought nor did I want to Chair the Vanderhoven Memorial Foundation, but that shrewd old woman had set me up in such a way as Chuck Vanderhoven's only progeny that the position literally became mine by right of birth – despite me having been born on the wrong side of the blanket on the wrong side of the ocean.

I was vociferously cross with her and argued against her little scheme only to be dumbfounded by her triumphant chuckle.

"Emily," I had told her, "I'm not a real Vanderhoven. If this were medieval Ireland I would have been named FitzVanderhoven."

"You know, Sugar," she quipped as she laughed with me, "I love fighting with you, it reminds me so much of the cat versus dog arguments I regularly had with your father before he went off to win the war."

What she kept drilling into me was that, because much of the principal that launched the Foundation had come from what would have been my portion of Chuck Vanderhoven's estate, and because I had a track record of successfully managing a respected business, it was not only appropriate that I be on the board but that I should also follow in Emily Vanderhoven McAllister's footsteps. Thus it was that I had now been publicly outed as Chuck's daughter and, that in this position, had a significant say about what would happen to my birth father's remains and those of his comrade-in-arms, and that continued responsibility of the Foundation's work for the betterment of society and the glory of God should be in my hands.

I may not bear the Vanderhoven name, but Vanderhoven blood flows through my veins – who else should chair her father's memorial? Not only that, but I had made sure that my daughter, both genetically and by marriage a Vanderhoven, be dragooned onto the board of the Foundation, and I was laying the groundwork for Amanda to step into my shoes when I was ready to lay the gavel aside.

At the beginning of 2012, I was formally installed as Aunt Emily's successor, only a few months before she slipped off in her sleep. The tributes at her funeral were fulsome, and it would have pleased her no end that, given her generosity to the Diocese, the bishop himself had preached the homily and been there at her graveside. In her will she had made lavish provision for Amanda, Carlos, and their two young sons. They inherited her lovely home, but she had already determined that the guest quarters of the house should be my home away from home whenever I was on the American side of the Atlantic. What grandmother could turn down such a bequest, making it easy for me to spend time regularly with my grandchildren, to dote on them and spoil them?

The Foundation was sometimes so demanding that it seemed I was spending far more time in Tennessee than Thorpe Beauchamp. Emily had once kept a couple of horses, so alongside my little corner of the house was a barn which we then had converted, among other things, into a dry warm home for the little silver Honda Civic that became my vehicle on what Amanda kept calling 'the left hand side of the Atlantic Ocean.'

Thus, in the years prior to the discovery of *The Rebecca Anne*, I had settled to a comfortable transatlantic existence.

● ● ● ● ● ● ●

Preceding the video conference, we had met with several members of the family of Chuck's co-pilot, Danny Gonzales. We wanted them to have the same say as we did in all that would happen, but we also wanted them to be with us as we received a whole day's briefing from members of the team that was involved with raising *The Rebecca Anne*. Not only were there salvage experts, divers, and maritime lawyers but also representatives of the Pentagon and the Department of Defence in London. Although our foundation is not as large or influential as the Ford or Rockefeller Foundations, the authorities clearly wanted the Vanderhovens involved because we came with some money attached. It would also make it less difficult getting funds from Congress and other charitable donors if the pilot and co-pilot's kin were involved and had already made lead gifts, and especially if the Vanderhoven Memorial Foundation opened its own checkbook.

The trustee conference call was set for early evening, London time, the day following the briefing, with Carlos, David, and me spending the whole afternoon together talking through possibilities and scenarios in David's office, the one that had been mine when I was the Director of The Quinn Galleries. Danny Gonzales' son and grandson joined us, and as an engineer, the grandson, also called Danny, had some very insightful contributions to make to the conversation. The Galleries was an easy place for us to be able to include in our conversation Amanda and Millie, both encumbered with their children and already having made a pact that they would not be left out of any decision-making.

The previous day's consultation had been both thorough and intense. We had been briefed on engineering challenges that I did not quite understand, so I sat back and listened as the men plowed through these. What had been emphasized was how important this find was. 12,731 B-17s in their various editions had been built to save the world for democracy, but only a handful had survived – maybe as few as forty-three were left. There were all sorts of questions that needed to be asked about preserving a complex piece of machinery that had been submerged in sea water for so long. However, salvage plans were well-advancing with a view to lifting *The Rebecca Anne* the next summer, hopefully in one piece.

After some lengthy transatlantic phone conversations between Quinns and Vanderhovens, we agreed that it was imperative that we do all we could to make this happen. The Gonzales family concurred. We also agreed that our participation should be neither token nor penny-pinching, for this plane had been heroically flown by the man who was the scion of our families and, more importantly, was my natural father, as well as my children's grandfather. This was the man whom Daddy had saluted as a hero when hearing that his only child was in fact the product of Chuck Vanderhoven's passionate love for my mother.

The big issue for us was not so much the plane itself but how we should deal with the pilot's remains. We had met with Danny Gonzales's son and grandson both before and after the day's briefing, having dinner together in the evening. This had given us the opportunity to talk through the family implications. The co-pilot's son and I were very happy with our final position. If they had not had to return to Texas I would have invited them to sit in on our video board meeting, and I hoped Danny Gonzales Jr. would consider joining us on a permanent basis.

A key talking point would be the final resting place of the pilots' remains and, as might be expected in any strong-willed family coupled with the board of a respected charitable foundation, the Vanderhovens were all over the show. Some Vanderhovens wanted Chuck back in Tennessee, a big funeral and celebration of his life at St. Francis Church, then that he be buried with other veterans going back to the American Civil War in the Nashville National Cemetery on Gallatin Pike.

Rather than burial, others wanted him cremated and the ashes to be scattered over the spot where *The Rebecca Anne* had lain for nearly three-quarters of a century. Their idea was that they should be scattered from the *Sally B*, the last serviceable B-17 in Europe, now stationed at the former RAF Duxford near Cambridge, home of the aircraft division of London's Imperial War Museum, the plane I had seen fly over all those years ago on my first Memorial Day visit to the American Cemetery at Madingley.

Amanda's sentimental side came out when she suggested that perhaps Chuck's remains should be buried alongside her grandparents' grave in Thorpe Beauchamp churchyard. This was a huge disagreement between me and my daughter – a *ménage à trois* is bad enough in life, but as Chuck's daughter I held the veto.

"Mumsie, I didn't realize you could be so cold," said my tearful Amanda, a recently naturalized American citizen who now sported an endearing mid-Atlantic accent. She broke down weepily when I gave my final ruling over the phone.

"No, sweetie," I had countered. "Let the remains of your grandparents rest in peace... they worked out their lives and marriage in the wake of Chuck and it is wrong to impose him upon them so long afterwards even though all three have now gone to their reward. Yes, he might have been my natural father, but the Daddy I knew and loved, and who always adored me, can never been anyone other than Jeremy Lisle. I want nothing to detract from him and his memory."

There was a silence on the phone line as she digested this then said, "I wish I could see your face at this moment because it might give me an idea of what you really want."

"The one thing I don't want is for him to be cremated and then scattered over that spot in the North Sea off the coast of the Low Countries – there seems to be something callous about this. Out of sight, out of mind – honored for a moment and then forgotten forever. A dozen years ago I would have been aghast to hear myself expressing such an opinion, and although I am proud of my Britishness, I am also delighted that even if I don't have two passports like you, I have become part of a distinguished American family."

"I agree that cremation and scattering is wrong, and when I talked to them earlier in the week so did Davey and Millie. I'm sure my Carlos backs us up 100%."

Amanda's way of always referring to Charlie Vanderhoven as 'My Carlos' was endearing. Rather than commenting on this I continued. "It would be appropriate for him to be buried in Tennessee among his kith and kin, but somehow that doesn't seem right. He died in the heat of battle after having saved the lives of his men. Your natural grandfather was honored by his country for bravery, and I want that bravery to continue to be remembered. I fear that if he was brought back to Nashville the media would go wild, and the grave would be gawped at by sightseers and may even require 24-hour security. I just wish I knew Emily's mind, wish she was still alive."

"The extended Vanderhoven family might not agree with you. They consider Chuck their very own war hero and there is a sense of heritage and pride that would love a decorated veteran's grave in the National Cemetery, or even Arlington Cemetery in Washington. D.C."

I felt myself bristle. "Chuck's *my* father, not theirs, and he's also your grandfather. I would have bowed to Emily's wishes – which, of course, we will never know, so it is ultimately going to be my decision."

"You want him at Madingley, don't you?"

"Yes, my darling," I responded quietly.

"What do you have in mind, Mumsie?" Carlos asked.

"There are two places in this world that are precious to me. One is the St. Andrew's Church in Thorpe Beauchamp. As a little girl growing up it always stood there calm and serene across the wall from *Honeypot Hill*. Now as an old woman it still stands there calm and serene, and I see it each day knowing that my parents are buried not many feet from the base of the tower, and in due course my remains will join them. I have spent hours tending their grave and talking to them – although I know their true selves are not there."

"And the other?"

"The other is the Cambridge American Cemetery. I feel such pride in my heart whenever I see my natural father's name there on the wall. Remembered by a grateful nation, and not forgotten. I wish I had known him."

After talking to the Gonzales family and then conferring more with my son and daughter and their spouses before the video conference, I told them what I was going to press for, and this was enthusiastically endorsed by Hector Gonzales, Danny's son.

As we sat there in the office at Quinn Galleries finishing our preparation for the evening's meeting, I told them, "What I would like, and I have agreed with the co-pilot's son about this when he and I had a nightcap together last night, is for there to be a traditional funeral service for the two men together at St. Andrew's Church, Thorpe Beauchamp, presided over by our Vicar, a Roman Catholic priest, and a USAF Chaplain, then for them to be buried side-by-side among their fellow veterans of World War Two, both men and women, at the American Cemetery in Madingley, and that they be buried with full military honors."

"Why at Thorpe Beauchamp?" David had asked.

"Going through the church records for that time, particularly the burials, we have discovered that several men who had died either at the US Army Air Forces base in Thorpe Beauchamp or whose remains were brought back following a mission over enemy territory, had funerals in the village church and were later reinterred at Madingley. The Vicar at that time and chaplains at the airfield cooperated with one another as best they could. As this was the pattern back when Chuck was flying, why not repeat it now?"

"Is there a marker around the church about these funerals?" David then said.

"Not that I'm aware of, and I do know the church and the churchyard pretty well – in so many ways it has been my church for seventy years as well as my playground as a little girl."

Then from across the Atlantic and from his chair beside mine, both my children said together, "Then we should do something about that…" I heard what they had said in unison then laughed.

I laughed too. "So, my children, whether you like it or not you are just proving that either genetically or by conditioning you find yourselves thinking very much alike."

Then Millie chimed in, "Mumsie, darling, you are Chuck's daughter, and when the foundation board meets in a couple of hours I think that you should shamelessly play that card – because it's what you want for your father."

I sighed. "I guess there aren't too many people who can say they've planned the funerals for *both* their fathers."

• • • • • • •

As much as I loved Thorpe Beauchamp, especially now that David, Millie, and their girls had taken over *Honeypot Hill*, there were things about London that I missed – especially during these early autumn days when the evenings were still light. Balmy breezes wafted down streets and across the parks, the late roses were blooming, and the bulk of the summer tourists had gone.

Our powwow over, David had work to finish at the gallery before the conference call, and Carlos needed to talk with his office in Nashville as well as catching up with Amanda and his sons on a more personal level, so I decided to walk to the video conference, taking in one of my favorite corners of London on the way. As I strolled down Piccadilly, past the Ritz, and into Green Park, I found myself wondering if my birth parents had perhaps taken this route on one of their lovers' trysts in London in the months before I was conceived, Rebecca clinging possessively to Chuck's arm, perhaps fearing that he would be taken from her on one of his perilous missions over Occupied Europe, yet immensely proud. The streets would have been thronged with other couples similarly grabbing a few intimate hours together.

I took the route I did because I wanted to sit for a few minutes on the bench in Green Park that Tim and I had once dubbed 'our special place.' It was here that he had proposed to me, embarrassing me by kneeling on the soggy walkway with people strolling past, craning their necks to see what we were up to. He then refused to get up until I said a definitive 'Yes.' As I sat in exactly the same spot, I wondered what he would have made of the journey my life had taken in those so many years that I had lived since he had been so cruelly taken from me.

Tim was a Londoner through and through. I used to tease him about the way that he would get fidgety if he strayed too far beyond the reach of the Underground system or the network of red London buses. He found weekends at *Honeypot Hill* irksome despite his great affection for my Mummy and Daddy. For my city boy the countryside was just too quiet, he was only really at ease when he was in what old Londoners used to call 'The Smoke.'

Despite being a Londoner born and bred, his son had evolved into something very different, leaping at the idea when, at Millie's prompting and my suggestion, they move to *Honeypot Hill*. I would have a granny flat built for myself on the footprint of the old garage, the place where Daddy had stored his precious archives – all of which had now had pride of place in the Archives of Anglia Ruskin

University in Cambridge. It was less than an hour by train to Kings' Cross Station in London, and we all knew Thorpe Beauchamp would be a far healthier and safer environment in which my two little granddaughters would grow up.

The years had not been easy for David and Millie. After the birth of little Charlotte Sarah, there had been all sorts of complications, two miscarriages, a stillbirth, and now, finally, toddling all over the place was their precious little girl Emily Elspeth. On top of these reproductive issues had been business worries associated with the near collapse of the world economy in 2008 followed by what Americans have been calling 'The Great Recession.'

I suspect The Quinn Galleries could have been forced into liquidation if David had not been impossibly stubborn, using their lovely home in the North London suburbs as collateral to keep the business afloat through the hard times. Those stressful years had taken their toll on both of them and may have been a reason behind their inability to conceive a second healthy child for so long.

They had sold their home in London a couple of years earlier and had jumped with both feet into the life of the village. David had always had this knack of making friends so quickly became a favorite at The Lamb and Flag pub at weekends. During the season it was rugby, rugby, and more rugby that was the main topic of conversation. Millie was one of the most reliable mothers when it came to chaperoning the children from the village primary school where Charlotte had flourished and would now soon be moving on to school in Cambridge. Best of all, the whole family came to church each Sunday, the five of us all squashed in the pew together – how proud Daddy would have been.

I wondered how Tim would have taken to being Granddad or living with me in the converted garage, which I had to confess was warmer and a lot more comfortable than *Honeypot Hill* itself. I had made sure I had an excellent view of what had once been the airfield from which my father had taken off for those thirty-five missions, coming home and landing following thirty-four sorties over

Occupied Territory. I would often find myself wondering what sort of man Tim would have become if he had lived, and what sort of shape my life would have had. Rather than becoming director of the gallery, I suspect I would not have become involved in the business until the children were older, but by being forced to take over The Quinn Galleries I had discover abilities and skills I never knew I had.

Looking at my watch, I stirred myself and walked past Buckingham Palace, my mind now on my American family. A couple of months earlier, when Amanda had been over to visit, I had taken the boys to see the Changing of the Guard. Andrew had been conceived almost as soon as Amanda and Carlos had married at Thorpe Beauchamp church toward the end of 2005, and Lawrence then appeared barely eighteen months later.

Carlos joked that, like the royal princesses, his wife had done her job well and that there was now an heir and a spare to continue the Vanderhoven name. This always infuriated Amanda's feminist streak, and she would regularly threaten to change her own last name back to Quinn, by which she was still known professionally, and that of the boys, too. "And remember this, my Music City boy, you might be the one who brings the Vanderhoven name to our partnership, but I'm the one who contributes the Vanderhoven genes."

Seeing the way Amanda and Carlos joshed one another made my heart sing. My beautifully joyful bouncing daughter was back after those angry years in the wilderness punctuated by the tragedy of that very first baby. She had thrown crockery at Carlos when on one occasion he had the audacity to call her Mandy, but he had supported her to the hilt as she had completed her book on the Virgin and Child in medieval painting and in her adjunct teaching at various of the colleges and universities in Nashville. More recently she had become a member of the Vestry, the church council, at St. Francis Church – quite a change for a girl who until meeting Carlos had preferred to spend Sunday mornings asleep in bed.

As I turned onto Grosvenor Place I found my heart bursting with gratitude. For a moment or two I needed to sit down and catch my breath on a bench in a little green area near the office to which I was heading and to thank God for the life he had given me. It had not been easy, but with an extended family spread across two continents and all the purpose added to my life by the Vanderhoven Memorial Foundation, I was doubly blessed. Standing up and hoisting my bag over my shoulder, I realized the time had come to turn my mind to the business in hand.

Twenty-five minutes later I found myself sitting at the head of that grand table looking across at our trustees eating their sandwich lunch on the other side of the Atlantic. Amanda, sitting among them, gave a little finger wave at her husband and her mother. I glanced at David and Carlos and both nodded that they were ready, each having a part of the presentation that we were just about to make.

"So, ladies and gentlemen, thank you for taking this hour out of your busy lives so that we can discuss how our foundation is going to respond to this exciting and surprising find in the North Sea. We've got a lot of work to do, some big decisions to make, so let's get on with our business…"

The author writes:

"I am a truly transatlantic person, and to see family members usually means a lengthy plane flight. Our children and grandchildren have a variety of English accents. Having been born and raised in England, the USA has been home for much of my adult life, especially the state of Tennessee.

Throughout life, I have at times turned to writing fiction for my own pleasure and, perhaps, my mental health! The time has come to share this avocation with a wider audience. *The G.I.'s Daughter* is the first out of the starting gate, more are likely to follow.

I use the pen name, C. E. Hollingsworth, as an apt way to separate my scribbling from my professional life."